MW00882908

MARK FOR BLOOD

MARK FOR BLOOD

NICK THACKER

Mark for Blood: Mason Dixon Thrillers, Book #1
Copyright © 2017 by Nick Thacker
Published by Turtleshell Press

This is a work of fiction. Names, characters, places, and incidents either are the product of the author's imagination or are used fictitiously, and any resemblance of fictional characters to actual persons living or dead, business establishments, events, or locales is entirely coincidental.

All right reserved. No part of this publication can be reproduced, stored in a retrieval system, or transmitted in any form or by any means—electronic, photocopying, mechanical, or otherwise—without prior permission of the publisher and author except in the case of brief quotations embodied in critical articles or reviews.

PREFACE

(Or: I wrote a book.)

Hey. Mason Dixon here. Thanks for grabbing this story about me, I know the guy who wrote me will appreciate it.

But I want to talk about me for a second.

I the pages to follow, you're going to have a lot of fun hearing about some of my adventures and escapades. You'll *also* hear about my drinks — some of which I've invented, and some of which you've heard of and I've just perfected.

I don't just use drinks to take out my marks, either. I *drink* them.

And, recently, I started writing about those drinks.

I just published my first book, called *Classy Drinks for Classy People*, and I wrote it for *you*, classy reader.

It's a recipe book, a how-to guide, and a humorous history book all rolled into one. I think you're going to get a kick out of it. So what do you way?

Want to learn to mix drinks the Mason Dixon way?

Go here to find out more: http://www.nickthacker.com/CDCP

...and then come back here to continue reading about me!

CHAPTER ONE

I KNEW I WOULD KILL him as soon as he walked in.

Not quite sure how, but I knew. That *feeling* was there. In all of my fifteen years behind the bar I don't remember a time when it was wrong — off slightly perhaps, but never flat-out wrong. There was that time it told me it was the guy, instead of the girl, but we got that straightened out (or rather, it didn't really matter much after I'd killed them both, as I found out later he was just as much a dirty schmuck as she was dirty all around).

There was also that night I went around a few times with a younger kid, a guy ten years my inferior, and I thought the whole time he was screwing with me. Took me until he had a knife at my throat, his huge bicep turning his faded *Semper Fi* tat into a bloated pig of a prior life's memory. I used that kid's own knife on him. *'Once a marine, always a marine'* doesn't hold a lot of weight when your side gig starts paying more than the US government, I guess.

But after a few times testing that feeling I started trusting that feeling. In my mind it's more of a *feeling* anyway. It's a knowledge — an instinct, really. I just *know*.

So he walked in, and I knew he was the mark.

He looked like he was in college — that shitty outfit, wearing pants that sagged to his asscrack, those shoes that said 'I don't give a shit but I care that you think I give a shit,' and that hair.

My God, that hair.

His hair would've made me kill him even if I didn't have another reason to. In some ways I think I even made his hair the *main* reason. It was poofed up, the pressed-down-to-his-ears, then teased in a not-accidental kind of way the way they do it up in a salon that's meant for men the same way a tampon's meant for men. The kind of hair that says, 'yeah, my dad's got the money to bail me out.'

I didn't have a plan for this kid — I never do. One of the reasons I'm the best at what I do is that I hate planning. Plans never go the way they're supposed to, and by the time you've planned through all the possible outcomes of a situation, the plan's useless because the situation's changed.

Another one of the reasons I'm the best is that while I hate plans, I'm the best with details. I know what people are thinking even before they do sometimes. It's not a superpower, but I guess it's a gift. Haven't met anyone else who's able to do it quite like I can yet. That's how I knew it about him. He was already shouting when he walked in, but of course he wasn't walking in alone. These types always travel in groups — a posse. His was right behind him, stumbling in like they'd already been drinking for a few hours with those huge dumb smiles on their faces but waiting until their leader approved of some invisible thing before they spoke or walked toward the bar. Four of them, altogether, but the main one came right up toward me at the bar.

He did approve, I guess, because he started toward me

and the others dispersed. I had the towel in my hand and I was moving it like I was supposed to, the universal sign of 'I'm cleaning,' even though we all know it takes more than a whitish towel and a *Karate Kid* motion to clean a bar top, when he gave me the nod.

'The nod,' meaning that half-assed head throwback that couldn't possibly get any lazier. I'm a classier type, so I returned with a full, deep, frowned-faced forward nod.

"'Sup," he half-assed.

"How are you tonight?" I asked, raising my voice just a bit to carry to him over the low roar of the other patrons and the clinking of glassware. There weren't many — the way I liked it — but there were enough engaged in a card game on one side and a few in a deep conversation on the other to create a steady din.

"Good, man. Scotch, on the rocks."

"You got it. Weapon of choice?"

His micro expression clued me in, but to his credit he recovered quickly. "Uh, yeah, sorry. How about Macallan?"

"*The* Macallan?"

He looked at me for a moment. I knew what he was thinking, too: *It's that important to you that you gotta give the weight of a 'the?'*

I shook my head. "No, it's part of the name. It's called '*The* —' never mind."

He laughed. "Good stuff, man. Yeah, I'll take one of those, or whatever. On the rocks."

"12? 18? 25?"

He frowned.

"Years…"

"Ah, right. Uh, 12? What's the price on those?"

I shook my head. Imperceptibly to him, but it was for me. Bartenders — real ones — hate that. If you know what you want, it shouldn't much matter how much it costs, right? This isn't a '$2-you-call-it' bar, anyway.

I raised my chin just a bit. "12 year is eight a glass. 18 year, thirteen. And the 25… not sure you can afford it."

"Oh?"

"Oh."

"Don't think I have the money for it, champ?" he asked.

Champ? Okay, now I really was going to kill him.

"No, I'm not sure I've met anyone who does."

"How much it gonna set me back?"

"Well it's been sitting on sherry-infused oak for twenty-five years, so, let's make it an even $700."

"A *bottle?*" he asked.

I shook my head.

"Holy sh—"

"Yo, Dawson, this the place that dude was telling us about? Seems a little run down."

CHAPTER TWO

ONE OF 'DAWSON'S' — THE MARK'S — lovely friends had decided that shouting from across the room was an ideal way to have a conversation. And 'the room,' in this case, was my bar. A single, small, one-facility building set back from the street a ways but still lit enough to see the front door. I had renovated it myself with the help of a contractor friend, splitting the empty building in half so I'd have a nice front chamber for the drinking and sitting, and a back half split in two again — one half for the office and kitchen and the other for the restrooms.

I fell in love with the place from the minute I saw the listing. A buddy dabbling in real estate set up the meeting, and I was his one and only client before he moved on to his true passion — marrying a rich lady from the bay area and moving in with her and her kids. Anyway, the contractor friend and I spent a few weeks gutting the old restaurant and cleaning out the fried food smell, then framing out and drywalling the separating wall, then I hired a team for the grunt work. Restroom, electrical, plumbing — no one wants to do those jobs.

It was a hit with the locals right from the start. Part of the appeal, I heard later, was that when it opened I had refused to talk to the town's paper and the three idiot 'food bloggers' who'd come down from Charleston repeatedly that week. I didn't like press, what they thought they stood for, and I certainly didn't like the tight-jeaned hipsters who came in with their phone cameras clicking away, expecting me to give a shit about some-odd 'thousands of followers.'

The older locals thought I was a hero, and the younger ones thought I was a legend. It was weird — I was certainly neither — but I accepted the attention in the form of greenbacks. They liked drinking in a place that was relaxed. A bit old-fashioned, but relaxed about it. I didn't smack the youngsters upside the head when they would ask for an old fashioned and then frown at me when I wouldn't squish a bright-red maraschino cherry into a red Solo cup before I poured the drink.

Likewise, I didn't argue with any of the older ones. Twenty-five years ago I was twenty-five years younger, and there were plenty of folks twenty-five years my senior coming in. They all have their ways about them, like I do now. Some of them thought the only way to make a daiquiri was with daiquiri mix, and some of them thought 'Scotch' meant anything distilled last century.

Whatever. As long as they paid their tab and left a decent tip, I was happy. Doing what you love is only surpassed by doing *two* things you love at the same time.

And tonight I was going to do two things I loved.

I poured the kid's Scotch, the cheapest of the options I'd given him, and thought about how I'd do it. Guns and knives were always traceable, and even though I wasn't worried about local authorities much I had a business to run. Any questions I got meant downtime, and not-working time.

Poison, chemicals, and other exotic treatments were just that — exotic. That meant they were more difficult to exhume from the corpse, but once they were it was almost a sure thing that the higher-ups would get involved. Ditto about the downtime in that case.

Thankfully it's left up to me to decide how it's done. That was the deal, and that will always be the deal or I'm out.

I repeat methods, but not often. Usually there's some story-building involved, as it makes for a more natural climax and a much smoother transition to normal life… and I like stories.

Dawson's unenthused buddy walked over, hovering over the bar like I owed him something.

"Yeah?" I asked.

"What you make my friend here?" he asked.

"Scotch. On the rocks."

"I'll take one too."

I poured it and then listened. They always start talking, when there are two guys at the bar next to each other. Even if they don't know each other, they always talk. *Always*. If it's just one, they're either silent or they try to bring me into whatever it is they're dealing with. Women, it's the opposite. They want you to draw it out of them, or if there's more than one they'll sit there and wait for the other one to talk. If they're drunk — man or woman — all bets are off.

This time I couldn't tell if they were drunk or not. They started yapping about 'some chick' one of them had seen and/or done some stuff with, but I wasn't interested enough to know the details. I hadn't thought they were drunk when they'd come in, but listening to their conversation really made me wonder.

Kids these days.

Wait. Did I really just think to myself the words, 'kids these days?'

I felt immediately disgusted and simultaneously amused. I felt like I was turning into my old man, the curmudgeon of curmudgeons. Here I was pouring drinks for kids half my age, silently judging them behind a half-wall I'd built with my bare hands.

Probably while I had to walk uphill both ways in the snow to get home at night.

I decided to take a bit more interest in their conversation.

"…Because they smoke the whiskey when it's done," Kid B — not the mark — said.

"How do you smoke liquid?" Kid A — the mark, or Dawson — asked.

"I, uh, I think it's… they just add like that liquid smoke stuff I guess."

I shook my head. Enough to give them a clue but not enough to give me a headache.

"What's that?" the mark asked, turning his coiffure my direction.

I smiled. "Sorry — no, it's — hate to interrupt, but it's before the distillation process. They smoke *peat* and then add that to the fermentation. Then it's distilled out, but that smokiness is still in there."

Kid B had the look of '*who the hell asked you?*' on his face, but the mark, to his credit, seemed enthused. So I kept going.

"They age it in charred oak barrels after that. That's the number you see on these bottles — how many years it's been resting on oak."

"And the oak gets in there, and, like, flavors it?"

"Yeah, exactly," I explained. "It enhances the flavors by —" I stopped.

What am I doing? Am I really this bored?

One of the oldies came to the bar and asked for a couple margaritas. I recognized her, but didn't know her name. I held up an index finger at the boys and busied myself with the lady's drinks while I looked over to her table to make sure that she was actually sitting with someone. She'd entered with a younger gal, perhaps my age, maybe a little younger, and they'd started talking deeply about some issue or another before they'd even started drinking.

I always like to make sure someone's not drinking alone, and especially not ordering more than one drink at a time. I don't really have a rule against it, necessarily, it just seems like anyone so excited to get going that they need to have two drinks for themselves on the table at once is a little too excited for me to not pay attention.

The lady who'd ordered asked if we kept tabs open. I made the universal sign of 'yeah, sure,' by tucking my open palm out to her and shaking side to side and she seemed to get it, leaving her credit card there on the counter for me.

I finished making the margaritas — old, traditional style with no mix — and came back to the boys.

"What brings you in here tonight?" I asked.

The first guy — the mark with the amazing hair — thought for a moment. Maybe hesitating just a bit. "Uh, yeah, we wanted to go out, you know? Hadn't tried this place yet, but I got a tip from someone that it's worth checking out."

I nodded. "Seems like your buddy knows where the hot spots are."

I waited to analyze his reaction. Both of them seemed to think I was joking, that drinking here was a bit of a *step down* from their typical haunts. I went with it, smiling.

"I know, kind of a dump, huh?"

"It's — it's not the worst I've —"

"Tell the owner it smells like catfish in here," the mark said.

I sniffed, good and long and hard, just to show him I cared, then responded. "Yeah, we have a tiny grill back there. Catfish is our main dish, believe it or not, and Joey cooks the hell out of it."

"Really? Way out here?" Kid B said.

"Really." 'Way out here' in this case referred to the fact that we were nowhere near the big city as long as you didn't zoom out too far in Google Maps. The town was on the coast, the main road actually backing up against the beach in most places. My bar was only a few blocks from the beach, but since there wasn't a direct road to the coastline and the town sort of wound around a bit before meandering its way to the sand, it seemed like this was the last stop on the way to the inland areas, rather than the way I liked to think about it: a *first* stop on the way to the beach, if you were from out of town.

"Makes sense," the mark said. "Hey, this isn't half bad," he said, rotating his drink around in the glass like a pro. His eyes flicked up at me, taking me in, calculating something, and it was the first moment I thought of him as anything more than an idiot frat boy between summer flings. There was depth there, something unspoken. Something he hadn't even told his buddy.

It also irked me in that I didn't know how to respond. "Yeah," I said quickly. "Took me awhile, but I think I mixed it pretty well."

We stared each other down for a few seconds until he burst out laughing. "Nice — good one, champ. Just pure Scotch and pure ice, can't go wrong with that, right? Unless you're mixing something else in there?"

He said it with just a bit of a lilt, just the slightest of questions. I of course didn't think he was really *asking* me, since there was no way he could know I was the one who'd do it, but it took me a split-second to recover. "Not this time, *champ*. Just Scotch and frozen water."

CHAPTER THREE

I DID THE *KARATE KID* thing with my towel all the way to the opposite end of the bar where a new couple had come to sit. I noticed them walk in a few minutes before the mark and take up a place at a table to my right, but I hadn't gone over yet to check on them. Since they'd moved up to the bar instead of waiting for me to walk over, I decided to make sure they weren't upset with me.

"Howdy," I said. I neither like cowboys nor am I from Texas, but it seemed like a good fit in the moment.

Clearly I was wrong about the moment and I needed to step it down a notch, judging by the man's wide-eyed expression. He had a ring on his left hand, so I assumed this was a husband-wife pair, in for an evening of drinking.

"Sorry," I said, "just getting a little bored. Thought I'd try to have a little fun."

He looked at me like I'd just insulted his mother in a language he didn't understand, so I turned to the woman. I was about to ask what they wanted when I realized this was *not* just a typical Wednesday night visitor.

The girl in front of me was absolutely *stunning*. Her hair

was light brown, woven around itself and gently perched on top of her head, streaks of lighter blond interspersed through it all. Small diamond earrings brightened her face but took nothing away from it. She had a petite, youthful look in her eyes, yet she couldn't have been more than ten years younger than me.

He, however, seemed just a bit older. Maybe there was something offset about him, or I was just imagining it, but he had a distant expression and stoic stance, even as he leaned — curled forward like an aging librarian — with both elbows on the bar top.

Finally I found the words. "What are you drinking?"

I directed the question at the space just between both of them, as I couldn't look at him without asking what was wrong, and I couldn't look at her because… well she just reminded me…

Stop it.

I wasn't sure I wanted to go down that train of thought, at least not yet. She had something about her that seemed familiar, and I didn't think I liked that. Her beauty wasn't the same as a supermodel's or that of a Photoshopped actress on a magazine cover. It was simple, unassuming yet confident.

The man spoke first, while she just smiled. "Uh, yeah, I — give me a — or give her a martini… no, a Cosmopolitan. I'll have — I'll have a water, for now."

I hate 'for now.' 'For now' means they're either afraid to drink in front of who they're with or they just read too slow. If they just want a water, without the 'for now,' they're probably a recovering alcoholic or they're sick, or they're just not wanting to drink that night. I can respect that, but a 'for now…'

I turned around to make the drinks, but the gal got in a quick order: "Make it up however you like it. I'm not picky."

Her voice danced around in the air, and I immediately latched on to her words. I respected that. Every bar has their 'own way' of doing things, and most of them aren't any good. I don't like messing with classic drinks unless they need messing with. I'll squirt a lime over the top of a whiskey smash just to bring some of the flavors out, and I'll kindly redirect an unassuming victim asking for one of the 'candy martinis' like a Lemon Drop or a Washington Apple to something a bit more respectable, but I'm not about to screw with a tried-and-true like a Cosmo.

I made it up perfectly, using a jigger just to show her I cared, and brought that and the water back to them. They'd pulled up at the bar now, each taking a seat on an old wooden stool I'd salvaged from a liquidation a few months back, and started sipping.

I watched, waiting to see if the man was truly content with the lukewarm H2O-on-ice or he'd man up and get something harder, but he was still off in la-la-land. She, on the other hand, followed my eyes and finally caught up to them.

"This your place?" she asked.

It was almost like she already knew the answer to the question.

"Yeah," I said. I flicked over to the frat boys to make sure the mark hadn't taken off, then came back to her. "Been here ten years almost. Built it myself, trying to pay it off."

She smiled. "We — we're just traveling through." She motioned to the guy next to her. "He's my brother. We're heading to a funeral."

"Sorry to hear that," I said. "Staying here in town?"

She laughed. "Is there anywhere to even *stay* here?"

I returned a smile, nodding. "It's not big, but it's got everything you need. Came here to settle down myself, but that sort of morphed into 'making myself crazy trying to run a business.'"

She sipped the cosmopolitan. "This is really good. Thank you."

I wasn't sure if that was intended to be the end of our conversation or not, but as the man was still staring at the mirror along the back wall of my bar, I decided to see how the mark and his buddy were warming up to the night.

"…She wasn't even part of the —"

He stopped talking when I came over, and Dawson turned to me. "'Sup, champ."

"'Sup." I gave a one-shot back nod, like I'd seen the kids do, and tried to feign nonchalance. "Ready for a second round?"

"Uh, yeah." Dawson cleared his throat. "Probably need to be going after this," he said.

"Yeah? Whereabouts you headed?"

As much as I'd tried not to, I had picked up some of the lazy small-town speak of the area when I'd moved in.

"We, uh — we're going to —"

Kid B cut in. "Just around. We were told this place had a decent nightlife, but…"

I nodded, smirking. "I get it. Bunch of old folks clogging up the place. No music, no ladies. That about right?"

Kid B laughed. "Don't be so hard on yourself, man. It's a nice —"

I grabbed his drink — still half-full — and sloshed it up onto his shirt. On 'accident.' "My bad, bud, let me get a new one for you. On the house, of course."

He seemed rightly perturbed, and not a little bit shocked, either with the speed with which I'd sloshed him or the fact that I had in the first place, but he did exactly what I'd expected.

"Let me — thanks, for that — let me hit the restroom. Back there?" he flicked his head sideways.

"Mm hmm, yeah. Back there. Drink's waiting for you when you return."

When he left I turned my attention back to the mark.

"So, what else can I do for you this evening?" I asked. It was a long shot, that he'd just somehow and for some reason jump into a perfect explanation of why I should kill him. I knew it was vetted as well, by the boss, and that anyone coming in here as a mark was someone they deemed worthy to be offed, but I always got more proof. Just a little will do it, but I have to get it.

For me.

A lot of times it's as simple as following them home. Sneaking in when they're not around, checking message threads, emails, hell — one mark even left a sticky note on the fridge with the username and password of their online alter ego. An alter ego, I soon learned, that they used to lure adolescent children into scenarios that would allow this mark to 'interact' with them in person.

I didn't need to know any more details than that — the boss had already done the research and given the orders, I just wanted to make sure it was the right mark.

It's a sick world out there, and the kinds of things that piss normal people off drive me to do things I'm really good at: the 'sticky note' mark, for example, ended up skewered inside the smashed, twisted metal of a horrific vehicular explosion. What can I say? He came in and ordered an Irish car bomb.

Another one ordered a Sidecar. Respectable, actually, but I had no idea how I was going to find an actual, real-life *sidecar*, and even then what I'd do with it. Do you attach it to a motorcycle? Does it have to be one of those German ones they drove around in WWII? So I improvised and just ran him down with my car. A few times over the lower back to wake him up, then once over the neck to put him back to sleep.

But as I'd suspected, this particular mark wasn't going to fall for any stupid tricks of mine. He looked at me with those big, dopey, frat-boy eyes and then smiled.

"Nah, man, you don't mean what I think you mean, do you?"

I cocked my head sideways.

"Like 'happy ending' stuff?" He made the finger quotes when he said it.

I shook my head. "Sorry to disappoint. This is a respectable pub. I just meant food — you want any food?" At least pivoting to another topic didn't sound awkward. We *did* serve food.

"You mentioned that catfish. Any good?"

CHAPTER FOUR

I HAD JOEY FLIP A few catfish fillets on the griddle, as the smell of a single one cooking usually earns us a few more orders. I have no idea what the man puts on those things, except butter — *lots* of butter — but they really are delicious. I keep getting the town's 'best catfish' award, but in a town of 400 with about five other restaurants, I'm not sure it's much of a compliment. I have a plan to one day pitch to the Chamber of Commerce expanding the award to 'best grilled food' or even just 'best food,' but for now, I'll be the town's official 'catfish king.'

I came back out to the bar to find that the half-lovely couple had vanished. *Weird.* Her drink was still sitting there, a few drops of condensation finding their way down the spout and onto the bar top. His glass was completely empty, save for the ice cubes and straw.

I glanced around to see if they'd just moved somewhere else, hoping for a view of the beach — (there wasn't one) or just better company (there wasn't any). A group of older folks, regulars, sat at two of the five tables on one side of the place, talking amongst themselves. No one sat on the other side; the card sharks had taken off a while ago. The center of the larger room was empty and cleared, partly because I liked the idea that we might do some dancing in here at some point, but mostly because I liked the lack of clutter.

Joey knew the old folks' orders well enough to handle them, so he usually took care of drink-running while I parked it behind the bar most nights. It had the best vantage point, and with the addition of a small three-camera closed-circuit system with a monitor just beneath the bar top, I could keep an eye on the entire facility with just an eye flick.

So it was pretty obvious the couple had left — ditched without paying, too. I thought about checking the restroom, but it seemed unlikely both would go at the same time. Their chairs were empty, too. No purses, sweaters, hats. They were gone.

What struck me as worse, however, was that my frat boy friends were gone. The two that had pulled up to a table in the corner near the door were gone, and my mark's buddy was gone as well. The main man, too, was nowhere to be found.

Something bugged me in that instant. I felt the 'it' I talked about before. The sense I have about this stuff, it was suddenly there. I hollered back to Joey to watch the place, generating a positive-sounding grunt from the kitchen area, then booked it through the front door.

I dash out like this from time to time, so I didn't need to stop and explain anything to the regular patrons. I recognized Jimmy and his wife, a starlet-turned-smoker who'd nabbed an old, rich, retired guy after her forty year-run in Hollywood. They were across a table from Roger Pennington and Jessup McNaab, another pair of fisherman who had nothing better to do when the sun went down than barhop. And being the only bar like mine in town, they 'hopped' down here just about every night.

They barely gave me a glance as I got up to speed and nailed the front door. It flew open, and I had that silent freak out of wondering whether or not there might be a person trying to come in at that exact moment, but once again I lucked out. The street was dark, the single lamppost long since overdue for a bulb change and bug cleanout, and it took a second for my eyes to adjust.

When they did, it didn't help. It was still nearly pitch-black outside, and there was no one around. No cars, no late-night walkers, not even a dog alerting my arrival.

I turned and jogged around the back of the building. A small alleyway for trash pickup and deliveries separated my building from the thick wooded area that ran to the beach. The alley ended at my building, but ran alongside the woods and a few other establishments before connecting to the main road once again. Which, in my initial scoping of the property fifteen years ago, I thought to myself would make a nice hideout for some bad guys.

I saw the silhouette of the woman, only now noticing that she was decked out in a relatively formal-looking dress, standing with her back to me on her phone. I couldn't hear what she was saying, but it sounded like she was arguing with the other person. Her voice was mostly a whisper, punctuated by a few gasps and surprised breaths. In my opinion, not a good phone call.

I slowed to a walk and cleared my throat, knowing that jogging or running up behind a person in a dark alley is never a good way to start a conversation. Still, she turned and looked for me in the darkness with a weirdly scared expression on her face.

"Hey," I said, "it's just me. Sorry, I —"

I saw movement off to the right, farther behind my own building, and assumed it was her brother. Maybe he'd gone outside to relieve himself, which was weird, but not the end of the world.

The guy started running, and from the tiny flickering of the small light I'd installed above my back door, I could see him reaching inside the back of his pants.

Now, there are really only three things you reach for in the back of your pants: the first is contraband, but we weren't in an airport and if he'd shoved something up there was no way he'd be running so fast. The second is a wallet, and I had the feeling he wasn't excited to show off his new ID picture.

The third is what I was preparing for. I wasn't armed — my closest piece was still in a drawer in the tiny office inside — so I pulled out the next-best thing.

The white towel I'd been using to swab the bar.

I wasn't sure if there would be any use for it, but it was better than nothing.

Maybe.

The pistol came out, smaller than a 9mm from what I could see, with a suppressor attached. Possibly a Glock 42. Not a ton of stopping power, altogether, but there was hardly any distance between us. Even a suppressed .380 from this distance would do some damage.

I started running, hoping I was still in the realm of 'the element of surprise' against the mark. I figured he'd come out after her, knowing she was alone outside and somehow sneaking out by getting past Joey in the kitchen.

This guy's here for her, I knew. I no longer needed to do my due diligence. I knew the sort of asshole I was up against this time around — not a pedophile, but far from a stand-up citizen. Probably the type that preys on women only, assuming they were weaker and easier to nab.

I should introduce him to some of the ladies I know, I thought. I almost smiled, but knew I had to focus. I pushed the thought out of my mind and hauled it toward the attacker. His hair was floppier now, no match for a gentle breeze and running at full-tilt.

The weapon rose, and I jumped. He wouldn't dodge out of the way because it might screw with his aim — an unfortunate truth I learned about long ago. Sure enough, he stood his ground and tried to recalculate his shot since I'd suddenly gained a few feet in the air.

My head landed on his chest, but my left arm was out, pushing his right arm up and away as best I could. I'd placed myself directly in the line of fire, hoping the girl wouldn't move — or if she did, that she would move *toward* the building to our right and not out to my left where the bullet would go.

Crack! The handgun fired — suppressed but still plenty loud — and we fell, tumbling end-over-end a couple times before stopping in a mud streak that cut across the alley's asphalt. I was on top, thankfully, so I wrapped his legs into mine and sat high up on his stomach. I bounced as high as I dared a few times, hoping for a cracked or bruised rib, but unleashed with a couple hooks onto any open skin I could find.

Many times in this scenario my mark, not typically a fighter or scrapper, forgets where they are and simply tries to curl up and make it go away. Sometimes they have a little spice to them and they fight back, but they always seem to forget that their weapon is still in their hand.

This time my mark was *not* unaware. He flicked the Glock sideways, pummeling me in the temple and effectively removing me from his chest. I rolled, in pain, but recovered and swept out with a leg.

He jumped but it caught his right foot and he started to fall sideways. I took the momentary advantage and ran at him again, tackling him into the picket fence at the back of the alley. His body cracked, or the wood cracked, but he sort of imploded into himself and ended up in a sitting position on the asphalt, his back to the fence.

I wasn't done yet, though. I kneed him in the face, feeling more than seeing the blood spatter out everywhere, and laid in again with my fists. He groaned, but turned his head at the right moment and sent my left fist through a picket.

This hurt, and it severely pissed me off. But in that moment I realized I had underestimated my mark. Dawson rolled over and came up swinging, hitting me in the groin and stomach in two quick shots, then finishing with an uppercut that nearly connected. I stepped back just at the right time to dodge the punch, then fell forward onto him with a punch to his gut, simultaneously wrapping my leg around his.

This time I was able to get him falling backwards, so I pulled up on my leg, then jumped, aiming the point of my elbow at his sternum. I heard a pretty satisfying *crack* sound when we landed and felt something inside him give way, but I wasn't going to take any chances.

I'd already underestimated him once, but I'm not one to enjoy making the same mistake twice. This was the mark, and this man would die. I wouldn't get the luxury of deciding how it'd be done, but that didn't matter now.

I wrestled the pistol from his hand and saw his eyes bulge out, either from the surprise of it all or the pain that was no doubt sending scores of signals through his body. I lifted the tiny thing up the side of his head and didn't hesitate.

Like I said, a .38 at close range — or no range, like in this case — will do some damage. He was lucky he died immediately, as I was still pissed he'd gotten the jump on me, and almost on the girl.

I shuffled through his pockets as quickly as I dared, trying to feel for anything that might identify him. Trying to find the token…

CHAPTER FIVE

I TURNED AROUND, STILL KNEELING on top of him, still hoping the token had simply fallen out and rolled somewhere close by. I searched around a bit, but I eventually caught her eye. She was there, watching. She'd seen everything.

The white towel I'd accidentally dropped lay nearby, right where I'd started my run. In my haste, I hadn't even been able to come up with a plan to use it.

"You… you okay?" I asked.

I wasn't exactly sure what to do — there was rarely anyone else around, and in the cases that there were, I just cleaned up the mess of the second person the same way I cleaned up the mess of the first. The boss never *tried* to send two marks at once, but sometimes things weren't as simple as they seemed.

Like right now.

This girl had seen me kill a man, in cold blood and right in front of her. *Was she going to be in shock?*

"I'm…" she didn't get out more than the single word, a useless contraction that told me nothing.

I waited.

She still didn't speak, but I did notice that she'd already hung up the phone and put it away, into a pocket on her dress or something. Hopefully the person on the other end of the call hadn't heard anything strange.

"I'm sorry about that," I said, trying to make the best of it. *Make the best of what?* I thought. *There's a dead guy on my back porch, and this woman saw me do it.*

She was shaking, but she let me approach her. "He was running at you with a gun," I said. "I just… wanted —"

"I know," she whispered. "I know, I saw it. I — I hung up the phone, but you had already started —"

I didn't know what else to do, so I grabbed her and hugged her. It felt weird, since I was still riding high on the adrenaline rush, but still oddly comforting. For me. And she let me, even sinking in a little bit as I held her.

"Who was on the phone?" I asked, remembering her scared expression when she'd noticed me coming out to her.

"It was just… sorry, I've been on edge lately. It was a lawyer — nothing to worry about. You just startled me."

I nodded. "Where's your husband?" I asked softly.

She looked up at me, those amazing eyes just sitting there, trying to piece things together. "Oh, you mean —" she actually smiled. "That's my brother. He's — he went to the restroom, I think, and —"

At that exact moment a man's voice cut through the night air. "Hey! What do you think you're —"

She whirled around, ripping free of my hold, and turned to her brother. "No, Daniel, he was helping me…" She had her phone in her hand, waving it around as she ran up to him. I followed along, hoping we could stop Daniel before he got to the corner of the building and saw around it.

"You were… you guys were —"

"Daniel," she said, cutting him off once again. "Look at him in the light." She yanked me to the side and toward some invisible light she thought she could see, and pushed my chin up. "He's from our *high school,* back home. Don't you remember? He was a few years ahead of us, when we were in school, but — Daniel, you *have* to remember him!"

She seemed almost frantic now, perhaps realizing like I did that Daniel was mere steps away from stumbling onto a murder scene that involved his younger sister and a disgruntled bartender that was *far* more than 'a few years ahead' of them. She started walking forward, toward the front door of the bar, and Daniel and I followed along.

"Oh," Daniel said, "yeah, okay, now I see it, I think." He studied me from his perch a head shorter than me, looking me up and down as if he did in fact see something in me he recognized. He reached out a hand for me to shake, and I returned with my own hand. His sister kept walking, even picking up her pace as she headed around the front corner of the building.

Daniel was obviously distraught, barely able to comprehend what was going on, but I wasn't about to complain about that. He'd come in that way and he'd come out to us that way, so I just went with it.

We returned to the bar, the same regulars curled up in their tables with fresh beers in hand, the smell of Joey's catfish mingling with the hoppy aroma of freshly poured ale. I guided the sister — still didn't know her name — to her chair at the bar, and shook Daniel's hand again before walking around.

"I need to take care of a few things in the back," I muttered. "You guys sticking around for another? On me."

She nodded, a slight smile on her face, but not enough of one to cover the fear in her eyes. "Yes," she said. "Same thing, please."

Daniel looked at his sister, seeming to notice for the first time that she wasn't okay, then looked back at me. "Just a beer, please. Something light."

I poured his beer and mixed her drink, then placed them on the bar and turned to the kitchen. I could see Joey's small frame standing at the grill. I announced my presence before walking in, then brought my voice down a bit. "You see anyone come through here?" I asked.

He frowned, then shook his head. "No, I don't think — shit, boss, you got another one tonight?"

Joey is one of the few people on the planet who knows what I *really* do, aside from my stint as a bar owner. He did a run in the Navy, but I found him cooking down at a street cart on the beach in the summertime months. One taste of his shrimp tacos and I offered him a permanent nightly gig.

"Yeah," I said. "He's behind the bar. In the alley."

"In the *alley*? Damn, man, you usually get them out in the woods at least, maybe —"

"I know, Joey," I snapped. "But I didn't. Almost got the jump on me and the lady in there. Think you can trust me with the flipper enough to head out and start cleaning up?"

He shrugged, but sniffed loudly. "Yeah, of course. And it's called a *spatula*. When you ever going to learn? What we doing, anyway? Fishbait?"

I nodded. "Yeah, might as well. Nothing to salvage." *Fishbait* meant he would be taking the body, after it was bleached, through the woods to a small skiff and out into the bay. He'd go as far as he trusted the old motor, then wrap the guy tightly and hang weights on him that would keep him down long enough to, well, become fish bait.

He grabbed the bucket of bleach by the back door, a few heavy-duty contractor bags, and a spool of rope, then kicked the back door open and walked out.

CHAPTER SIX

BACK AT THE BAR, THE brother and sister were whispering softly to each other when I returned. I raised my eyebrows, asking a silent question, and she gave me a quick nod.

Everything okay?

Yeah.

It was all I needed, but I knew she'd need more. She would want closure, or an explanation, or just someone to process it with. I knew she wouldn't be telling her brother. Whatever that man was dealing with, he didn't need this dumped on him, too.

I figured I'd have to wait around for them to finish, get tired, and leave, then another hour or so for her to figure out how to ditch him and come back here, so I got comfy. I poured a finger of an old standby bourbon, local to the area, over an ice cube and added a bit of simple syrup and a couple dashes of homemade bitters. I was a bitters addict, and had about two-hundred varieties between the bar and my apartment. This one was a standard-issue herbal, tasting similar to Angostura's main issue with a little more spice, and it went perfectly in an old fashioned.

I gave it a stir and brought it to my lips, then noticed that the brother, Daniel, was gone.

"Went to get a hotel," she said. "We were just driving through, but someone at the airport mentioned we should check this place out if we had time."

I frowned. Both because there weren't many outsiders who actually *recommended* stopping in Edisto, but also because we were at the end of the map. No one is 'just driving through.' Edisto Beach is a town of about 400 situated at the end of highway 174, which itself is a meandering small highway stretching twenty miles down from 17 that bends out of Charleston. I told her as much.

"We flew into Charleston and were going to try to make it all the way to Hunting Island, but the rental car company at the airport was about as competent as TSA at the airport. But we saw a sign for a bed and breakfast, and we didn't know how far it was to town."

I nodded. I'd seen that sign off the side of 17, just before the exit onto 174. "Yeah, that place is old Marley's and his wife's. Decent stay, I hear."

We let the pleasantries die and suddenly I felt the weight from her gaze.

"Are we… are we going to talk about that?" she asked.

"I just want to know if you knew that guy."

She shook her head, looking down. "No, I've never seen him. I thought — I thought he just came out to smoke or something, but then…"

"Hey," I said, "it's okay now. I'm going to take care of it."

"You called the police?"

I scoffed. "*Hell* no." Realizing I'd picked my voice up a few too many notches, I glanced around to make sure the oldies were still satisfied with their brews and looked back at her. "Sorry. No, I didn't. And I won't. Something like that happens around here, in a town this size, it'd be the end of this place."

"But —"

"But *nothing*. I'm not asking for your input on this one. I said we're taking care of it, and —"

"You said *you're* taking care of it."

I sighed. *Dammit.* "Yeah, Joey's helping. He's… good with this stuff."

"He's *done* this before?"

"No, I — I meant…" *Shit, this girl's going to break me.* "I meant he was in the Navy, and had a rough background. I don't know, I guess he's just not as uncomfortable with stuff like this."

"And you?" she asked.

"And me *what*?"

"Are you *'comfortable?'* with stuff like this?"

I squeezed one eye closed just a bit as I stared at her. I didn't want to give her anything, but it seemed like she'd already pulled it out of me.

"No. You're never *comfortable* with shit like this. You just do it, because, well, that's what you do."

"That's what *you* do."

"Yeah, that's what I said."

She studied me for a few more seconds, then smiled. "You were good out there."

"Well, good thing, or we'd both be dead."

"No, I mean, did you see the way he fought? It was calculated, like he was… like he was a professional."

I stopped, putting the drink back down.

"Yeah, I picked up on that. Wasn't as easy to put down as some of the stray dogs we get."

"You do this a lot?" she asked.

She was in now, and she knew it.

"I do. More than I'd like, but I'm good at it."

She nodded slowly, processing. She brought the cosmopolitan up to her lips and took a deep, long sip. "Okay."

"Okay what?"

"Okay," she said again. "You're hired."

"I'm sorry," I said, confused. "I'm *what?*"

"You're hired. This is what you do, right?"

"I don't think you really know anything about what I do."

"That guy was going to kill me. You stopped it. Then you said you'd take care of it, and you won't get the cops involved."

"Yeah…" I said.

"So," she replied quickly, "I'm looking for someone like you. Someone who can help me. And I've got money."

I took in another swig of the cocktail, enjoying the perfect balance between the ingredients. Even the ice tasted great, releasing the water into the drink at just the right tempo. *Man, what I wouldn't give to just sit here and drink these for the rest of my life.*

I sighed again, then looked longingly into the top of the glass. "I'm not for sale."

"I have a *lot* of money."

This time I looked at her, trying to figure her out. She winked at me.

"Not interested. I don't even know your —"

"Hannah," she said, interrupting. "Hannah Rayburn, and you already met my brother Daniel."

I smiled. "I like that. Always have liked that name. We used to think… maybe if we'd —" I stopped. I didn't know her too well, so I didn't want to get into it now. Hannah had been the top of our list of girls' names, but we'd never had a chance to settle down and procreate.

She smiled back, seemingly knowing what I was trying to say. "Thanks. My father, Bradley Rayburn, apparently loved that name. He liked word games, puzzles, things like that, so he wanted me to have a name that reminded him of that. 'Hannah.' It's a palindrome. Spelled the same backward and forward." She choked up a bit, but kept plowing ahead. "That's actually why we're passing through. To get to his funeral."

"Sorry to hear about your old man," I said.

"It's okay. I mean, we weren't too close. He and Daniel were closer, and they worked together. He — my dad, I mean — he wasn't the best role model, I guess."

"Yeah, seems like that's one thing we got in common."

"Yours is still alive?" she asked.

"Yeah, for now."

I stood there, across from this gorgeous woman, drinking together and just sitting in the... *whatever* it was we were feeling, for another five minutes. There were questions I had, like why they'd *really* stopped here on a whim, coming all the way down from 17 instead of plowing on another hour and getting to Hunting Island. Or, for that matter, why there was a funeral on Hunting Island. Last I'd checked, the island was nothing but a state park, no houses or private property anywhere on it. I kept silent, trying to maintain a bit of distance. It was an old habit I had, and it had worked out for the best more often than not.

She almost dropped her glass, as if realizing that her brother might return at any moment and catch us in the act of catching up.

"Listen," she started again, "you can't say *anything* about this to him. To Daniel. It'll crush him."

"I don't make a habit of sharing the details of my moonlighting gig."

"Good. Thing is, and this is what I want to hire you for, I think… I think my father was murdered."

I cocked my head to the side a bit.

"He was in with some people I don't think he trusted. It was kind of the nature of his work, but I always just thought no one at that level trusted anyone else. It was sort of the cost of entry."

"And what was his line of work?"

"Importing."

I waited, expecting her to continue. She didn't.

"So will you do it?"

"What exactly do you want me to do? I'm not a private investigator, Hannah. I can't just — just start *looking around* and hope to find some guy that killed your dad."

"I know," she said. "I know that's not what you do. But if we could find them, if we could just figure out who *did* do it, then you could…" She looked at me those damn eyes again.

"Yeah," I said. "If we find them, then I could."

CHAPTER SEVEN

DANIEL CAME BACK IN FIFTEEN minutes later, ready to collect his kid sister for their trip to Marley's B&B for the night, but she met him at the door. They exchanged animated whispers for a minute, then she came traipsing back over to the bar while he departed.

I raised an eyebrow.

"He wasn't terribly enthused about my staying out late," she said. "But I told him you and I wanted to catch up a bit."

"How'd he take it?" I asked. I wasn't sure how much she told him, or how she pitched it. I didn't want to push it, but I also wanted to play the part.

"He thinks something's up," she said.

I raised the eyebrow even farther, adding a little head cock to underscore my confusion.

"He think's something's up with *us*," she said. "I didn't tell him anything about that body in the back."

I knew Joey would have cleaned up the body by now and would be just about to the center of the bay, ready to fishbait the sucker, but something else she'd said caught my ear. "Something's up with *us*?"

"Stop. I let him believe that. You know, old high school flame or something. Younger gal takes an interest in a *much* older guy. Never was okay back then, but now? It can pass."

"No, *you* stop. *Much* older? And what do you mean, 'it can pass?' If I wanted…"

This time she played the part of confused bystander. "If you wanted to *what*, mister…"

I realized I hadn't told her my name. I thought for a moment, wondering if I should give her a ruse, just to make sure we were safe. I examined her face once again, looking for any tell that she wasn't who she said she was. Like I explained, I'm really good at figuring this stuff out. So when the 'examining' became nothing more than 'checking her out,' I decided to go with the real deal.

"Mason. Mason Dixon."

She waited. "Wait, really? *Mason Dixon?*"

I nodded.

I thought she might launch into a tirade about my name, but she loosened her expression and went on. "And I didn't mean anything by it, I just don't appreciate the 'old guy' jokes. You don't even know how old I am."

"I'm going to guess you're thirty-eight."

I almost spit out my drink. For one, she was ten years off. Second, I *knew* I looked ten years older than thirty-eight. Hell, I might even look older than *forty*-eight. I had pockmarks from long-ago scars, scratches that even lit napalm couldn't smooth, and a nose that could sink the Titanic. And that was just my face.

"So, no?"

"No. Not even close. But thanks."

I took a moment to take stock in what was happening. There was a girl, a woman, a lady with the southern charm and common decency I typically find lacking in modern society, apparently with money, apparently with a request only someone like me could fulfill, and she was standing in my bar. In a town of 400 people, interested in me.

Interested in me.

That's when I knew I was off-base. I was assuming things that weren't true — they *couldn't* be true. She'd said it herself: I was way too old for her and the only reason she'd stayed behind after her brother left was that we'd had a shared experience. That experience, of course, had been a potentially life-changing and traumatic one.

I backed it down a notch. No one's ever accused me of being a 'nice guy,' but I've definitely been labeled a flirt. It's just my nature, though. I'm going to joke with the waiter or waitress, and I'm especially going to appreciate any attention tossed my way by the opposite sex.

"You want to guess mine?" she asked.

"Not really, no."

She scrunched up her face in a way I assumed she thought would make it uglier, but it backfired horribly.

"I have a rule that I don't guess ages and I don't guess if they're pregnant."

"I'm not pregnant."

"I wouldn't have guessed you were."

"Come on," she said. "Give it a shot. You'll be surprised."

I listened to her voice and watched her eyes. Of course I wanted to guess; I'd already started. I just didn't want to guess *out loud*, as that's when we get into the most trouble. But the voice and the eyes usually tell you everything you need to know about a person — not just age.

Her voice wasn't high like the schoolgirls, or thin like the city chicks, but somewhere deeper and thicker than those. It sounded like she was from somewhere nearby, like she'd grown up in this hellhole and escaped at a young enough age to go have a life and experience the world.

And her eyes — those eyes. My God, if my nose could push a laser-guided missile off course her eyes could correct it. They were big, fluffy, and brown in a way that I didn't know brown could be. They had a sadness to them, not surprisingly, but they also had a sharpness. A wit I knew I matched with my own baby blues.

"Twenty-five," I said.

"You're an asshole. Give me a real guess."

"Twenty —"

"No," she said. "Come on."

"Fine." I sighed. "Thirty… *three?*"

She laughed. "I'm thirty-nine." She said it and then looked away and peaked her upper lip in the corner like she was disgusted with herself. "Ugh. Thirty-nine. Almost *forty*. Can you imag —"

She cut herself off, but I was laughing. "Yeah, I can imagine. It's not so bad, really. Feels a lot like the other ones. It's really about who you're with."

"Who were you with that prevented your midlife crisis, then?" she asked.

I took a sharp stab at the remaining old fashioned in my glass, then mopped up an invisible spill with my trusty rag. "My wife," I said.

She didn't say anything, so I thought I should clarify a bit. "I buried her on my fortieth."

She opened her mouth, but then closed it quickly. I liked her; she didn't like to be rude. She came up to the bar and sat; I hadn't even noticed that we were standing close to each other, on the side of the room, until she started moving. She pulled up and dropped her head down a tiny bit, just enough to let me know.

"It's not a —"

"It's a big deal," she said. "I'm so… I'm so sorry."

"Really," I said. "I'm over it." *That was true.* "I'm a different man because of it." *That was not true.*

She pushed her glass out and toward me. I guess without even realizing it I'd come across the bar and took up my post, the drink sentinel once again. I grabbed it and started mixing.

"Wait," she said. "What's that — what are you drinking?"

"Old fashioned."

She frowned.

"Historically it was just whatever spirit the bartender has on hand, sweetened up a little, with a dash of bitters thrown on top and some cool water. Folks would come into the tavern and ask for 'their medicine' — the bitters — but they'd need it smoothed out a bit to help it go down. I like them, but I've tweaked the recipe a bit from the good 'ol days, since we're working with far better spirits. And we have ice. Still, it's a good drink. 'Sposed to be medicinal."

She smiled at me again. "I could use some medicine. I'll take one of those."

CHAPTER EIGHT

I POURED THE DRINKS AND we spent the rest of the night at the bar, just talking. Talking in a way that brought me back to the first days I'd opened, fifteen years ago, when the oldies weren't nearly so old and they'd come in asking for drinks that made my soul grow.

'Whiskey Smash' *meant* something back then, and it wasn't just a name on top of a description on a menu. It had *oomph,* real *impact,* a true drink that meant something. 'Martini' came with a set of preferences. James Bond would have gotten an earful trying to get me to shake his vermouth and gin, but he'd have eventually listened because I would have *made* him listen.

The conversations back then were as pure as the drinks. Even ten years ago. They would come in, heading right toward me — they never knew me — but they knew what they wanted, and I respected that. They had it in mind and on taste buds already. I could see it in their eyes. They salivated, knowing I could whip it up 'just the same way so-and-so used to,' and they tipped me well for doing it that way.

It was never about the money. It helped, but money was always a grace note to the larger orchestra hit. Seeing them swoon over a perfectly poured cocktail after I'd slaved over it, never grabbing for the unopened bottles of mixers (cheaters) that lay within reach, never allowing even a minuscule piece of pulp through my juice strainer into the glass, was what I did it for. I knew they'd appreciate the taste, even if they couldn't understand the process, but back then a few of them even asked about that, too. They wanted to know how I did it, how I took an egg white and some fruits and made them mad about a new whiskey I'd just gotten in.

Talking to Hannah brought me back to that. I knew I'd help her even before we discussed price. Most people can't afford me since I'd never done this sort of thing, but something told me she could, even if I changed my mind and *did* decide to charge her. She brought me back to the days when I could just stand at my tower and look out, talking to those who understood, ignoring the idiots who didn't.

Most of the marks were idiots, and I told her that. They came in confused, not really sure how they'd gotten there, but that was to be expected. I knew, but they didn't. Simple as that. They'd walk in, frown a bit as their eyes adjusted to the brighter light than outside, then they'd sit down and start drinking. Or talking. Sometimes both, if I was really unlucky.

But I didn't tell her about the token.

I couldn't — how could I?

The token was the coup de grace of it all; it was the last piece of the puzzle. The requisite designation that told me what I needed to know, even though I always tried to verify it for myself. Most of the time they'd slump it onto the table like it was an archaic gold piece, capable of getting them whatever they wanted. In their minds they lived in a world in which they *could* get what they wanted, and this was just another form of currency.

I didn't tell her about it because I was terrified of it. The token hadn't been on the mark's person. That was a first. It was *always* on their person. Somewhere, even if it was wedged between a sweaty sock and the sole of a shoe, it was always there. They sometimes forgot to 'spend' it with me, but they always had it.

I told myself Joey would find it — he knew to look for it — and focused again on the woman who had stolen my evening.

She asked about the way they were, the marks. If they were smart about it at all, or if they fit their stereotype and were driven by something other than the head perched on top of their neck. I laughed and told her that stereotypes were there for a reason, and you could tell by what they drank.

The idiot marks always drank something out of their league. They never really understood *what* they were drinking, they'd just seen someone — their father, their older brother, that 'cool' friend they wanted to be — order it and pretend to like it.

Micheladas, dry martinis, Jack and Cokes, these all fit the bill. Most guys had no idea *why* these were their drink choices, they had just always sidled up and ordered them. Sometimes it would be disguised a bit, like Bond's own 'shaken, not stirred' style. Wrong, but he liked it that way. He was fictitious, too, so it's hard to fault the guy.

I always figured that the first rule of not following the rules is you have to know why you're not following the rules. The marks never knew *why* they ordered things the way they did, and that's always the easiest tell.

I thought about the mark tonight, the one Joey was

taking care of. He'd ordered scotch, but he had been hesitant about it. Not in a way that meant he was drinking above his pay grade, but in a way that led me to believe he was just doing it because he thought it was the right thing to do.

"What did you think of that guy?" I asked.

"The... dead guy?"

"Well, yeah. Before he was dead." I am admittedly bad at making small talk, but I really had no other option at this point. "I mean, did he have any reason to kill you?"

She looked at me strangely. "You do realize that normal people don't talk like that, right?"

"I guess... yeah, sorry. Did you have any enemies? Anyone who might want you..." I stopped.

"Every sentence has the word 'dead' in it."

"I'm not trying to —"

"I know. Still..."

"Sorry. Anyway, you didn't recognize him?"

"Never seen him before in my life."

This was a typical answer, actually. The marks we dealt with in my line of work were the kinds who preyed on women they'd never seen before. Something about the unfamiliarity of it all made them think they could get away with it, I guess. I wasn't surprised she had never seen him, but I wanted to make sure I did my due diligence.

"You don't think he was a friend of your —"

"My brother doesn't really have friends."

I filed this statement away for later. If she was telling the truth, then her brother was something of an enigma. Everyone has friends, or at least people who know you well enough they'd call you a friend. Her brother, while obviously distraught after the death or murder of his old man, was still somewhat of a loner. He had barely spoken to me, and when

I'd gone out to find them, he was holed up in the restroom while his sister was outside on the phone.

"Your brother's married," I said, a bit abruptly.

She nodded.

"His wife?"

I wasn't sure what the question was, but I figured that any answer I got would be good enough for some information.

"His wife… what?"

Okay, I thought. *Maybe not.* I changed tactics. "His wife is… they're still married?"

She nodded. "Unhappily, in my opinion. She's a loose cannon, seems to be one of those that's in it for the money. None of us ever really liked her, but she's nice enough, most of the time. No kids, but they keep talking about it like we should all care." She made a face that implied she didn't really care much about when she might become an aunt, but I didn't press into it. "He's a bit 'out there,' as you've probably already gathered, but he's a good man. He's always been interested in making sure we — our family — are taken care of."

"Tell me about your old man."

"My father?"

I nodded, pouring some more whiskey into my glass. It was a diluted old fashioned now, the components all out of whack and hardly worthy of being called an old fashioned, but I didn't want to interrupt anything she might be willing to explain.

CHAPTER NINE

"MY FATHER — BRADLEY RAYBURN — HE'S a businessman," she began. "Always has been, for as long as I can remember. He currently runs — or used to, I guess — an importing business."

"You mentioned that already," I said. "What sorts of things did he import?"

"I'm not really sure," she said. "But he was *always* working. He owned the company, but I don't think he actually did much of the work. I mean, he was always talking to people and meeting with them."

"Sometimes talking to people is work."

She smirked. "You know what I mean."

"Where did he work?" I asked. "Did he have an office?"

She nodded. "Well, sure. Different places over the years, in different states and even overseas, I think. But he always worked from home, too. Down in Hunting Island, where we grew up. Daniel and I moved away for college and never came back home. Dad had a huge office there, off the east wing of the house, overlooking the dock and the ocean, and his yacht."

I cocked an eyebrow. Anyone who described a portion of their home using the word 'wing' and 'yacht' didn't live in a small place. "You grew up in a mansion?"

"Not a mansion. Well, it's big, I guess, but I wouldn't call it a mansion."

I laughed. "I bet I would."

"Fine," she said, smiling. "But growing up my mother, until she died, did a good job hiding from us the fact that we were wealthy. I only figured it out when I started having friends over. Their faces told me everything I needed to know."

"So your *mansion*, on Hunting Island, next to where he parks his *yacht*. I thought it was all state park down there?"

She considered this. "Yeah, I guess it is. We're on the northern tip of it, right across Johnson Creek from Harbor Island. I think he bought the land a long time ago from the state, or something like that, but it was always pretty hush-hush. Only house on the entire island, I think."

"Yeah, I would've sworn there were *no* houses on the island. Your old man must have been really close with some state bigwigs to swing a deal like that. So why would someone want to kill him?" I asked.

She shook her head. "I honestly have no idea. Money, I'm sure."

"How could someone get money from your father if he's dead?"

"I guess, I don't know… maybe they would get money *because* he's dead."

I nodded, taking another sip of the watered-down mixture. I was about to trash this round and start over, but I had her going on her father. I was in this now, so I decided I'd better sit up and pay attention. For the time being another drink could wait. "So you think he was into some... *questionable* business?"

"I know he met with some shady types, but I never thought..."

For a moment I thought she might break down and lose it, but she held it together. It was essential for me to get whatever I could out of her during this first phase of grief, as they'll often shut down completely within a day, and it could take months to open them back up again. Again, I'm no PI, but I'd seen this before. She was dealing with a whole slew of emotions — anger, disbelief, loss, fear — and I needed to dodge those mines and navigate through it to her core, where she could tell me the truth.

"I know this is hard, but if you can give me *anything* that might help me figure this out... It's a tricky business, but it's crucial that you're honest with me."

"You think —"

I held up a hand. "No, I'm not accusing you of not being truthful. You have been, and I appreciate that, but you're going to start feeling all of this a lot harder in a day or two, and it will potentially get... trickier."

She nodded, sniffing quickly. "I understand. Okay, I can tell you that he was into importing, and the company is called Crimson Club."

I frowned. "Crimson Club? They have a logo or anything? A website?"

"Yeah on the first one. Not sure about the website. He was always old fashioned."

"Sounds like I would have liked him."

"Well, you'd be the only one. He was kind of a jerk. When I was really little he was a great dad, taking us to the park, going to school functions, that sort of stuff. And he was funny, too, always tricking us with puzzles and making up terrible puns, but the more money he made the more distant he became. He got more and more serious, and aside from the obligatory birthday and Christmas gifts — always some sort of puzzles — he pretty much detached from me completely. He'd make sure I knew he was still there, I guess. Always telling me things like 'you're the key to it all, my Hannah.' Just an absentee father trying not to feel too estranged from his daughter, but we both knew we had nothing in common. He started working in the yacht all the time, just camping out there on the water. By the time I was in high school he had all but told us Daniel was the favorite, and besides giving me a chunk of the business and paying for school, he rarely reached out to me."

My ears perked up and my spidey sense started sending me signals. "Okay," I said, "hold on. Your father gave you a portion of the business?"

"Yeah, Daniel and I both have an ownership interest. But he never gave me any authority or even voting power. It was a 'tax decision,' he told us. But I'm pretty sure his plan was to bring Daniel in and have him run the business eventually. He was always by Dad's side, under his wing."

I had finally reached the floor of my glass, and tossed the cubes into the sink behind the bar. Hers was nearing completion as well, so I listened to her for another minute, talking about her home life, her relationship with her father, and how her brother was the 'chosen one' to him. It all seemed rather normal, at least for a wealthy family, in my opinion. I didn't know anything about wealthy families from firsthand knowledge, but I thought I had a decent enough idea from the people I'd met over the course of my life. Well-meaning parents, caught up in their business, slowly drifting away from their kids. Seemed to me to be nothing out of the ordinary.

She eventually drained her own glass and handed it to me. "Thanks — tell you what," I said. "It's late. I have some tidying up to do in the back, and then I need to touch base with Joey. Can we do this again tomorrow? You want to give me your number?"

"Sure. Do — do you think —"

"Yeah, I think you'll be safe. Actually, that was what I was going to have Joey do. He's got a good head on his shoulders, and I trust him. I was going to have him drop you off at Marley's and park it outside, then watch the house for the night. Kid can go a month without sleeping."

She seemed to like this plan, but I saw another question in her eyes. "What about you?"

"Me? Hell, I'm old. I can't go an *hour* without sleep."

She smiled, but I could tell she wasn't convinced.

"Look," I said. "I haven't been in the 'hunting people down' game for a long time, and even back then it wasn't like this. I've never been a detective. These assholes always come to me. I verify they're the mark, I take them down. That's it. So I have some brushing up to do, a few errands to run, and I was hoping to make a few calls."

"Okay," she said.

"Okay. Let's talk tomorrow. 5pm?"

She nodded, and I offered her an arm as I walked her to the front door. I heard Joey banging around in the kitchen, back from his errand already.

CHAPTER TEN

JOEY WAS SHORT, BUT NOT in a tiny sort of way. He was stocky, like a boxer, but built like a horse. He'd even boxed a bit in the Navy during his short time there, which meant he was a solid scrapper. I had sized him up when we'd first met five years ago and thought he'd make a good sidekick, so I pitched the idea to him. I told him a little about what I did, explaining the tokens and the marks. 'Find the token, take out the mark.' Really wasn't that complicated.

He did his characteristic shrug and asked a few questions, and that was that. When the first mark came by, apparently hearing about us from a 'business associate,' Joey was the one to spot him. I was in the kitchen when he came back and tapped me on the shoulder. "Yo, boss," he'd said, "I think I got a token. Guy came in from the city and slapped it down on the table saying it was so he could drink free. We don't do that, do we?"

I remember smiling and shaking my head. These idiots were always so bold and blunt about everything. Like they owned the world and it was their playground. "No, Joey, we don't do that."

I told him the play — I'd go serve him, giving him what he wanted for the night, then lead him out back when he was hammered enough to not care. It went *mostly* to plan that first time, but Joey did a bang-up job. He was cool, collected, and professional, even when the mark started throwing punches (he wasn't nearly as drunk as we'd thought). Joey gave him a solid sucker punch to the nose, sending him to the asphalt, and I finished the job.

Joey ended up having to burn the shirt he was wearing — blood doesn't really come out well, and you don't want anyone asking questions — but otherwise he was no worse off. He had taken the mark out and turned him into fishbait, then came right back in and started cooking up some catfish he'd caught that morning. During our late-night debrief, I couldn't tell which I was more impressed with: his catfish or his attitude.

I increased his hours on the spot, and raised his take on what I brought in from the marks.

It made a lot of sense to have him actually working at the bar while we waited around for the marks, instead of having him just stand around and look awkward.

Joey was in the kitchen now, the morning after our frat boy debacle. "Hey, kid," I said, getting his attention. "How'd it go last night?"

He was groggy, and rubbed his eyes, but otherwise seemed fine. "Need a nap, but it was good. No one else staying there, so no one came or went. I saw both of them head into town this morning, but I stopped following them when they hit the grocery store."

"Good stuff. Yeah, I doubt any of that loser's friends will be around. They probably had no idea what he was into."

"What *was* he into?" Joey asked.

"No idea," I answered. "But it's always one of the three

— pedophilia, pornography, or pimping." All of the marks were the types who stayed under the radar with the law. They were upstanding citizens in every way except one, and that *one* was the *only* reason our paths ever crossed. Most of them were into the former two categories, either buying and selling photos and videos of underage women (or men), or buying and selling the women (or men) outright. They had networks and circles that traded this shit, but they were the ones I was told to bring down.

Joey made a puckered face. "Ugh. Man, this world is messed up."

"Damn right it is," I countered, "but that's why we do what we do. Keeps me sane. Hey, by the way — you find anything on him?"

Joey frowned, then made a face. "No, I mean besides clothes and a wallet he didn't have anything."

"What was in the wallet?"

"Just a fake ID. Couple hundreds, three twenties."

I nodded. The deal was that Joey got to keep all that extra 'stuff' he found — I didn't need it, and there wasn't much we could do with it anyway. I considered it a tip for doing his job exceptionally well. "Good," I said. "The regular payment will hit your account tomorrow."

It was beneficial that Joey was on my payroll as a bar hand and kitchen staffer; he worked his ass off, so I had no problem paying him what I did. The IRS typically left me alone, as we had long ago established a chain of trust funds and nonprofits that satisfied the grayer areas of their abomination we call the US tax code. I figured that since we used the same loopholes used by the fat cats in Washington, they'd rather let anything fishy slide than open up that can of worms.

So far, so good.

"Nothing else, though?"

"No, boss, why? You —" he stopped mid-sentence like he'd just figured it out, so I hushed him before he started getting antsy.

"It's not that, Joey. I'm just making sure we didn't cut any corners."

"I *never* cut corners, you know that."

"I know that." I waited for him to ask again about the token, but he seemed to get the point.

We looked at each other for a second — the young, stocky cook and the old, grizzled assassin — then starting smiling like idiots.

"We need to get some sleep," I said.

"Bullshit. *I* need to get some sleep, old man. You didn't have to watch a bed and breakfast all night. What's with her, anyway? You hoping to hook me up with her?"

I squinched an eye closed and gave him my best Clint Eastwood. "The day I hope that is the day you fishbait me."

He laughed. "Well, she's a looker. You interested?"

"She's been through a *trauma*, Joey. I'm just doing my due diligence."

He had a smug look about him, and I knew what he was thinking.

"And she's married."

"No she ain't."

"Well she's got a boyfriend."

"Nope."

"Well I'm tired."

"Go get some sleep," he said, still chuckling. "I got this. Get back before four if you can — I'd like to catch a nap before the evening shift. That okay with you?"

"Of course," I answered. "Thanks, Joey."

CHAPTER ELEVEN

I HAD A LAUNDRY LIST of things to take care of between my chat with Joey and his 4pm ultimatum, but there was one item that sat at the top of the list. I grabbed an antacid from the back room, washed it down with some orange juice, then pulled out my phone.

I dialed the number I'd memorized years ago.

It rang.

Nothing.

No answering machine, no message.

Not surprising, considering the circumstances.

I considered throwing the phone across the room, but it was my only one. And I would never get through using Joey's. Instead, I grabbed a phonebook — the most useless object in the entire building — and chucked it over the shelf I'd set in the middle of the back room.

But the chucking I'd wound up for was far less powerful than I'd hoped, and the phonebook flapped open, caught the air, and slammed against the five-gallon bucket of sugar on top of the shelf. Problem was the bucket wasn't full, so it fell sideways easily and dumped its half-full contents of pure white sweetener onto the tiled floor.

I thought of a string of curses that would pair nicely with the situation and instead let out a long, slow, sigh.

Getting old sucks.

I wasn't even that out of shape. I knew the problem, and when I have a problem, there's really not much I want to focus on until I've solved it.

This problem was bigger and *much* more important than some spilled sugar.

I need to find that token.

I tried again, knowing what I would hear. Sure enough, no answer. "Dammit!" I slammed it shut— I still use an old-school flip phone because the thing just can't be killed and, let's be honest, I'm somewhat of a curmudgeon — and tossed it into a pocket. Heading for the back door, I grabbed my car keys off the hook and opened the door to the alley.

My car was parked across the small access road that goes to the alley, the same one Hannah had been standing in talking on the phone last night. I made it a point to check out the spot where I'd taken out the mark, to see how well Joey had cleaned it up.

As usual, there wasn't even a circle of clean asphalt where the body had been previously. Joey had taken the time to do something he called 'futzing up' the area, moving leaves and sticks around to make it blend in once again with the rest of the road. He'd even tossed a crushed beer can onto the spot, for effect.

And of course there was no sign of the mark. Once again Joey had performed his duties exceptionally well. Still, I glanced around once more, hoping that in the daylight I'd be able to see the sparkle of a token that might have rolled away.

I found nothing.

My car, a beat-up 1995 Toyota Corolla I refused to replace, sat waiting against the wall of the building next door. I hopped in, still frustrated, and started driving away.

I needed this money, and I needed it yesterday. My mortgage was due, and while the bar itself brought in plenty, I had planned on paying off the balance twice as fast as the bank required. Not to mention I had a place to live — a small rental on the other side of town — that needed to be paid for.

My retirement account was a joke at this point. I had taken the bulk of it out to afford the downpayment on the bar, and the rest of it was my collateral for the improvement loan I had taken out for the repairs and to flip the place into what it was today. There was still plenty more to do, but there would be time for all of that, I hoped. Some day.

I drove in silence, refusing to allow any music through the speakers that might accidentally improve my sour mood. Sometimes you just needed to be pissed, and this was one of those moments. I wanted to *feel* that I'd messed up, instead of just knowing it. I'd never not gotten a token before I'd taken out the mark, so I was already in uncharted territory. The fact that Hannah and her brother were hanging around while I helped her look for whoever killed her dad was just icing on the shitstorm cake.

I knew the *real* reason I wanted to help her. *It was her.* She was… what was she? I didn't know her, but I felt like I wanted to. I needed her in my life right now, even if I didn't fully understand why.

Best of all, I was sane and lucid enough to know that my feelings for her were exactly *why* I shouldn't have anything to do with her. Still, I knew I'd wrap my life around hers as much as she'd let me, even after knowing her for mere hours. I really am a desperate fool.

I finally gave in and turned on the radio, hoping something there would jumpstart my thoughts onto a different path, but an old Johnny Cash crooned out into my ears and solidified everything I'd been churning through.

First things first, I told myself. *Get that money.*

I made it through the one-street town and up into the backcountry, heading northwest on 174, away from the coast. About two minutes up the road I pulled the Corolla off and drove along the shoulder for a half mile, going slow, until I found it: a small opening in the stretch of trees that perfectly masked a tiny old dirt road. I turned onto it, making sure there weren't any cars in the rearview mirror or coming over the road in front of me, then kept driving.

The old Corolla had been through hell with me, but I'd rebuilt it twice and had a friend in town who helped with smaller repairs when I got too busy to do them myself. It was a solid, reliable, easy-to-fix piece that got me where I needed to go, but every time I drove this path I felt my knuckles tighten up. I always thought that I'd be walking home, leaving the old ride dead somewhere along this road, the engine finally used up and the suspension wasted.

Surprisingly I made it through the trees yet again, and brought it to a stop just in front of a massive boulder. The rock was one of many that had somehow been strewn around here from something during a previous epoch in time, and the whole of them together formed a natural opening in the forest, large enough to walk around in yet small enough for the trees to pull back together high above my head.

I hadn't found this place — the boss did, I assumed — but I liked it. To me it wasn't only a place to find my money, but it was a place of solitude. I likened it to Superman's Fortress of Solitude, except a bit warmer most of the year.

Sometimes I came out here even if there wasn't money waiting for me. It was nice to get away from things, even though the town I lived in now would have no trouble making their city's slogan 'the place you go when you want to get away from things.' My fortress was even more away from things.

I don't know how the path had ever gotten there, but I'd never seen anyone else on it. I assumed it was cut by a moonshining outfit from years ago, using these rocks as a perfect hideout as they made their liquor. Still, there wasn't a water supply anywhere nearby that I knew about.

I took a minute to smell the air and enjoy the perfect calm of the woods. It was still, but not quiet, the sounds of small mammals and the godforsaken seagulls penetrating the walls of my fortress and into my head as I stood there. Finally, I started walking.

Past the huge boulder, around two more smaller ones, and toward a fourth that sat at the back of the line, along the perimeter of the circle. I came to the side of it and knelt down. Feeling around in the leaves, I looked for the loosely packed pile of dirt that meant I'd found it.

When I did, I started digging. The dirt was loose like it always was, the only sign that someone had come through here and tampered with a bit of Mother Earth. About a foot down, I found what I was looking for. The top of the metal box was rusty, but it worked well enough to keep out the majority of the moisture and crap in the ground.

I pulled it up to my lap, greedily hurrying as I reached for the small padlock and began to unlock it. I knew as soon as it was resting on my thighs that there was something wrong.

I finished unlocking it and swung open the lid, hoping that I was wrong and that the weight was throwing me off.

It was empty. Even the silk bag that kept the money out of the weather was gone.

"Shit." I didn't yell, but I didn't need to. Inside, I was screaming.

I said it again a few times, all while looking down at the empty box.

What happened? I hadn't found the token, but there was no way the boss would have known that and come back to remove the money. There was no way he could have known that I didn't have the token on me *now*.

"Shit."

I flung the box into the hole, kicked a bit of soil on top, and stood up, brushing my palms off on my jeans. *This is not good.* I didn't even bother making it look natural. It didn't matter now.

I'd left the Corolla running, knowing I wouldn't be long, and I always did like the idea of making sure I had a fast getaway plan. As unlikely as it might be out here, I didn't want anyone getting the jump on me.

Getting back into the Corolla once again, I took the phone out of my pocket and dialed the number a third time. I shut the door and listened to the ringing over the sound of the engine.

This time I didn't even make it through a full cycle. The ringing cut off after two and a half rings, and I knew the boss was sending me a message.

You screwed it up.

I knew he was right. *I screwed this up.*

CHAPTER TWELVE

THE END OF THE DIRT path seemed farther away this time. I wasn't driving it any slower than normal, but there was something that felt *unending* about it. Maybe it was the deep feeling of dread in the pit of my stomach, or that I was just paying extra attention to every tree root and shrub I drove over.

Still, the end came, and I was about to pull out onto the main road and head back into town when I saw them.

Two cars, going slowly along the shoulder, coming my way. They were about a hundred feet away, but I made the mistake of stopping and staring at the first car to see who was in it.

They sped up, and I didn't get out of the way in time. I reacted slowly, smashing my foot on the pedal, and the Corolla lurched forward and up, nearly catching air as it sailed over the edge and out onto the road.

The first car reacted with me, though, and turned just a little bit to make sure he was still heading straight at me.

I felt the impact at the back corner of the car, heard the

crunching of the metal-on-metal, and braced myself. In that instant I realized I was not wearing my seatbelt.

I flew sideways, smacking the side of my head against the window, then flew the other way, this time coming up out of the seat. The car was spinning, but there was plenty of momentum to carry me into the passenger seat and nearly through that window.

The car stopped moving, and I took a quick second to take stock. Nothing felt broken, but nothing felt good, either. I groaned, forcing blood back into my head so I start using it. *Think, dammit.* Nothing useful happened, so I sat up to get more information. I looked around, seeing only the second car driving by. The car that had hit me was gone.

I crawled back over to the driver's seat and started working myself down into it to see how bad the damage was when I saw the first car again. It had gone over the hill and was now bearing down on me again, aiming for my dinky beater once again.

I smashed the pedal down once again and found that my trusty ride still had a few lives left, and we shot off down the road. A glance in the rearview mirror told me two things: the second car was turning around to join the chase once again, and the first car, apparently having suffered zero damage from its earlier impact, was going to catch up to me *fast.*

The car was a Buick, I think, and it was much larger than mine. I knew them to drive like boats, but I also knew they could take a beating. If there was ever a tank built for consumer use, it was made by Buick.

I gave it everything my little Toyota had, but it wasn't enough. I had just enough time to strap in and buckle the belt when the Buick smashed into my back. I pushed hard against the steering wheel just before impact, hoping it wouldn't buckle my arms in half.

My arms were fine, but I screamed in pain anyway when my head crashed backwards into the headrest. I tried to recover, but the second car had somehow found its way in as well, and it hit, a bit softer, but threw me back into the headrest once again.

I blacked out, for how long I don't know, but I blacked out and then woke up and they were there around me, walking toward the car's window. I opened my eye, just one of them, to check it out, and saw them.

They weren't thugs, but they didn't strike me as seasoned professionals. Maybe hired guns. They wore street clothes, but both had cargo pants that seemed loaded with something and shirts that were tucked in. They were even wearing belts. Sunglasses, caps, and boots to finish it off. I smelled ex-military or off-duty cops all over them.

I felt the blood on the back of my head, but it was a minor injury and would have to wait. My right shoulder throbbed, and I thought my wrist might have a small fracture, but still I ignored it all. I focused only on my next move: I had to get out of there, but I wasn't sure I could still drive. I wasn't sure the *car* could still drive.

The guy tapped on the glass.

I pretended like I was still blacked out, hoping they'd give me at least something before I was forced to do something.

"Just take him out," the second man said.

"I will," the guy at the window replied. His voice was lower, a bit gruff. "I want to see if he knows anything."

"That ain't the job, remember? We don't need to know *shit* about this guy. Just do it, and let's go."

I knew that 'just do it and let's go' meant a couple things: for one, they weren't interested in making it clean, like I always do. That meant they were being paid to do it, but they didn't care about any more details than their employer gave them. They might do it to make sure they weren't somehow discovered, but they weren't going to spend any more time with my cadaver than they needed.

It also meant they were in a hurry. Again, money. These guys got to be in a hurry when the money was good, and it was quick to acquire.

I waited, my heart starting to pound. I was taking a major risk, a *stupid* risk, waiting. But it was the only way to figure out who they were.

Unfortunately, the exchange seemed to be over. The first man fumbled with my car's handle and I heard it creak open. I squeezed my eye open just enough for the cloudy outlines to give me a rough idea of what was happening.

I saw a blurry pistol coming toward my head, and I knew it was time. I clocked the second guy at about five or six feet away, but I couldn't see any weapon on him. Either he didn't have one pointed at me or my blurry squeezed-eye vision was useless.

I waited until I felt the steel hit my temple and I jerked my left arm upwards. The man's forearm smacked the top of the Corolla and the pistol flung out and down, landing right in my lap.

He tried to get out a few choice words, but I already had it in my left hand and was pulling the trigger when I started the engine again with my right. Aiming for the spot just above his hip, I fired. Twice.

It wasn't intended to be a kill shot — kill shots tended to kill people, and I didn't want more loose ends to tie up. It hit right where I'd intended, and he stumbled backwards as the second guy grabbed at his own piece. It was hidden behind his back, tucked into a belt, but I got him before he had it out and around.

Again, aiming low, I fired. I missed the mark, hitting him

in the thigh instead, but I wasn't going to give him a chance to fire back. I watched him fall to the ground, nearly landing on top of his partner, when I peeled out and took off.

I found that my damaged ride was good for about forty miles an hour before it started to shake violently, so I eased up and let it sit there, checking impatiently in the mirror to see that they didn't get back up. I had been shot through the shoulder a long time ago, and I knew any bullet anywhere in your body was not a happy feeling. They should be down for a while, and even if not they'd have a difficult time driving home.

There wasn't a chance in hell they'd go to the *real* cops, but there was a small chance the cops would come to them. Highway patrol was out here every now and then, checking things out, and it would be just my luck if they happened to be out this way and saw two bleeding bad guys on the side of the road.

Even then, I figured it was still unlikely they'd just start telling the cops the local bar owner was a murderer. These guys were professionals, hired by someone to take me out, and they wouldn't just give the police free information.

I had time, but not much. I needed to get back in town and get started. This was all connected somehow, I could tell. That *feeling* was there again, and I knew to trust it. I had to get back to the bar, to check in with Joey.

And I had to get back to *her*.

I checked the clock in the car, noticing it was a few minutes past four.

Joey would be pissed.

CHAPTER THIRTEEN

"HEY, BOSS MAN," JOEY SAID as I entered through the back door. "Where you —" he cut himself off when he saw me. Our eyes locked for a moment.

"I'm going to need to ask a favor," I said. I explained quickly about the guys who'd attacked me, leaving out the part about what I was doing out that way.

"Yeah, I figured. No nap for me, but that's all right."

"We need to get Hannah and Daniel out of Marley's and back here."

"Here?"

"Well, somewhere besides Marley's. We can't watch the entire place with just two of us, and still stay out of sight ourselves. Plus, I have to get started finding her old man's killer."

"You're still doing that? Should we —"

"Yeah," I said, "we'll still get these assholes who attacked me, but we still have to figure out who was out to get her father."

"Why?"

I sighed. He was on to me, and it was only going to get

worse unless I had an ally. "Because, Joey. We need the money. And now that my car's hanging on by a thread…"

"You having it fixed up?"

"It's getting towed sometime within the hour. I'll have Billy look at it over at the shop, and tell him to get it rolling again. Hopefully won't be putting me out any more. All the more reason to get some money coming in."

I waited for him to ask more about it, but I think he understood. He walked over to the grill and fired it up. "Well, I guess I need to eat if we're going to do this. Catfish?"

"No, thanks though. I'm good."

I reached into my pocket and grabbed the flip phone and started dialing Hannah's number. I still had over half the battery charge remaining, and the phone was still in perfect condition even after slamming it around in three car crashes.

She picked up after a few rings. "Hello?"

"Hey," I said, "it's me. How are you?"

"I'm… bored. Been holed up here all day. We still on for 5?"

"How about right now?"

There was a pause. "What happened?"

I shook my head, as if she could see it, then added. "Nothing. Well, nothing much. I'll fill you in when you get here. You think you can borrow the car?"

"It's a rental. My brother has it. He left a few minutes ago to get some wine, I think. Only thing we didn't grab at the grocery store."

"Okay," I said, looking at Joey. He flashed me a thumbs-up sign and I put the phone back up to my ear. "Okay, Joey can let me use his car. I'll come grab you. Leave a note for your brother."

Joey's car was blaring godawful rap music when I put the key in, so I pressed scan on the radio until I found some oldies. Wasn't a great song, but it was oldies, which meant it was automatically better than anything post-1980.

I drove fast, pushing it up about ten over the 55-mph speed limit until I reached Marley's. He was out on the porch doing some gardening, and he waved when I pulled up. I gave him a single nod, hoping it came across as 'I'm-pretty-busy-but-certainly-not-rude,' but truthfully I didn't care. I could patch up any hard feelings later over a free drink. Marley and his wife were staples in this town; they had always been here and it seemed like they always would be.

The bed and breakfast, Marley's historic old plantation home, was gorgeous. I'd never been inside, but I'd lusted over photos of the interior many times, jealous of the century-old crown molding, attention to detail, and overall perfect appointment of each of the rooms.

I wasn't much of an artist, but if I had to be, I'd choose architecture. Something about the way things are put together on a large scale, retaining their natural beauty while still providing function, has a lot of appeal to me.

I called Hannah and told her I was outside. She told me she was finishing up her shower, which I took to mean she was just starting it. I told her to take all the time she needed — I had to make a call.

This thing had gotten out of hand, and while I didn't really have anyone but Joey I could bring fully up to speed on the situation, I still needed to call in someone that had more resources. In this case, I needed information. I dialed.

"Hello?" the person on the other end said.

"Hey — Truman?"

"Shit, Dixon? Is that you?"

I chuckled. "Better believe it. Wasting away down here in the south."

"How far south? You moved away from the big city, then?"

"South Carolina, on the beach." I didn't need to go into details; technically the beach *was* close. "Listen, Truman, we definitely need to catch up. The bar's doing well, and it's all-you-can-drink on the house for you if you ever make it down this way, but I need a favor."

"Yeah, of course. Anything for an old friend."

"Not as old as you." I paused for him to laugh. "It's — it's hard to explain, actually, but I'm trying to track someone down."

"Uh, Mason, you know I can't —"

"No, no, I understand. I'm not asking you to get into any trouble. Let *me* get into trouble tracking this guy down, you won't even need to know the name. I'm just trying to put the pieces together, find out who he was working with, that sort of stuff."

"Ok, yeah, I guess. I can only keep it general. High-level, you know? Unless you have a warrant…"

He left it hanging, as if he meant he could only look the other way if I had a warrant — even though he knew I wasn't in a position of authority that might allow me to use one. He was an old friend, and wanted to help out, and I appreciated that.

But I wasn't about to get anyone else caught up in this mess.

"No, again, it's not really a search like that. Just 'casting the net,' see what I pull in."

"Got it. What is it?"

"Organization, probably a corporation or partnership. Called 'Crimson Club.'"

Long pause.

"You there?"

"Uh, hey. Listen, Dixon, get out of whatever it is you're in, man. Not worth it."

"Wait, what's up? You've heard of them?"

"Dammit, man, *everyone* up here's heard of them. And every other department as well. They're blowing up right now."

"What — what are they? I was told they were in importing."

He snickered, then actually laughed. A full-fledged laugh, right in my ear.

"Yeah, importing. Sure, I guess. That's what would be on their manifest, anyway. But *no*, they're not *just* importing. You probably picked up on that."

"I picked up on that. That's why I called you. Can you help me or not?"

"I'm telling you, honestly, *stay away from this one*. It's bigger than you are."

"Most things are."

"I don't think you get my point. Let me be as clear as possible: This is out of your jurisdiction. Whatever you're wrapped up in, fixing it by digging into these guys is *not* something you need to do. I've got a case file on them open on my desk right now as thick as my arm. And it's not just us — DEA, CIA, hell, even Homeland Security's got a file."

"Shit."

"Shit's right. These guys aren't just priority uno, they're priority uno for *all of us.*"

"Why?" I asked. "Why now?"

"They've been blowing up. Doing *massive* business."

"Importing, still?"

"Importing, exporting, buying, selling, whatever you want to call it. But Crimson used to operate mostly overseas, targeting third-world and emerging nations for their 'unique offerings.'"

I knew 'unique offerings' was a government term Truman had used before, and I was pretty sure I knew what it meant. But I had to know for sure. Something was nagging at me about this whole thing, and I needed to know. To hear it from him.

"What kind of 'unique offerings,' Truman?"

"Hell, man, what do you think? Pedophilia is the big one, and I don't just mean media escalation, either."

Media escalation was another term he threw around every now and then, and it meant something that was outlawed or criminal becoming sensationalized into the worst possible form of the root issue. In the States, when someone just below the legal age had willing intercourse with someone just a little bit above it, it was considered statutory rape. It could be consensual, even, but that didn't stop the news from reporting it as 'pedophilia,' or 'rape of a child,' which conjures up far different images than a high school romance taken too far.

But I knew what he meant. There was no media in these parts to escalate anything — the reports he was reading didn't need to be escalated any further.

I sighed.

"Yeah," he said. "It's bad. We've got a few low-level ringers in custody, but we're hoping for the big fish. The head of the company itself is likely behind it, even. I can't tell you his —"

"Bradley Rayburn. He's dead."

"How — do you —"

"Wikipedia."

Another pause. "Okay, yeah, I guess that's an easy one. "But still. Stay out of this one."

"I can't. I'm in it. Anything you can do to help me —"

"You can get out of it. You're out-fielded on this one, man, I'm serious."

"I understand. Listen, I'll deny calling you. I know you've got fancy stuff for that and everything, but it's the least I can do. Hate to see you getting in trouble with the boss."

He laughed again. "I *am* the boss. You know that."

"Right," I said. "Thank you, again. Talk soon?"

"You got it."

We hung up, and it was the same moment Hannah emerged from Marley's house.

CHAPTER FOURTEEN

SHE LOOKED *STUNNING*. HER HAIR was wavy, slightly curled so it bounced as she moved.

And I couldn't help but notice it wasn't the *only* thing that bounced as she moved. She had a skirt and a white blouse on, frilly on the edges — not sure what else to call it. The skirt wasn't too short, but it certainly wasn't too long, either. Her legs, thin and tanned, melted down to her feet, just long lines of perfection. Her shoes were those expensive burlap sacks I see younger women wearing these days, but somehow she made them work.

I didn't want to seem like a creep, but — dammit she was *beautiful*. I forced my head back up to a reasonable height.

I couldn't tell if she was wearing makeup, which probably meant that she was, but she was *really* good at putting it on. No lipstick, unless it was the same tone as her lip color, but in that case, why bother?

She came around the other side of Joey's car and I stumbled a bit, realizing I should have gotten out and opened the door for her. Instead, she'd caught me gawking.

The best I was able to do was flick at the inner handle a bit with my right hand fingers, catching it just as she pulled on the outside handle.

And preventing her from being able to open it.

We did it again a couple times until she was laughing and I was all but ready to break the damn thing off and kick it open, and finally she got it. She swung in and fell into the squishy seat, then closed it and turned to me.

"How you doing?" she asked. Then, "what happened to you?" her face soured.

"It's… nothing. A scuffle." I would explain — maybe — but not right now. Right now, I was focused on *her* face. *My God, she's stunning.*

I tried to change the conversation back again by answering her first question. "Good — uh, good." *Doofus.*

"So you don't know how to open a door for a lady?"

I felt my cheeks flush. I was embarrassed, a feeling I'm not sure I'd felt since junior high. "No, I, uh, I'm sorry. It was just…"

She raised her chin a bit and gave me a smirk. "Was it just *me?*"

Damn.

"No, I was admiring Marley's handiwork by the garden. You see those —"

Suddenly I felt my face pulled to hers, and her hand on the back of my head. She pulled me in and kissed me. Just a little one, like promise of more to come, then it was over.

"I — uh…" my cheeks were going nuts.

"That was for last night," she said.

"Um, thanks?"

She laughed.

"Usually my clients just leave tips, but I guess I could get used to this."

She was still holding my head, but she turned serious. I thought I could even see her eyes glossing over. "I'm not joking. Thank you. This — this has all been so *crazy*. We have the funeral in a few days, and — "

"I know," I said.

"You know?"

"I know what it feels like to be forced into something. Something that breaks the chain of expectation. Your father, now this traumatic experience. Yeah, I know."

She nodded, let go of my head, and looked straight out the front window.

I matched her gaze and started driving. "So," I said, "we have something to talk about."

"Yeah, we do. My dad —"

"Not your dad," I said.

She flicked her head back and stared at me. I kept my eyes focused on the road.

"You. We need to talk about your *real* involvement in your dad's company."

"I told you, I don't have any — I don't know what they *do*. He always kept me out of it, and my brother only knows a little bit of it."

"What *do* you know? You're a part-owner of Crimson Club, aren't you?"

"Yes, but… but I couldn't even tell you the names of the other board members."

"Fine," I said. "Let's start there. It was — is — board-run?"

"Yeah, they manage it. But my dad was definitely the most involved one. Probably the most powerful. That was important to him, I think. We always had a great house, and he was always entertaining, always taking people out to his yacht. Wanted to show off a bit, I think. He used to tell me all the time, 'the secret to a great business like mine is in the yacht.'" She laughed. "Like that was it — you just buy a fancy yacht, and immediately your business is successful."

I didn't know anything about multi-million dollar businesses *or* yachts, so as far as I knew, the old man might have been right. "Did he ever talk about what sort of importing they did?"

"No," she said. "When I was a kid, I thought it meant exactly that — like he was buying stuff in other countries and bringing it into the United States. He used be gone for weeks at a time, but then he would come back and he wouldn't have anything with him except the luggage he left with. So I didn't understand what it meant."

"But later?"

"As I got older I figured out that it was a business, not a one-man operation. He could have been doing just that, buying things and getting them into the country, but doing it through his company instead of actually carrying stuff with him. Still, I never knew what he imported. I asked him once, and all he said was, 'whatever pays the biggest margin,' like that was supposed to mean something to a nine-year-old."

"But he treated your brother differently?"

"Yeah, definitely. When he was getting through high school they were nearly inseparable. They hunted just about every weekend during the season, and they camped throughout the year. My brother always liked him, but it was a respectful sort of 'like,' not really a typical father-son relationship."

"And what does a typical father-son relationship look like?" I asked.

She smiled. "I have no idea. I guess I mean it seemed like my brother was always afraid of him just a little bit, like he was trying to please him or make him proud."

"You know, actually, that sounds *exactly* like a typical father-son relationship."

"Yeah, but most dads aren't doing illegal importing."

"Why do you think he did anything illegal?"

"Well, like I said yesterday, I got the impression he was in with some bad people. I know it's a big world out there, and there's a lot of money to be made, and I knew my dad to be the kind of guy who wouldn't really bat an eye at the *how* as long as the *how much* was big enough."

"Yeah," I said. "I know the type. But he never said or did anything that made you think that?"

"Not really. Not directly. Just… a feeling, I guess."

"You have a good gut about this stuff?"

"Yes, sure. Maybe."

"Well, I'd trust it. Your old man was *your* old man. No one probably better to say that than you."

She sat, silent, for a minute. I swung by the single gas station on this side of the road, stopped, and filled up. I liked to do things for Joey like this every now and then. I'd had a boss a long time ago that did this sort of thing, and it always made me feel so much better about my job. And it made me like him even more.

She waited inside while I did it, then I jumped back in and started the engine.

"Hannah," I said. She looked over, and our eyes met. "I like you. Probably not a secret, and I'm probably not the only one who's said that to you. You've got — you've got a 'special something' about you, and I promise it's not just that you're a knockout."

She smirked again, then raised her eyebrows, silently asking for the 'but…'

"But," I continued, "I *have* to trust you. I need to know

if you had any involvement in what Crimson Club *really* does."

She swallowed, then nodded. This time, she started to cry for real. "No," she answered. "I don't have any involvement in what they do. My name is on a few documents that give me an eight-percent share in the company, but I can't even do anything with it. I am telling you the truth."

"Okay," I said. "I trust you."

I sped up, heading for my bar just past the end of town and around a slight bend in the road. We were a minute away.

"You wouldn't ask me that if you didn't already know," she blurted out. "You asked me that question because you *already know* what my father's company was up to. It was one of the calls you had to make this morning, wasn't it?"

I clenched my jaw, wondering what to say. I was obviously going to tell her, but I hadn't quite worked out the how or the when just yet. In my world, sharing deep secrets with people just wasn't something I did often. I heehawed for a moment, trying to figure out a way I could tell her something else entirely, maybe just for the time being.

In the end, I did the right thing.

"I'll tell you what I know, and what I want to do about it, but it's the kind of telling that needs telling over a drink."

She seemed to agree. "I can get behind that," she said. "Old fashioned?"

"No," I answered. "Not this time. I've got something else in mind."

CHAPTER FIFTEEN

SHE SNIFFED IN THE GLASS and did the scrunch-nose thing that I'd come to adore. "That's disgusting," she said. "What is it?"

"I'll have you know that this is a *fine* cognac. A brandy from the Cognac region of France."

"But there's nothing else in it? No ice, no — what's that little thing you squirt in there — or anything else?"

I sighed. "You mean *bitters?* And you don't 'squirt' it in there, you 'dash' it. Just a couple dashes. And no, this isn't a cocktail. No ice because the warmth of your hand is meant to get around the cognac and let the bouquet open up."

"You're kidding me, right?"

She looked at me like I was trying to tell her that her car was out of blinker fluid.

"It's meant to be had *straight*, like a nice bourbon or Scotch. An ice cube is acceptable for some people, but not to me. Fermented just like wine, using grapes or another fruit, then distilled. You still get the graininess of a solid whiskey sometimes, but there's that grape hit in there, too."

"I'm not sure I'm a fan of straight liquor."

"That's just because you don't know how to enjoy it."

"Yeah, that's exactly what I'm *telling* you," she said.

"No, but you can learn this stuff." I walked across the back of the bar again and grabbed four snifter glasses I had cleaned and dried earlier. I placed them next to one another on the bar top, then walked over and made some selections from the massive oak cabinet that housed my nicer stuff.

"It's easy, really," I began. "We can *smell* all sorts of cool things, but we often can't make the connection in our brain that a particular smell is called a particular thing. For instance, you can imagine the smell of lavender, right?"

She sniffed, pretending. "Sure, yeah."

"Okay, so that's easy. But what about coriander?"

She closed one eye as she thought about it. "I guess — I know I've smelled it before, and I've cooked with it, but I don't think I'd be able to pick it out of a bouquet."

"*Right,* exactly. So it just takes practice to be able to *say* what you're *smelling* and *tasting.*" I gave her the first of the snifter glasses, and I took the second. "Lift it up, spin it just like wine, and then let it rest a second or two. Then smell. Keep your mouth open."

She did, and then looked up at me. "I don't smell lavender *or* coriander."

I laughed. "No, I guess you wouldn't. That's an American whiskey. But how about caramel, vanilla, oak?"

She tried again. Her eyes widened a little. "Okay, yeah, I think I got that."

"Perfect. Now taste."

She did, she made the same face she'd made before with the brandy. "Sorry — she said. It's strong."

"It's *perfect,*" I answered, raising my glass and downing the shot.

"You're a nerd. But thanks."

I gave her a wink and settled into the bar seat next to hers. "So — want to get started?"

She nodded. "Yeah, I guess it's about time I hear what my old man got himself into."

I jumped in, telling her everything I knew about Crimson Club thus far. I started from the beginning, explaining that I had a contact who might have some information, and how he desperately asked me to back down. I told her that meant this was something the feds were already neck-deep into, and it was highly likely I wasn't going to be able to find anything they couldn't. I explained that I had never been in a situation quite like this before, and although I truly wanted to help, there would be a chance I wouldn't be able to do anything of value.

She looked at me quizzically, and I waited for her to talk.

"That's a pretty solid disclaimer," she said. "Now get to the point."

"What are you talking about?" I asked. "I'm trying to make sure you understand —"

"Look," she said. "I know what you're trying to do. It's admirable, even. But there's no way you can back out of this now."

I raised my eyebrow so high I thought it might jump up and land on the top of my head. "Whoa, slow down. I ain't trying to back out of anything. I'm just making it clear that all of this stuff we're about to get into has multiple layers, like an onion. And when you cut an onion, it stings. The deeper you go, the more it stings."

"I just found out my father was killed and he might have been involved in a much bigger and messier situation than I could have imagined. How much more do you think this can sting?"

I looked her up and down, sitting there next to me on

the barstool. Her legs were crossed, and she had her elbows drawn in where they touched the table, as if she was cold. She didn't have goose bumps on her skin, but I knew what was happening.

She was bracing herself.

She knew that I was about to cut this onion in half and look at the center of it all, to bring out into broad daylight what her father had been poking around in. She knew that I had more information than she did at this point, and she wasn't going to let me off the hook easy.

"Okay," I started. "Let's do this. Your father — remember, I didn't know him — your father was in some deep shit. I don't know much about the details yet, but it's all going to surface when the feds get done investigating whatever they are looking at. All I know at this point is your old man was sitting on an absolute fortune, and I believe it made him a pretty massive target to someone who wanted it."

"A fortune in importing? I mean, we were always very well-off, but…"

"No, Hannah, I'm not talking about importing anymore. You probably saw the wealth built from that enterprise, but at some point during your father's career he got into some pretty nasty stuff."

She was nodding along silently, so I continued.

"The guy I talked to said they are investigating the overseas accounts of an organization called Crimson Club for illegal activities including the selling of underage pornography, sex trafficking, and other similar affairs."

I watched Hannah's face very carefully as I dropped the bomb. This incident would tell me something crucial about her character: she either had no idea what her father was involved in, or she did. Or, I guess, she was in on it the whole time and would fake one of the above two scenarios. I trusted my gut, so I watched her face as she reacted to what I said.

First, her mouth opened and closed like a fish a couple times, slowly, like one that had been laid out on the dock and was still in shock, wondering if it was really unable to breathe or not. Second, she turned and did a full circle in the barstool, bending her neck around to take in the entire place. Finally, she swiveled back around and stared at the mirror behind the bar, her eyes locked in place even as I stood up and walked around.

I intercepted her gaze and waited until she focused on my face.

"Hannah, I'm sorry. I —"

"Don't," she said quickly. If she hadn't been whispering I would have thought she'd snapped at me. "Just don't."

CHAPTER SIXTEEN

SO FAR, MY GUT WAS telling me that this was a woman who had just found out her father had been involved in some very reprehensible activities. Hell, they weren't even questionable activities. If what my contact had told me was true, her father was guilty by association even if he had never set foot outside the country. If Crimson Club was in fact engaged in this sort of crap, he would have known about it. He would have had something to do with it being set up under his nose.

What's more, the man had set up his own kids with a portion of the business, likely to make it seem as though they were all equally responsible, or at least to diminish his own role in it all. To even the blame a bit, among the man's own children.

Reprehensible.

I was disgusted already, and if it weren't for the drinks I'd already poured down I might have had a harder time with breaking the news to her. But she hadn't had the luxury of being able to sit with the information for as long as I had. I had the benefit of not only knowing about her father for a few hours longer, but also that I dealt with schmucks like this every day.

But my gut was definitely not wrong about this one. Hannah Rayburn had had no idea that her father was dabbling in — or running — a sex-trafficking ring. I could imagine the emotions running through her mind. Hell, I could see them on her face. Posted up there as plain as day. And she hadn't struck me as someone who wore their emotions on their sleeve.

We waited, me standing inside the bar area and her across on the stool. She swiveled left and right slowly, just a bit, still letting the information marinate. I wanted so badly to interrupt her, to ask how she was doing. To try to help.

If being married had taught me anything, it was that these next few minutes of silence were crucial for her. She needed to be alone with her own thoughts for a while, to let her own brain sort through it all and figure out heads and tails of it. Then, and only then, would I be in a position to speak.

So I let her be. Just walked away, down to the other side of the bar. It was still early, so the place had been empty, but a youngish couple had walked in and sidled up, waiting for me to notice them. I served them, a couple martinis, then checked in on Hannah.

She was still swiveling and staring, so I came back to the couple. Found out they were on their way to the drive-in movie theater that had opened last summer. It was a new thing around here, except way back when during the times when a drive-in theater wasn't so much a new thing. But the city folks especially, who were lucky enough to find a solid theater that sold them popcorn for three times the price of their ticket and their feet didn't stick to the floor, a drive-in theater was all the rage. So I'd seen it before, plenty of times, and I certainly wasn't arguing with the additional business it brought in.

My bar sat right on the main road — a small road, but a main one nonetheless — in a tiny town outside of Charleston. It was really a town outside of a smaller town outside of a suburb of Charleston, but for folks not from around here, 'outside of Charleston' seemed to give them the geographic satisfaction they craved.

Thanks to the beaches and all the golf, our area would eventually be consumed by a metropolitan district, but the ebb and flow of modern society told me not to start counting down the date. Who knew when the trend of the throngs of people moving into the larger cities would reverse, and everyone would have the age-old desire to connect with their Americana roots and move out here to the sticks, like me?

So I set my bar up the way I wanted it, did my business the way I wanted it, and lived my life the way I wanted it. Didn't much care for how I was 'supposed' to run a business, and I certainly didn't follow any trends. They build a drive-in theater out in the middle of nowhere, fine. I'll serve beers to anyone wanting to make the trek.

The couple was busy laughing at some inside joke, so I watched the door and cleaned, keeping a peripheral gaze on Hannah as she swiveled.

Then she stopped swiveling. I was on her fast, like I'd been waiting for it. I *had* been waiting for it, but I'd forgotten to give the obligatory few seconds to not make it creepy.

She looked up at me as I arrived, her eyes wide and surprised.

"Sorry... I —" I didn't know quite what I was supposed to say. Couldn't make a joke about watching her and waiting around for her to be done. Seemed insensitive. "You okay?" Good a thing to say as any, I guess.

She nodded, frowning. "Sure, yeah. I guess deep down I knew it was something like this. Like it had to be about more than just the money."

Now it was my turn to frown. "I'm sorry, what do you mean? Isn't that *exactly* why they offed him?" I kicked myself for saying it so nonchalantly, like I was a detective discussing a case with a fellow officer.

"I'm sure, yeah. I mean ultimately that's *why* they did it. But there are plenty of rich people, you know? Plenty of people who make more than him. More than us. So there has to be more to it. There has to be something at the heart of it, and that's it. He was in a line of *business* —" she said it with contempt, saying the word the same way I thought the word — "that has to be pretty under-the-radar. Something that would have safeguards in place, so they won't be caught."

I understood her reasoning. "So they targeted your old man because they thought it would be easy enough to get him to sign over the business to them. No one would bat an eye, because no one knew to look there in the first place?"

"Right," she said. "I obviously don't understand the details, or how the business stuff would work, but you can't blackmail a Fortune 500 CEO too easily, I bet."

"Probably not."

"But if you're doing the kind of business my father was in, it's *already* got to be shrouded in secrecy. You wouldn't be submitting a form to the IRS letting them know there's been a change in management, and here's how much they're getting paid, and oh yeah we're still just in importing."

She chuckled a bit at the thought of it.

"Yeah, true," I said. "Still, seems a bit out of line. To just kill him? Why not threaten him first? Force his hand? Once you've got his approval, what can he do? He can't go to the authorities with it all, blow it all wide open. *He'd* be the one convicted."

"I know," she said. "That's why suicide makes sense. But it doesn't. I can't see him doing that."

I took it all in, thinking. I wasn't a detective, and she knew that. But at the moment, I wished I was. Here was a woman worried, scared, and probably not a little bit angry with what her father had been involved with, and the fact that he was now dead because of it. She was trying to piece it together, and the only person she'd placed her trust in was a bartender.

My skills weren't in the deduction arena, but more the physical harm arena. The problem was, I couldn't figure out who I needed to *harm*.

"Okay," I said. "Let's talk this out real quick, then I can maybe figure out what we do next. Sound good?"

She nodded.

"Your old man was killed, made it look like a suicide. Whoever killed him wanted something from him, probably control of his business, or the portion of it that deals with overseas sex trafficking. Something under the table that would already have a circle of protection around it, making it difficult for anyone else to trace. You guys — you and Daniel — would think it's a suicide, go to the funeral, move on. So far so good?"

She nodded again.

"But something doesn't add up. You suspect it was *not* a suicide, which means there's someone who is now better off because your father is dead. So, and this is the million-dollar question: who is that person? Who stands to gain if your father is dead?"

She made a distressed face. "That's just it," she said. "I

don't know. I have no idea. I wasn't privy to business information, financial records, nothing."

"But was there ever anyone at the house? Anyone who came by to meet with your father?"

"Sure. He worked there, early on. Had the office off one of the wings. Huge space, well-appointed, the works. He was pretty gung-ho about that space, too. But there were people in there all the time. Day and night, even. But then he started working from the yacht a lot, like I said."

"Right," I said. "So back to square one."

CHAPTER SEVENTEEN

THE SCENE AT THE BAR heated up, and I had to leave Hannah to her swiveling and drinking. She'd asked for another round, but specifically asked for it to be something *mixed*, so I scratched the idea of getting her into straight cognac. *Oh, well. Maybe another time.* Instead, I poured her another standby favorite: a traditional whiskey sour, just whiskey and lemon juice and simple syrup, complete with an egg white shaken in.

She was initially repulsed by the thought of a raw egg white in her drink — one of the main reasons bartenders are a bit leery to give out their recipes — but I told her to trust me. She did, I made it, and she sipped at the foam on top. I watched her reaction from in front of the newer couple on the other side of the bar. Her face brightened just a bit, then she dug in for a *real* sip.

Mission accomplished. I smiled a bit to myself as I served the other patrons.

After the new couple had come in, a set of oldies walked to their usual seats on my left, gave me a head-nod wave, and took out a deck of cards. Sometimes they liked to play a little bridge on the weeknights, poker on weekends. *What it would be like to be retired and have nothing to do all day but wait for the bar to open.*

I served them their drinks, loading up a tray for Joey to take over. Another party of oldies, this one with a couple of people I didn't recognize among them, had walked in and chosen a booth on my right. I knew I'd need to wait on the newcomers, and I liked to do that personally.

"Evening," I said.

"Sonny, it's nearing six-o'-clock," one of the geriatric members of the crew said, matter-of-factly.

I half-smiled. "Yep, that is correct. I'm assuming that means you'll be needing your night-cap? Shot of cough syrup chased down by whatever half-open beer I've got in the fridge?"

There was a moment of looking around as the ninety-year-old processed my comeback.

Suddenly he burst out laughing. He turned to one of the oldie regulars, man named Chesson, I think, and slapped his arm. "You weren't kidding, pal, this kid is a riot!" I was immediately taken by their excitement and happiness, and started laughing along with them.

Chesson looked up at me. He winked. "I didn't tell him you were the only bar in town."

I laughed even harder, playing along. The guy had some out-of-towners visiting, I would make sure they had a great time. This was my element, my MO. I also didn't counter with the fact that there were no less than *three* other bars in town, technically speaking.

Caviar's, a weird and off-putting name, was (I think) trying to tap into a nonexistent French nightlife appeal, but they closed at 9pm on weekends. I'm not even sure they served caviar. If they did, I'm not sure where they got it.

Jake's Sports Bar was the typical sports bar, minus whatever appeal typical sports bars had. I figured most sports bars featured sports, chicken wings, and D-cups, but I don't think they even had a cable package and they certainly didn't have anything better than a C-team running the place on weekends. Not sure about the wings — maybe those were killer.

Finally, there was a place 'downtown' that I actually really liked. There weren't too many nights I wasn't here at my own place, but if I had an evening to kill, I didn't mind spending it at the Wobbly Barstool. It was a dive bar, the kind of place that had the best hamburger in a 200-mile radius just because they refused to ever clean their griddle, and it had the cheapest beers in town. I'm not a huge beer guy, for different reasons, but there's no other option at Wobbly Barstool. The owner, a nice guy named Steve, was also their cook and head bartender. I appreciated the effort he put in.

So for a town of 400, it was a bit surprising that there were already two bars up and running when I moved in. Caviar's came after, and I had a feeling it wouldn't last a decade. But the others were well-established when I set up shop, and I got the impression they weren't too keen on an outsider coming in to steal their business. I made it a point to make friends with their owners — worked with Wobbly Barstool, didn't so much with Jake — but whatever.

I wanted this place, and I wanted to do it my way. If they didn't like it, they could close.

Guys like Chesson, his friends, and the other oldies, they liked tradition. They liked the same thing, all the time, no matter what. When I'd first opened, I drew them in not because I was something new to them, but because I was something *old*. I don't pipe in loud music much. I've got a jukebox, and the dancing floor, but both are hardly ever used. I keep the jukebox set on a low volume, so anyone who sticks a quarter in it gets pissed they can hardly hear their selection. I serve cocktails, the way I was taught by my granddad over a quarter-century ago. Simple, easy, no frills. I've got beers, too, more than just the crappy mainstream variety, even though those are the only ones that sell.

I finished with Chesson's group, wrote everything down — the oldies aren't impressed by memorizing their orders, they're impressed when I get them right — and took it back to the bar to get them started. Hannah was still there, still swiveling.

Whatever she was feeling she was going to be feeling for some time.

"How you doing?" I asked.

She just nodded.

"Your brother coming by later?"

"Yeah," she said. "He's still getting some last-minute arrangements done for the funeral on Sunday. Flowers today, I think."

I was surprised he had been gone this long, considering it was well past typical business hours, but I didn't press. "You staying in the bed and breakfast tonight?"

She looked up. Her eyes were asking a question, but her mouth was a straight line. I suddenly felt like I was nine years old, getting scolded by Grandma for sneaking a bite of a cake that was resting on the countertop. I really didn't mean anything by it, other than making small talk, but I could tell she was actually wrestling with the question.

"I, uh…" she started, then stopped. She looked up at the ceiling. Then down at the top of the bar, finding a spot I hadn't yet cleaned and beginning to try to chip off the crusty part with her thumbnail. Obviously letting her mind wander. "I think, you know, it would be hard to tell Daniel…"

I started laughing, bringing my head down and trying to conceal it. "I'm sorry," I said. "I'm just — I'm just making talk. You know, passing the time."

"Yeah?" She had that line on her mouth again, but this time her eyes matched. "Really."

"No, really. I'm just making sure you're okay there with him, at Marley's. He seems so, you know…"

"Preoccupied?"

"Yeah, preoccupied. With the funeral and all."

Her hands stopped fiddling with the crusty mark on the bar top and came to rest on top of one another, idle. Calm.

She's made up her mind.

I turned to help the couple getting ready to leave, the ones who had enjoyed a couple martinis each to loosen themselves up before the movie. I longed for their ease, their ability to swoop in, pay some money to an unknown agent who would deliver them an elixir of relaxation, one that could carry them innocently through the next few hours.

"I'll come over, if that's what you're asking," she said.

It was loud — she'd had to raise her voice a bit to reach over the oldies' conversations — but it wasn't frantic. Controlled, but not thoughtless. I turned around.

As I turned, I caught the eye of the man who had paid the tab, the male half of the couple. He gave me a knowing look, then nodded slightly. Satisfied, encouraged.

I kept turning, pretending I hadn't seen him. I raised an eyebrow. "What's that?" I asked.

"I'm not repeating it," she said.

"I have a little trouble hearing, these days," I said.

"Oh, bullshit." She was smiling now. "You heard me. First and last time I make the offer." She paused, looking around, a bit of horror creeping onto her face. "You *do* have a 'place,' right? One that's not here?"

CHAPTER EIGHTEEN

I DRIFTED TO THE LEFT, away from Hannah a bit, leaving her grinning to herself. I didn't want her to think I was too eager. I wasn't sure exactly what she'd meant by it, anyway. Could be what I was thinking, could be she just wanted to feel safe. I tried to rationalize against it. If she wanted to 'feel safe,' she should go to a police station, see if they'd hole her up in a cell for the night. That was ridiculous, so I stuck with the first option.

I was feeling pretty high on life by the time I'd gotten my mind around the idea that she, of all people, might be wanting to come over for the night. I couldn't help but smile a bit, then I turned up to watch Joey.

Joey was hard at work keeping the oldies happy, and I even saw him engaging some of Cresson's out-of-town friends in conversation. They seemed to be enjoying his company, but he was a professional — he waited for a polite moment to duck out, thanked them for coming in, and came back to the bar and kitchen to continue serving the other guests. He waited for a lull in the orders, then walked over.

"Remind me to give you a raise sometime," I said.

He tossed it right back. "That's the fifth time you've said that, boss. Where's my money?"

I Clint-Eastwooded him until he broke.

"Fine," he said. "You know, I love working with you because I can tell you're going places. So trendy, so up-to-date. I'd do this job for free. Maybe even consider —" he stopped when he busted out laughing.

In spite of his poking fun, I couldn't help but compliment him. "You really are a hard worker, Joey. I appreciate that."

"It's good work, honestly. I worked in a kitchen up in the city. Man it was rough. All hours of the night, you know? At least here it's about half a day, maybe less."

That was true. I employed Joey at the bar between thirty and forty hours a week, but we were closed Sundays, and he didn't come in on Mondays. Too slow of a day. The other hours, the ones he got paid nearly double for, totaled about fifteen to twenty hours.

Still, I tried to do my best to make sure he wasn't ever working *nonstop* that many hours. I'd done it, plenty of times, but it was no fun. Come in, do your work, then get some sleep. Maybe have a little fun on the side. That was how I wanted things here, and that was mostly how they were.

He knew, though, that the 'extra' component of his paycheck — the portion paid in cash — was something that required a little more, a little bit different set of skills. It came with a slightly different set of expectations.

"I'm going to need you more," I said out of the corner of my mouth as we side-by-side threw back a couple shakers of whiskey sours ordered by a couple locals. He was fully capable of making the drinks himself, but I wanted the regulars to see me making a drink, and I had a hankering to shake the crap out of something anyway. "I'm going to need you a *lot* these next few days. Any big plans?"

"Getting married, but other than that, no."

I nearly dropped my shaker. I swung around to find his big-ass wide toothy grin jutting out at me, mocking me.

"I'm kidding. You're too easy, you know that?"

I wasn't *too easy*, and I knew it. But Joey seemed to have me all figured out, which was part of the reason I liked him. Trusted him. You didn't want a guy like that against you. He knew how to dig in at me when I was most vulnerable — a very rare thing to be vulnerable at all, but there were moments.

"It's her, isn't it?" he said, finishing his drink and pouring out the top of the strainer, just like I'd taught him.

"Yeah," I said. *Let him figure what that means.*

"She invite you over for the night?"

I sniffed. "Nope."

He turned to me and stared, forgetting all about his drink. "No shit, boss. You *caved*?"

I looked at him, admittedly a bit confused. "What are you talking about?" I tried to feign innocence, suddenly focusing so intently on my whiskey sour I was sure it was going to blow the minds of whoever had decided to order it.

"You caved, right? You invited *her* over. You *can't* invite them over, boss. You should know that. It's a cardinal sin. *They* have to invite *you*."

"Joey," I said, trying to summon my best fatherly voice, "this wasn't a casual bar conversation, featuring a typical run-of-the-mill dame and lad. This isn't a college drinking game, either. This is complicated."

He wasn't buying it. He had turned back to his drink, now shaking it out into the chilled old fashioned glass. I didn't like drinking whiskey sours out of snifters — focused the wrong aromas toward the wrong places — and I liked the texture and long-term appeal a few well-placed small cubes brought to the mix, so I had trained him to use lowball glasses for nearly everything. Old-fashioned glasses, rocks glasses, same thing. It was a go-to around here. I was a David Embury believer, so my style was simple, tried-and-true, basic. Typically an 8-2-1 ratio for a lot of mixed drinks, don't stir the fruit juices, that sort of stuff.

"So she wanted to stay with you?" he asked.

I looked over at him, but found he was concentrating on the drink in front of him. He rolled a lemon peel against the edge of the glass and placed the drink on the tray.

"Any day, old man," he said.

The jab didn't hurt. It never did. For some reason, I didn't think of myself as an old man. I said things that led others to believe I thought of myself as old, but I didn't *actually* buy it. Age is a construct; age is a state of mind. And I wasn't old. No way.

I laughed. "Yeah, *she* wanted to stay with *me*." I emphasized the pronouns to make sure he understood that it was a choice *she'd* made. Something that proved my worth and my youth.

At this he stopped making the drink, grabbed the white rag he'd slung over his shoulder, and took up the unofficial bartender stance. Arms crossed, the rag draped over his elbow, his feet shoulder-length apart and his head tilted back just slightly. He was ready to diagnose my situation.

"You don't say."

"I don't say," I responded. I tried not to look him in the eye. If I did, I would have to explain. Who the hell was I to have to explain anything to a kid half my age?

I caught his eye. I sighed. "Fine," I said. "Yeah, that's what she told me."

CHAPTER NINETEEN

WE LEFT JOEY TO TEND the bar and kitchen for the few people remaining in the tables along the sides of the place. There was no one at the bar when we left, and I had a feeling that there wouldn't be too many. It was Thursday, which meant that anyone from the town who usually went out would head to the city, and anyone from the city who wanted to go out would stay in the city as well. Only on weekends would people trek more than twenty or thirty miles from home to drink. And we weren't exactly a destination bar.

I had plans to change that, of course. This was a dream of mine since my college years. Not sure why, but I'd always been fascinated by mixology and business, and specifically how the two might be combined. Buying my place was a huge milestone, but there had been some setbacks over the years.

The town was good to us, and even though there weren't too many kids around of hirable age, there weren't too many drinkers either. It was a quiet operation, but it was inexpensive enough to maintain that I didn't need a packed-out $2-you-call-it night to get the riffraff in just to keep the lights on. It also gave me time to practice my craft, mixing new drinks and getting to know the regulars, and it gave me time for the *other* line of work I was in.

I trusted Joey to run the place as long as he wanted, but I also told him to shut it down in a couple hours if it died so he could get some sleep — I'd still pay him for a full shift. I owed him at least that, and not just for taking out the trash earlier. He was a rare breed these days, a man willing to work his ass off and not expect much more than some respect and a decent day's wage in return.

Hannah and I drove through the town toward Marley's. I knew she would want to grab her stuff and talk to her brother. She could have called him, I guess, but telling her brother she was going to stay the night at the new guy's house might have been the sort of thing she wanted to do in person. Still, I didn't mention either thing during the drive. There was a small part of me that was hoping for more than just 'keeping her safe,' and there was another part of me that seemed to think I would ruin any chances I might have if I opened my mouth and talked about it.

It's a weird, inexplicable component of being a guy, but I bought into it that night. If I said anything, it would screw with the alignment of the planets or some other voodoo and she would change her mind and want to stay at the bed and breakfast tonight.

I chuckled to myself as I thought through the irrationality of the man's lizard brain. She looked over, trying to figure me out.

"What?" she asked.

"Uh, nothing. Just…"

I didn't know what to tell her. I couldn't say I was excited, that sounded sleazy and expectant. Nor could I say nothing at all, that would come across as overly confident and, again, expectant. Why couldn't I just be James Bond, and look at her with that mystical look in my eye and then squint a little with one of them and have her just *know*, without saying anything at all?

Hannah, I want to kiss you again.

That's what I 'thought-spoke' to her, across the car. I don't think she understood.

"You worried about something?" she asked.

"Sorry," I said, "I — I just don't know what I'm going to be able to do to help you out. This whole thing is out of my jurisdiction."

"But I told you everything I know. There's nothing else I can tell you about my father that would be any help."

"I get that, but I don't think it'll be enough. Whoever it was, they don't want to be found, I'm sure. And I'm not trained to be able to dig around like that. If you were to hire —"

"What happened earlier?" she asked, her voice suddenly ratcheting up a couple of notches.

I frowned.

"Before you picked me up and took me to the bar. Your face, and you've been babying your shoulder a bit. And when you called you said something had happened. Is that what this is about? You don't want to help me because you found something out that scared you?"

I was in multiple car crashes, back-to-back, and nearly died. But aside from that, no.

"I was paid a visit by that guy's friends. Not the same ones who were in the bar — those idiots were just his *actual* friends or maybe hired stooges, hanging out with him while he was on the clock. But two other guys, I think who might have worked with him."

"I take it they didn't like what you did to their friend."

"Not so much, no. They tried to ambush me when I…" I drifted off as I realized I didn't want to tell her about what I was doing out there. "When I was driving. That's why we're in Joey's car. Mine's just about toast. They hit me out of nowhere, then stopped to finish the job."

She put a hand over her mouth. "Did you…"

I shook my head. "No, I didn't kill them. Didn't want to. I guess I was wanting them to feel it, you know? I was pissed they caught me off-guard like that, and I was hoping they'd get the message."

"Or they'll get the message and just pass it along to their bosses," she said. "Whoever they were, if they were with the guy from last night, they were organized. So they'll have someone they're answering to, and I'm sure they're not going to like what you did to them."

"Won't matter. If I'd have killed them, their boss would still be fuming that they failed, and now he doesn't have two of his grunts. This way, I figure, maybe the boss decides I'm not worth it — he has to patch up a couple goons, but then he'll just move on to an easier target."

"You really think that'll work?"

I snorted. "Not even a little bit." I knew the truth. Whoever they were working for wanted something from me — they wanted me to be dead. Out of the picture. I had no idea why, except that I'd done it to one of theirs.

We pulled up to Marley's place and she got out, walking around the car to start up the steps. I watched her for a few seconds, taking in her figure one more time as she neared the front stoop, next to where Marley himself had been gardening earlier that day. There were no lights on in the house, which gave the mansion a gloomy sort of feel, like something out of a horror movie. Deep, long shadows converged on Hannah and my car, casting the entire front yard in shades of black.

Something moved out of the corner of my eye. Just a flash, a lighter black against the black backdrop of the hedges at the edge of Marley's property, but it was enough. I was on high alert in milliseconds, and I knew it would be only a few seconds after that when I'd feel the first stab of adrenaline hit me. I made sure Hannah was still heading toward the front door of the house, but kept my peripheral vision focused on the moving threat at my side.

I clicked the handle and swung the door open. They were coming right at me. A guy on the left, and another on the right, just behind the first guy. I lifted my fists, instinctively, hoping they'd at least give me a fair fight.

They didn't. I saw the brighter flash of a blade, glinting the glow of a distant streetlight into my eyes, and it was the only warning I had. I twirled around, catching the outstretched knife hand with the crook of my right arm. I pulled it toward me, locking it in and squeezing with everything I had. I aimed my own hands at the knife, waiting for a change in the attacker's grip so I could shimmy it out of his hand.

Meanwhile, I looked around in the dark for a foot. Finding their right foot just outside my own, I slammed my heel onto the bridge of it, feeling the satisfying crack of bone as the foot was pulverized under my own. It was a brutal attack, one that dealt far more damage than its simplicity let on. The man howled, a combination of rage and pain, and the knife fell away. I caught it, as my hands were still wrapped around his wrist and close enough to the handle to snatch it, and turned it around in my palm until it was at the right angle.

I thrust my right hand forward at the dark shape that was

rushing over. The man behind me had at least a few seconds to himself to recover, and judging by the wail of agony, he'd need them. I focused on the bear of a shadow running past me.

Past me.

Not at me.

I ran, unable to tell how far away the second attacker was, but I quickly realized he wasn't focused on me at all. I was gaining on him, but he wasn't even aware that I was behind him.

He was running toward the house.

Toward Hannah.

This was the moment I realized I'd made a significant mistake. Possibly more than one. First, these men were here to grab Hannah, but they didn't want to kill her — at least not yet. Had they been instructed to take her out, they could have (and should have) just done it quietly, from afar, without getting me involved. They may not know what I'm capable of, but it's never worth the additional body count or the risk of things not going the way they're planned. Second, I realized that the man from last night had been one of these guys — maybe not part of their group, but certainly hired by the same group. He had a handgun on his person, then, and I'd assumed he was going to use it to force her to acquiesce, but now I realized what I'd missed then: he was hoping to use it on *me*, to get me out of the picture so he could grab her and take her back to his employer. He wouldn't have needed a gun to snatch her. She would not have seen him coming, and besides, he was a far cry from a disturbed psychopath hoping to prey on an innocent woman.

I processed all of this in the time it took me to change direction. I didn't stop, or even slow down. I thought through the ramifications of my realizations as I chased the two of them. All of it had a startling repercussion, one I wasn't sure I wanted to admit. It was true, but it was something I couldn't believe.

There were *two* groups after Hannah. That much was certain. I had no idea who the second group was — the group behind the men chasing her now, and the man I'd offed last night — but I knew, without a doubt, who the *other* group was.

The other group was *my* group.

I was after Hannah. She was the mark from last night.

I had been caught up in the sight of the man's pistol, and his trajectory toward the woman, and my instinct that he was something other than a well-fed college-aged lowlife. I had been caught up with *her*, smitten even, and I had placed any logical rationalization my mind had been prepared to offer into a deep corner of my brain, subconsciously refusing to believe the truth.

I had been given a mark last night the same way I was always given one: they'd walk in, sit down, order a drink, and I would know. Then, after some back-and-forth and my suspicions leading me to feign letting my guard down, I would say something that let them know I was the guy they had been told to come see. That I was the guy that could give them their next 'hookup.' They'd slap the token on the bar, knowingly, and I'd wink at them with my eye but I'd already be killing them inside my head. The problem was that I had called it wrong. The token was nowhere to be found, and my gut had led me to take out the wrong mark.

I ran, but my mind was racing even faster than my legs. I was shaking slightly, even as I pumped faster and faster up the walkway toward the front porch. I had made a mistake, and it was going to be a mess to clean up.

Hannah was the mark.

CHAPTER TWENTY

HANNAH HAD REACHED THE STEPS and turned around when she'd heard the scuffle and scream of the first attacker, and she was trying to see in the dark. I had a better line of visibility to her, and I had the backlight of a dim streetlight working to my advantage, but I knew it was also helping the second guy see her.

She couldn't see it coming. The guy nearly flew the last few feet and wrapped his beefy arms around her waist, lifting her completely off the ground.

I pumped my legs harder, but the stretch of paving stones between the car and the house was getting longer. Time itself was slowing, but the distance in front of me, separating me from Hannah, was lengthening. I forced even more through my body, hoping it would be enough.

He didn't even slow down. Hannah had just opened her mouth to scream, but the shock of the impact and the devastating blow itself took her breath away, so she just stared back at me, not seeing me or anything else, her mouth silently moving up and down. The man sped up, apparently not at all slowed by the woman's weight, and he bounded over the old wooden porch and around the side of the house.

I was on the porch, running, leaping over twenty planks at a time, rounding the corner. Forcing as much as I had down through my feet, up through my arms, everywhere.

It wasn't enough.

The man had me beat, and he knew it. He didn't slow, but he didn't look back either. Hannah was still frantically silent, but there was something in her face that told me what I knew.

She knew.

She understood what was happening.

I saw the van too late. It was an obvious one, a blank, white van contractors use, and the door was standing open. Had I seen it as soon as I rounded the corner and started down the western side of the great house, I would have immediately ran back to Joey's car — it was still running — and started off after the van. It was parked in the long driveway behind Marley's. There was a road that connected all these larger old houses together, like an ancient neighborhood, but each house had their own hidden driveway that wound around their properties before finding the central road that would lead them to town.

This van had parked behind the house, waiting, a perfect escape vehicle. By the time I could get around the house and down the road that led back there to the driveways, they'd be gone.

She'd be gone.

I had to act, and I had to act fast. It was too late to get to Hannah, but there was something else I could use as an asset. I went through it in my head, trying to work out all the pieces, trying to get the plan to make sense. It was a long shot, and I was paddling upstream, but there was one possible solution.

One in the van, ready to drive them away. One with Hannah, taking her to the van.

And one behind me, recovering from the shot I'd given his foot.

I whirled around, silently pleading to Hannah to not be mad that I'd given up the chase. I wasn't giving up for good, but there was no way I would reach them and get her back. Instead I tried to make out the location of the first guy who'd attacked me, the one I'd left writhing on the ground outside Joey's car.

Seemed like he was trying to get to me as much as I was trying to get to Hannah. He was nearly on me, and as I spun around, sidestepping to my left, he almost ran past me.

Almost.

He was limping just a bit, so I knew it was mostly adrenaline providing him with whatever speed and agility he had remaining, but the limp and my quick movement was enough to cause him trouble. He teetered around a bit, losing his balance, and nearly crashed onto the hardwood planks of the porch. I had hoped he would do exactly that, so I brought my right leg up, using the momentum of my spin to help, and sent my foot flying into his face.

I'm no NFL kicker, and I've never been a martial arts guy, so my legs don't typically reach too high. This time was no different — I didn't even get close to his face, but my kick was still hard, and he was still soft. It got him right in the side, right between two ribs, and I heard them both crack.

He crumpled in a bit as he fell backwards, slamming up against the outside wall of the house. He looked sort of like a crunched-up aluminum can, but floppier. It made me a bit happier inside to see him like that, but not nearly happy enough. I was still pissed, and I still intended to let him know about it.

You take Hannah, I take you, asshole.

I meant it.

He would die, but not here. Not right now. I needed one more thing from him.

The van pulled away, clearly deciding that their main goal was retrieving Hannah, and not necessarily returning with their entire party. The man I'd attacked sat there against the wall, just beneath a massive curtained window, and glared at me.

"Feeling's mutual," I said.

He couldn't move. His side was crushed, and he was holding it like he'd been shot. He didn't seem to be in a position to offer much resistance, but I wasn't one to take stupid chances. Before I knelt down to grab him, I walked over and crouched in front of him. A little to his side, so he wouldn't be able to get a leg up into my groin, and I made sure it was his injured side so he wouldn't try to punch me.

I waited, hoping he might just give me what I wanted. I had sized him up immediately as someone who had some training, so I knew he wasn't an idiot, but I didn't know if he intended to draw this out or not. He knew what I would need — where are they taking her, what are they going to do, who are you working for. He knew that's what I wanted from him, and he knew the answers.

The question now was whether or not he'd give them to me.

I cocked my head sideways a bit, opened an eye a little wider. *You gonna tell me?*

He just sneered.

I shrugged, then lashed out with a hand and grabbed onto a chunk of his short hair. There wasn't much to play with, but it was enough. I yanked my hand forward a bit, taking his head with it, then slammed it as hard as I could against the wall.

It was a standard southern-style estate, and the outside paneling was wood. Old, soft, and painted with a thick layer of light-blue. The blow wouldn't kill him — far from it — but it would rattle him up some, at least until he knocked out.

It worked the first time, and I saw his eyes close and his weight sink into the edge of the wall, like he was trying to melt into the space between the planks and disappear down under the porch. He was out cold.

I quickly grabbed his arm and slung him over my shoulder into a fireman's carry. He was heavier than he looked, but not unmanageable. I walked him over the porch and down the steps, toward Joey's car.

"Dixon?" I heard a voice say from behind me. "Hello?"

Marley. The old man himself had come out to see what the commotion had been, and he'd caught me in the act of hauling away the remnants. It was dark, and I knew he wouldn't be able to see me clearly, but it would be abundantly clear that I was struggling with some sort of human-sized weight on my shoulder.

"H — hey, Marley," I said. "How are you tonight?"

He paused, and I could just barely see his face in the shadows, twisted up in confusion as he tried to figure out what was going on.

"Well, I heard a noise," he said. "Big bump outside the living room. Everything okay out here?"

Marley was a sharp guy, considering his age. Nice man, ran a tight business. I respected him. I also didn't want him getting involved.

"Marley," I said. "Listen. "I — I need to take care of

something, and I hope you can understand that I can't really explain it fully right now. But I give you my word, I'll swing by tomorrow and sort things out, okay?"

He frowned, but nodded. He either didn't want to become another human-sized weight on my shoulder or he actually trusted me. Didn't care one way or another — I just needed to get the hell out of there.

I turned and started walking again before he could respond. "I'll give you a visit when I can, Marley."

As I got to the car, I shouted a thanks over my shoulder, balanced the man's weight with one hand, and fumbled with the trunk release with the other. It popped open and I kicked it up fully with a foot, then tossed the man inside. There wasn't an emergency release inside Joey's trunk, so I wasn't worried he would get out.

Instead, I was worried about Hannah. I didn't have a lot of time to make my move, and I had the feeling I was already in over my head.

I slammed the trunk shut — might have clipped him a bit, but whatever — and got into the driver's seat and started driving away. Marley was still on the porch, watching me head out into the shadows.

CHAPTER TWENTY-ONE

I WAS SEETHING. RAGE DIDN'T begin to describe what I was feeling. Rather than a mixture of emotions — anger, defeat, confusion, betrayal, fear — they were all wrapped up into a singular, individual force. A single feeling that consisted of everything I'd felt that night.

I wasn't a revenge-driven person. Instead, I vouched for justice, longed for a world without the perverse style of hatred I fought so hard against. I wasn't retaliatory, nor was I the kind of person to get caught up in pettiness.

But this. This was different. This wasn't revenge. This wasn't retaliation.

This was removing a piece from the chessboard. This was taking out a threat, once and for all. It was getting information, and then figuring out how to use that information to my advantage to get Hannah back. And then destroying the thing that gave me the information.

The man in the back of the trunk had woken up. Either his head was harder than I'd thought or I hadn't clocked him well enough, but he wasn't going anywhere. Joey's trunk could be broken out of, but I doubted the man had anything on him he could use to pick the lock. Plus, it would be nearly pitch-dark in there, the dim lights from the old streetlights outside wouldn't be enough to allow him to see anything useful.

On top of that, we were only a few minutes away from the bar, and I knew Joey and I could handle him well enough once we were in the alley. I spent those few minutes thinking through the plan.

Hannah had been taken, but she had been taken by a group that was trying to exploit her father's death. They wanted what they thought she had — control of the company. That meant her brother would also be in danger. Hell, he was probably up in the room when they'd snatched his sister.

I still didn't have a token, but it was clear to me that the mark had been Hannah all along. She was the one I was supposed to off, since her father had been the one at the head of the company. It was simple — Mr. Rayburn was dead, so the only thing left to do was remove the other owners of the company from the picture. My mark was his daughter, and I could bet that if I'd accomplished my mission correctly the first time, my second mark for the weekend was her brother.

But there was still… something. Something I couldn't place. I drove on in silence, the radio killed long ago, and churned through the options. I tried to place the motives on the other group, the ones who had gotten to —

I stopped. Literally pulled the car up short. The brakes grabbed and stuck, hard and fast, and I heard the man tumble forward in the trunk and slam up against the indentations toward the back of the trunk. I heard a muffled groan, but I didn't stop to revel in the slight satisfaction that sound provided.

This group didn't take out her father.

I knew it, even as the words fell through my mind. I knew it, without a doubt. This group, the men who had taken Hannah and tried to kill me earlier that day, was not the group that had offed her father. They weren't the ones who had forced the man into a noose, told him to stand on a chair or a desk, and held a gun to his head until he walked off the side of it. They weren't the ones who had done that, because their *motive* told a different story.

They would have told the man what they wanted, and they would have threatened him or tortured him until he complied. They would have beat him until he bent and gave them what they wanted: control of his company. Specifically a very *profitable* portion of his company. The portion of the company my friend in high places had been looking into.

The schmuck would have given them what they wanted, and they probably still would have killed him, but then they would have had no need to come after Hannah.

But they *had* come after Hannah, and I was pretty sure it was a convoluted argument to assume they'd done so just to get back at me for offing their frat-boy from last night. They'd come after Hannah, but not killed her, because they *still needed the company.*

They still needed her to comply. She controlled some of the company. Enough of it, apparently, that they were interested in what they could gain if they took it from her. So they took her, and they would, I knew, do whatever it took to wrench it from her hands and then toss her away like a discarded piece of trash.

So that left me with the nagging thing I'd noticed from earlier, but couldn't quite place. The nagging had been there since I'd thrown the asshole in Joey's trunk, but I hadn't — until this moment — realized what it was nagging me *about.* This was it.

The timeline didn't make sense, and the motive didn't either. They had come for Hannah *after* her father had died. They had tracked her movements, watching her from afar for a few days, a week maybe, and they'd just followed her down here to Edisto, where they had a beach house and a yacht, where they would bury their old man.

They followed her down *after* her dad had been killed, but *they* hadn't been the ones to kill him. They had only shown up on the scene after the playing field had been leveled a bit — after the key piece was removed from the board. It made their job easier, having the old man gone, but they hadn't been the ones to do it.

No, it hadn't been *them*. Instead, it had been *me*. Not me, specifically, but my *employer*. He'd had the old man killed.

It was the only thing that made sense. Old man dies, my mark shows up at my bar looking for Hannah to kill her off, too. The playing field was being leveled.

I was responsible for his death. *I* was the reason he had been killed. He had been a mark, I was sure of it. The token always had a way of traveling through a set of people who were related by a single, unifying element of their lives. It traveled through until there were no more people in that group we had identified as being bad people. Then, and only then, was the token retired temporarily, until it was needed again.

These travelings happened in spurts, from one person to the next, each one a mark for me to kill, to take out and deal with, with or without Joey's help, until I'd made it through all of the people the token had deemed worthy of its attention.

But there was a huge, glaring problem. While I was completely sure the old man had been a mark, I had never even heard of him before I'd met Hannah.

I had never met him, nor had I been the one to kill him. He had been given the token just like they all had, I was sure of it, but it hadn't been me to pull the trigger.

My employer always sent them to me. Always. And this time I hadn't been the one to do it.

Which meant I now had a coworker.

CHAPTER TWENTY-TWO

I WAS STILL STOPPED ON the side of the road, so I fumbled around until I found my flip phone. I yanked it out and turned left to head back down to the alley behind my bar. I didn't want anyone to hear the conversation I was about to have, but I didn't want the man in the trunk to hear it either.

I jogged over to the fence and walked along it, away from the bar, until I found a narrow gate that had been installed far too long ago. It was just barely hanging on, a few pieces of warped rails all that gave it the support it needed. It had sunk into the ground a few inches as well, so I had to finagle it and shake it around until it pushed the leaves and junk on the forest side of it away enough for me to squeeze through. I walked into the woods about twenty paces, knowing I was pretty much as middle-of-nowhere as I'd get, and started dialing.

This time the phone connected on the first ring.

"You've had a busy day," the deep, gravelly voice said.

"We need to talk," I snapped.

"I imagine you do think that."

"We need to talk *in person.*"

The voice paused, then chuckled. "That is never an acceptable —"

"I don't *care* about protocol," I shouted, with the shoutiest whisper I dared. "I don't give a shit about your rules anymore. You know I want out, and we need to talk about that."

"We need to talk about what you've *screwed up*," the man said.

I hesitated. Too long. *Any* hesitation was too long, and he knew that I knew it. He reveled in it. Took pride in it. He'd won. "I can fix it," I said. "I can make it right. The mark —"

"The *mark* is gone!" he yelled. "You *missed* the mark. You hit the wrong one!"

"I know that — I obviously know that. There was no money, and —"

"Stop." The voice — my boss' voice — had returned to its all-too-controlled level, its calmness and coolness. A ruse, meant to get the listener to comply, no matter what. And most of the time, it worked.

I waited. He didn't speak. He was thinking about it. Considering.

"Come see me," I said. "You know where to find me. Hell, you're less than an hour away."

I heard breathing on the other end. A cough. Finally, a simple word. "Fine."

CHAPTER TWENTY-THREE

I TRIED TO SPEND THE hour napping on a thin mattress I'd long ago tossed in the back of the office, catching up for lost sleep and storing whatever energy my body would give me, but it was pointless. I had closed the bar early, which really meant I just had to give a free drink card to two oldies I hadn't seen before on account of 'feeling under the weather.' It wasn't something I'd never done before, either. A few nights out of the month, typically, I had 'other work' to take care of, so I'd had printed up a few thousand of those little 'free drink' coupon cards. Business card sized, nice and shiny, the works. Cost me about forty bucks, and it bought me the ability to run the hours I wanted to run.

Edisto is too small a town to really care, after all. The competitors' places all felt like kids' lemonade stands compared to the regularity in the hours I kept, so most of the oldies and regular attendees had no beef with my needing to change things up on them last minute. They were in here, night after night, and they got it. A man's got other responsibilities, I heard one of them say.

It was the out-of-towners that I had truly made the cards

for. I needed the money of my side gig, but I wanted more than anything to make the bar my life. So I couldn't afford for any of the city folks to go back to their big cities and write a nasty review on one of the weirdo online review sites they were always yapping about. I had plans — big plans — and I didn't need my reputation to suffer before I'd even started implementing them.

So a few free drink cards were well worth the additional hours I could buy at a moment's notice, so Joey and I tended to keep stacks of them on hand on both sides of the backbar area.

The oldies took off, making sure to finish off their beers, and left a tip before exiting and heading home. I dispatched Joey to deal with 'the issue' in the trunk, telling him to do nothing but make sure the guy didn't escape. He took to the task enthusiastically, as watching a closed trunk with a loaded handgun in hand was a far easier job than cleaning the kitchen after an evening of flipping catfish and mixing drinks.

I'm not sure I slept even a minute. I was thinking about it all, trying to make it make sense. The whole time I was concerned for Hannah. How long would they give her before they… started in? What would they threaten her with? I even thought about her brother. He was probably fast asleep back at Marley's, but in a matter of hours he would realize something was wrong. I made a mental note to check on the guy later. From what I'd seen of him yesterday, I had a feeling he'd be scared shitless when he found out Hannah wouldn't be coming back.

I lay there, thinking, trying to force the thoughts out of my mind and get some sleep, but it was hopeless. Finally I heard the tiny bell above the front door. It opened, the ringing sound hanging there in the air for a second, then it rang again as it closed. The sound petered out slowly, menacingly. Even after it was completely silent again I could still hear it, pinging around throughout the inside of my head.

I didn't hear the footsteps on the warped hardwood floor, which meant he was here. I checked my watch — nearly an hour after we'd hung up.

I stood up and sniffed a few times. I coughed, twice, then walked over to the industrial sink on the back wall across from the office, then checked myself out in the mirror. It wasn't a pretty sight — I'd been run through the ringer from the car accident, and the exertion from earlier that night hadn't helped. My eyes were bleak, reddened from a lack of decent sleep, and they looked hungover from knowing they weren't going to get any more anytime soon.

My neck and face was a topographical map of scars and pockmarks from old wounds, my nose hinged left just a little off-kilter, and my lips were fixed in the permanent sneer that for some reason had made Hannah feel like kissing me wasn't the worst idea she'd ever had.

My left shoulder sagged down a bit, and I could feel my chest rising and falling deeply, breathing heavily as I tried to compensate for the anger and exhaustion.

I shrugged, then walked out of the kitchen.

He was at the bar, waiting for me. He'd already helped himself to a glass of Jefferson's Ocean, carrying the lowball and the bottle of booze back around to the guests' side. He had poured it — an ocean-aged, lighter bourbon I actually enjoyed quite a bit — nearly halfway, with no ice.

As I turned left as I passed over the threshold, he winced and held up the glass.

"You look like shit," he said.

It was funny, really. He said it, all the while looking at me through those same eyes, that same sneer, that same mess of a face I called my own.

In a way, it *was* my own.

I poured my own glass of the same stuff, reaching across the counter for the half-empty bottle. I stared down to the bottom of the rocks glass, not ready to look up.

"Hey Dad," I muttered.

CHAPTER TWENTY-FOUR

"GET YOU A DRINK?" I asked.

"Besides the bourbon?"

"Besides the entire bottle of something I'd normally be able to sell at a four-hundred-percent markup." I said.

"Well, if you think about it, I bought it. So…"

"Well, if you *really* think about," I shot back, "your *benefactors* bought it."

He sneered at me. "I could use a glass of water. What's the markup on that?"

I spritzed some water into a glass and slid it across the bar. "Free. Ice is ten bucks."

He raised his eyebrows. I didn't have to imagine what he was trying to say. *Want to play, boy?*

"Seems like you'd be asking a whole lot more than ten bucks for the water, considering."

I clenched my jaw. "Yeah? Considering *what*, asshole?"

He stuck his tongue down into his bottom lip and stared at me with those beady little eyes I used to fear but had come to despise. He turned his head a bit, just slightly, letting me know he was in. He wanted to play.

I wasn't some idiot kid anymore. I wasn't the same little dweeb he loved to hang out to dry when I messed up. I was a guy who'd been through a hell of a lot more than he'd ever hoped to live through, and for some damn reason, he didn't seem to get that.

I waited, knowing he'd play along. He wanted to play, otherwise he wouldn't have come down here. Thought he might be able to stare me down like he used to, look me in the eye and wait until I came crashing apart around him, letting him stew and wait and stew and burn until he decided enough was enough and he'd help pick up the pieces.

Bullshit. I wasn't going to play that game. I'd invented a new game, and I was calling it 'I'm out.'

"How's Joey?" he asked. His lip was still out, his head still cocked, and he was still playing the old game. Trying to rile me up. Didn't matter. I didn't need to play the same game.

"How's Mom?"

His tongue went back into his tiny mouth, and his head righted itself. Quickly, but then shook just a bit as if he had been trying to hide it. His nostrils opened and shut once, again quickly. I saw his finger come out, start to bend into his characteristic gnarly point, and I almost smiled.

"Listen here, you little piece of —"

"Language, Pop," I said. "My place, my rules."

"You little prick."

"Takes one to know one."

We waited. Sat there for a minute, the tension building. This was a guy who had given me everything — a purpose in life, the funds to afford it, and a living that I tended to like. At the same time, he'd taken absolutely everything from me. Stripped away whatever semblance of a decent citizen his ugly genes had been able to pass on.

He'd made me, and he knew it. Trouble was he thought he *owned* me because of that.

"You called yesterday. I was out. Sorry I missed it."

I stared at him.

"What was it you needed?" he asked, innocently.

I rolled a nonexistent ball around in my mouth. "Wanted you to pay more for the water, I guess."

"Well I pay what it's worth. This water tastes like shit."

I nodded. "Fine. Pay what you think it's worth. Your mark's been taken out."

He glared at me. "You really think that?"

"That kid you sent in? The frat boy, with the hair? Took him out last night."

My father gave me that look that told me he knew I was playing him, trying to feel him out. He gave me the look until it changed into one almost resembling respect, gratitude. He wanted me to know, to *feel* that I'd screwed up — I still believe that's the biggest high he can ever get — and he wanted to watch me screw up all over again and admit it.

This was the second-best thing. At the end of the day, I was still his son. He had trained me as much as the Army had, but his training was in far more practical arenas. We were waging a war right now, and I was winning. He was proud of that.

"Sounds like the kid had it coming," he said.

I nodded. "Two other assholes as well. Came at me on the road, like they knew me or something. You know anything about that?"

I wasn't accusing my own father of trying to get me hit, but I also wanted to bring him in. At arm's length, but in nonetheless.

His gaze shifted. Stared off a bit, looking at the mirror on the wall that was surrounded by the liquors I stocked. Most expensive closest to the mirror, cheapest and most-often used on the outer perimeter and on the bottom. "Who were they?" he asked.

"No idea. Tried to run me down."

"You take them out?"

I shook my head and poured another bourbon. "No, I was hoping they'd get the point and head out. Didn't know the two events were related at the time."

"Okay," he said. "Makes sense. I guess. Seems like you should've taken the shot when you could."

"Seems like it."

I didn't feel the need to tell him about the rest of it — Hannah, her brother, the other men involved with her abduction. He probably already knew, just from looking at my face. If I was intuitive about people, able to tell what their motives were, he was an absolute prodigy. He could probably read on my face every detail of the night, including where it had happened and who was in my trunk at the moment.

"What do we do?" I asked.

"We? We don't do anything, son. This isn't a problem I'm involved with anymore. I gave you a mark, and you screwed it up. It happens, no hard feelings."

"It *happens?* What are you talking about? It *never* happens. The mark *always* brings me a token, and I verify one way or another that they're the one you meant to send. That's *always* been the case."

"Like I said, no hard feelings."

"What do we *do*? The mark *you* sent is with another party. I don't know who they are, but —"

"Doesn't seem like that's our problem anymore, does it?" he fired back. "I gave you a mark, a job. You failed, someone else got to her first. Fine. Takes it off our hands."

"But they're —"

"But *nothing*. You know the protocol. The drill. The rules are —"

"You *made up* the rules, Dad. You *invented* all of this. It's an arbitrary system, one that you put in place just so you could swing your dick around and feel like your world is bigger than your head."

He sucked in a sharp breath. Poured another drink. I wasn't sorry, never have been. Not with him.

"Listen to me," he said. "Lean in, and listen the hell up. 'Cause I'm only going to say this once."

I leaned in. Couldn't help it.

"You are going to forget this ever happened," he said, speaking through the top of his glass. I could see the fog dancing around the lip of the glass as the words tumbled out. "You're going to forget it, I'm going to forget it, and for God's sake, you're not going to tell that shitty cook about it."

That was the moment. I had been waiting for it, poised even, leaning in intently just so I could revel in the moment as soon as it transpired. It happened, and I'd caught it. Part of me wished I didn't have a dinosaur flip phone in my pocket, so I could have recorded it too.

He'd screwed up too. He knew it, now I knew it.

He had messed something up, something major.

I had a feeling I knew what it was.

"Who was it, Pop?" I asked, trying to feign nonchalance.

"Who was what?"

"Who'd you hire to do it?"

He shot me a glance that almost worked. I almost backed off, for a moment feeling like a little kid again. But nope. Not this time.

"Who did you hire? Who killed him?" I asked again.

I knew I had a few minutes, possibly more. He would sit

there, stunned all over again as he realized how big of a mistake it had been, sipping and thinking and stewing and thinking all around in circles until there was nothing left to stew about and he'd just be pissed he was still stewing.

I had minutes to spare, so I got up and poured yet another drink. I wasn't satisfied with the remnant fire of the bourbon he'd chosen. It wasn't quite top shelf, at least not to me, but it certainly wasn't the worst I'd had. Had a bit of a kick to it that I didn't like — a great bourbon should slide down like a spoonful of cough syrup but have the aftertaste of licking a caramel-coated oak barrel. His choice wasn't it. It made a fantastic old fashioned, whiskey smash, and a passable julep, but I was in the mood for something a bit more sophisticated.

A spirit that would match my own lifted spirits.

The thing about our company — *his* company, technically — was that it only worked because there was very little overhead. No office space, no secretaries, no admin assistants, no employees. Besides me.

And that was his mistake. He'd brought someone else in. Someone else on the payroll, and even the little my old man would have told him, it would be too much. Too much information was a mistake, as it led to too many questions, too many unknowns, and too many new variables.

He'd made a mistake bringing in an outsider, but I wasn't going to rush in and save him the embarrassment. He knew, and I meant to string it out of him like a long, slow drag on a cigarette. Let it burn, nice and slow, and only take in enough to keep that cake alive.

He stared me down. Glared. Begging me to jump in and speak.

"Who was it?"

He sneered. "That's what matters to you, isn't it?" he

barked, whispering at me from over the top of his glass. "That's *all* that matters to you. Making me look like dog shit."

I glared back. "Had a great teacher."

His head fell back a ways and his chin lifted. "Well, whatever award you think you're winning for being bigger than me, it's going to look pretty miserable next to the one you're getting for the shitstorm you caused."

"It was the wrong mark," I admitted. "But he was far from an innocent. Why didn't you pay me?"

"You get paid when you take out the mark," he replied quickly, anticipating the question. "You haven't taken out the mark yet."

"The girl?"

He gave me a look. He didn't need to confirm anything.

I sighed. "Fine. We both messed up. I missed the mark, but at least I didn't bring in a third party to —"

"You think that's what happened? You *really think* I would be stupid enough to bring in someone from the outside?"

I could tell he noticed the confusion on my face.

"This is why *I* run the show, son," he said. "This is why it's *my* company, and not yours. You want to make something of yourself, start thinking. No, of course I didn't *hire* someone to take out the old guy."

"Then —"

"*I* did it. I did it myself, son. Not someone else, not worth the liability. *I* did it."

CHAPTER TWENTY-FIVE

I SAT BACK, NOT CARING any more that my face was broadcasting how I felt. I was stunned. Completely blown away.

"But… why?" I asked. I pushed the glass around in front of me on the bar top, suddenly not feeling very thirsty. "Why would you do it?"

"He needed to go," he said, as if that explained everything.

"Fine," I responded. "But why *you*?"

"It was a business decision, son. You can understand that. There are three people with ownership interests in the company. The old man, his two kids. That's it. Take them out and you take down the company. That's what we're doing here, right?"

I nodded. "Sure, yeah, but that's what you pay *me* for. You… you made a *mess* of it."

"It was going to be a mess either way. Once we hit the big one, the two little ones would get suspicious. The brother and sister would start asking questions. So I gave you the sister, and I was going to focus on the brother."

"I just don't see how it would have —"

"This is *my* area of expertise, remember? You're the grunt who does the dirty work. Nothing more, nothing less. I've operated this business for thirty years, and you've been there for half of that. But don't you ever forget how I started."

"You're too old to be going out on hits, Dad."

"I'm as old as I say I am."

"No, you're really not. You're as old as you *are*, and you're *clearly* too old to be —"

"To *what?*" he yelled. "To *not screw it up?* I *hit* the mark, son, remember? You were the one who let her slip out of your hands. Now what? Now that *my guy's* dead, you've gotten your guy all tangled up in something else. You lost her, and that's on *you*. Not me."

I was furious, but I took a card out of his deck and played it cool. I rotated the rocks glass around in my palm, enjoying the cool dampness on my hand. He had wanted back in, and he'd done it without letting me know. It had created a few hiccups, but nothing we couldn't overcome. Nothing *I* couldn't overcome.

"You need to get back to the office," I said. "Head home, get some sleep, forget this ever happened."

"But there's still —"

"There's still work for *me* to do," I shot back. "*Me.* As in, 'not you.' You've done enough. Get back, get down, and stay out of it. I'll clean up my mess *and* yours, and you know that's the truth. So stop arguing with me about it and let me work."

His nostrils flared, but he didn't speak. He knew it was the right call, and I knew there was a small part of him that was still trying to cover his own ass, making sure I'd be the one to take the fall for anything that came out of this. It pissed me off, but it seemed better than letting him screw with the rest of the operation. As I said, he'd already done enough.

"Fine," he said finally, "do it. Finish this, and make it right."

"I will. You know I will. But I'm going to have expenses. I need a car, as my last one was destroyed on the job. You'd have just told me you weren't going to be paying me, I could have skipped that trip altogether, but as it is, you owe me a vehicle."

He clenched and unclenched his jaw a few times, considering and trying to come up with a pseudo-valid excuse. I could see the slight dimples in his cheeks every time he sneered, just small blips on a scarred face, nearly invisible against the years of wear.

"Fine," he said again.

"Enough to get me there and back again, wherever that is."

He nodded once and stood up to leave. He didn't reach in his pockets for a wallet or any cash.

I waited until he'd turned around and started toward the door. "I'll pick it up tomorrow morning. Usual spot."

CHAPTER TWENTY-SIX

I CHECKED ON JOEY IN the back after I'd rinsed out and stashed the rocks glasses we'd used. He was seated on the steps descending to the street behind my place, whistling low and slow, an old folk song he'd remembered from childhood or something. The air was cool, and it floated around me but left its sticky humidity behind. I stood there, the door swung open, until Joey turned around.

"How long you think he'll be okay in there?" he asked.

I shrugged. "Long enough. Can't suffocate in there, if that's what you mean. There's airflow from the cracks around the back seat. Worst case he'll starve or go thirsty, but that'll take a few days."

"So what do we do with him?"

"Not sure yet, besides trying to squeeze him for information." I wasn't really into torture, as it nearly always took on a sadistic excitement. I didn't need any more hobbies, and sure as hell didn't want to start enjoying the line of work I was in. So I really didn't have a plan, other than to tie the guy to a chair and rough him up a bit, mostly because

I was still pissed he'd taken Hannah. If he decided to talk about his employer, great.

"Let's leave him in the trunk a bit longer," Joey said. "He's going to make a lot of noise out here, unless we can get him tired out. Or maybe we can just get him out now and *make* him shut up."

I nodded, liking that last idea, and walked over to the trunk. I wasn't armed, so I waited for Joey to join me in case the guy had some crazy scheme he'd cooked up.

He didn't. The trunk flew open and he was just laying there, staring up at us, surprised.

"Who are you working for?" I asked, calmly. I figured I'd give him three chances, then we'd fishbait him. I didn't want to clean blood off the floor of my kitchen, and there was still the feeling that my anger and frustration would get out of hand and we'd end up getting ourselves all sticky with an interrogation style I wasn't comfortable with.

He didn't answer.

"I'm going to ask you two more times," I said, explaining it simultaneously for Joey. "Then we're going to kill you. Nothing fancy, nothing unnecessary. Just plain and simple, you die. Got it?"

"I'm dead anyway," he growled.

I thought for a moment. "True," I said, shrugging. "Fine. Joey, go grab my —"

"I'll tell you where they took her, but it should be obvious already."

I held up my end of the ruse. "I already know where they took her. I asked you a different question. *Joey*. Go grab my 9mm. Doesn't matter which one. Doesn't need a suppressor."

The guy glared at me, but didn't speak until Joey had left. "You're in over your head, pal."

"You know, that's not the first time I've heard that today.

Thing is, when you're in something, you gotta get out of it, you know?"

"Then walk away. Leave the trunk open, and walk away."

"I suppose you'll tell your people to leave me alone, never come back this away again, that sort of thing."

"Yeah, exactly. That sort of thing."

I could almost taste the lie falling off his sneering lips. I didn't even need to say the word 'bullshit' out loud. I just smiled.

Then I punched him in the nose.

"You took the girl, asshole. Hannah Rayburn. Why?"

There was blood falling out of his crushed nose, but he didn't even try to wipe it off. "Why do you think?" I lifted my fist again, threatening. He flinched, but then recovered. "You haven't figured it out yet, you're not going to."

"Okay, fair enough. I've figured it out. What's the end game? She die, too?"

"If she doesn't give him what he wants, yeah. Sure. And it won't be pretty."

"She doesn't give *who* what he wants?"

He ignored me. "He's got a whole string of guys that'd love to take her out, if you know what I mean. They ain't gonna make it pretty at all. Told me all about it. Girl like that, you don't waste it."

I saw him lick his lips in the dim light. There was blood on his tongue, but I couldn't tell if he liked it or not.

Joey returned, checking that the pistol was loaded and ready to go. He handed it to me.

"One more time, like I promised. Then you're fishbait. Who are you working for?"

"You know, cute little thing like that, I doubt they'll even wait to get started, and who knows if he'll be able to keep his goons off her. Probably all sick about it already, wanting to jump in. One of them's a legs guy, I think, from what I can remember. Probably start at the bottom and work his way up. Other guy… well, I'm not sure exactly what to call it, but…" The guy shook his head, then laughed. "I'm into some pretty kinky shit myself, but he — man, he's gonna really give her a ride."

It took every ounce of strength and mental fortitude not to shoot the guy in the kneecaps, then the elbows, then the head, maybe a few minutes later, just to watch him suffer. It wasn't about the handgun, either. Even though the pistol would attract unwanted attention if I discharged here, it was about more than that.

It was about Hannah.

I'm not sure when I'd stopped caring about the money and started doing it just because it was her, but I knew it was the truth. Staring down at the hired hand of a man who now had Hannah Rayburn in his possession, I could think of nothing else than getting her back.

I didn't care about my own father, I didn't care about his money, and I didn't care about this guy enough to even make it painful for him.

"Get out," I said, forcing the words out through my teeth. I turned and nodded to Joey.

The man struggled a bit, trying to wake up a sleeping appendage or something, then pulled his neck and shoulders sideways and started to lift them up.

I waited until his head had gotten out of the trunk and up a little bit, then I reached up and slammed the hatch door as hard as I could.

There were two bumps, one from his skull on the inside of the hatch door, and another for his body as it slumped unconscious once again. I checked that the trunk was closed tightly, then watched Joey come over with the keys.

"That ought to do it," I said, reaching for the keys. "You know the drill. Take him out, string him up, and dump him. Be clean, be careful. Put one through his head if he whines too much, but otherwise keep the gun out of the picture."

Joey was already in motion, taking the pistol back from me and guarding the trunk when I opened it. The man was bleeding from two spots now, but he appeared to still be breathing. We rolled him over and picked him up out of the trunk, and Joey threw him over his shoulder. He was heavier than the kid from yesterday had been, but Joey didn't even seem to notice the massive, sloppy weight that had been added. He was stocky, and wide enough to make it work.

I walked over to the gate I'd used for my phone call earlier and forced it open, this time kicking out the earth that had piled up on the other side so it would open wider. Joey navigated through with the unconscious man's body on him, then started back toward the bar. There was a path, barely noticeable unless you knew where to look, starting there somewhere and winding around to the coast. It was the path he'd taken when he'd gotten rid of the first guy, the younger kid, so he probably had the bleach and other supplies down there already, stashed in one of the cupboards inside the skiff. The bleach helped remove anything that could be dredged up later, like fingerprints on eyeglasses or shoe leather, and even though the ocean did a more than fine job of that itself, I always erred on the side of caution.

I watched Joey until he disappeared into the woods, nothing but a black shadow swirling around and becoming one of many. In another few seconds, I couldn't even hear him.

I walked back to the steps, sat down where he had been waiting earlier, and watched the fence, hoping that I wouldn't soon be hearing a gunshot.

CHAPTER TWENTY-SEVEN

THE LONGER I WENT WITHOUT new information, the further out of reach Hannah would be. I had told her the truth; I wasn't a private investigator. I wasn't a cop, or a detective. I wasn't trained to put pieces together and hunt down a killer, or find a kidnapped child. I knew what I knew — I was good at that stuff, always had been. But I also knew what I *didn't* know.

The problem was that I'd exhausted my options. Joey was good for a sidekick, but he needed direction and assignment. My father had proven how helpful he would be, and it had gotten us nowhere. Possibly even made things worse. And my contact in Washington had already explained to me that to meddle with his investigation was going to get me killed. Or worse, locked up.

So I was out of assets. I had myself, and I had the small amount of knowledge of the situation. I was running low on money, as my bank would start auto-drafting the month's mortgage payment early next week and my utility payments would be due shortly thereafter. My apartment had a rent as well, and even though it was cheap it wasn't nothing. I couldn't exactly afford to build an arsenal anywhere, pay for help, or spend the money traveling around and figuring things out.

Hunting Island was just a little over a stone's throw (if you could throw a stone exactly five miles) from Edisto Beach, but there were no bridges that spanned the five miles. Instead, 174 connected to 17, then to 21, which shot east and south again, reaching through to Hunting Island and the Atlantic Ocean just beyond. It was a two-hour drive that could be crammed into one-and-a-half if one was dedicated and lucky enough to miss any police.

Didn't matter how long it took, I'd decided, Hunting Island was in my near future. I was already making plans as I headed out to Joey's car. I needed to leave him a note, letting him know the next steps I wanted him to take. Mainly it was keeping the bar open and afloat, but there were some other things as well. There were people after me, so I didn't want to let him continue on without a watchful eye on the door. If he saw anyone suspicious hanging around or asking about me, I instructed him to call me immediately. Likewise if he got any strange questions or looks in general while tending the bar.

The plan was to head to my place, to get a couple hours of sleep before heading down to Hunting Island to snoop around. I was hoping to still get to Hunting Island early morning, before it was light, so I'd be able to walk around the property without being seen if the need arose, which meant I had only a couple of hours of sleep available.

Before I drove southwest across town to my place, however, I needed to stop by and check on Hannah's brother. He hadn't ever spoken to me, but I felt somewhat responsible for getting his sister kidnapped. She'd sworn me to secrecy about the details surrounding her father's death, which meant for whatever reason she didn't think he could handle the disturbing truth of her father's business.

Which meant she thought he was as innocent as she was. That was fine with me — I had no interest in trying to explain the details to anyone else, so I figured I'd just check in on him, see if he'd started to worry about his sister yet. I would tell him a little bit about it, just so he understood the magnitude of the situation and to try to get him to understand that calling the cops was a very bad idea, and I would stand there in his doorway and wait until he agreed with me.

I didn't think I'd need to rough him up at all, as that might be counterproductive, but my feeling was that if he was actually as fragile as he'd seemed in the bar and as innocent as Hannah was portraying him, he wouldn't really be in a state of mind to offer much help or resistance. So I needed to get to him, make him understand the basics, and give him the instructions. Don't call the cops, don't try to get involved, don't even leave the apartment.

He'd nod his head, solemnly, and tell me to get her back. He might even be shaking, trying to push down the fear.

Hopefully.

That was if everything went the way it was supposed to. That was if he cooperated.

I hated third parties when it came to stuff like this. Previous victims, siblings, witnesses, they all created problems and extra variables that I didn't want to deal with. They were sometimes loose cannons, trying to do things they weren't trained or prepared for.

In all, it created a hell of a mess, and I was hoping Daniel Rayburn wouldn't be a mess.

CHAPTER TWENTY-EIGHT

I DROVE UP TO MARLEY'S for the third time that week and parked along the curb. I got out of Joey's car and started up the steps, heading toward the porch. I involuntarily relived my previous experience as I saw the same shrubs, the same garden, the same dark shadows falling in the same way across the wide lawn. The two grunts who'd come at me, at us, and had taken Hannah.

I shuddered, then stepped onto the porch.

Something didn't feel right — I knew it as soon as my hand reached out and grabbed at the handle. The great wooden door was leaning a bit, closed but somehow crooked. I focused my attention closer on the wood around the door until I realized what was wrong.

The old, dried wood frame surrounding the door was cracked and splitting just about all over it, a symptom of age and lack of upkeep. I'd never been this close to Marley's front door, but I figured it was a typical feel for a door that was over a century old. The problem was that there was *another* crack in the door. I could tell that it was newer.

The crack started at the top of the jamb, near the ninety-degree joint that started into the horizontal framing, and fell straight down and widened, opening up to almost a half-inch across where the handle and strike met. The strike itself was fractured, and had slid backwards on a screw and was partly visible.

I reached for the handle, turned it, and pushed. The door wouldn't give, but it wasn't locked. I could see the strike, which meant the door wasn't even fully closed, so I pushed again. It was stuck hard, so I backed away and gave it a shoulder-jab on my right side and felt the splintering wood crack and bow a bit, then finally give way to the large door. It fell open then on a single hinge, smacked against the floor as it slid open, and a few pieces of wood that had been previously broken fell away into the house.

Someone had come in here already, taking the brutish break-down-the-door approach, and they'd left me with a partly closed door that was held together only with its own weight and the pressure of the slot the door had been designed to fit in. As soon as I'd forced it open once again, the structural integrity of the whole thing had been compromised.

The door fell away, losing its balance on the single remaining hinge and it twisted away from me, buckling the last hinge off its screws and falling with a huge thud onto the entranceway floor.

I waited, listening.

No one yelled or responded. I stepped farther into the house. The entranceway was immaculate, just as I'd seen it pictured online. The spot I was standing in offered me the best view of the majority of the layout, including an unobstructed view of the top level. The entranceway split off both directions, a small sitting room on my left, and a tiny open den area on my right. The den had a fireplace, one of three I remember seeing pictured. The other two were alongside the back wall of the house, one in a large master bedroom and the other in a larger, spacious living area on the main floor.

There was a stairway to my right, inside the front room there, and I knew there was another one on the other side of the house, starting in the main living area and ascending right up to the left of where I was standing now. The top level of the house was all bedrooms, each accessible by the square-shaped hallway that ran around the second story. A wraparound porch gave each of the bedrooms double doors to outside. It was a perfect example of the southern-style homes I loved.

I felt the urge to scrap the plans I'd made and just sleep here for the night. It seemed like no one was home anyway, but I knew better. Whoever had come in here had done it wanting something. Wanting something bad enough they had decided it wasn't worth waiting for the old man to let them in. They'd come barging in, destroying the front door, and had done something inside.

The 'something' was the part I was beginning to wonder about.

"Marley?" I yelled. "You in here?"

I had never met his wife, but I'd always heard the locals say he was married, so I assumed there was a Mrs. Marley somewhere inside as well. I called out again, and didn't hear anything.

I walked toward that room now, still listening intently for any out-of-place noises. Or any noises at all.

I walked by a small vase, seated atop a tiny four-legged table against the left wall. It was directly beneath a portrait of a woman seated in front of Marley. He was standing, smiling at the photographer, but she was stoic and expressionless. The picture was on a textured canvas, the raised paint perfectly spread on the canvas, the telltale sign of a photograph that had been rendered as a painting for economy purposes.

Mrs. Marley, I thought as I stared at the painting and the vase on the table. I didn't need a look inside to know where the old lady had ended up.

That meant there were at least two more people in the house unaccounted for.

I walked on, stepping down once to get into the main living area in the back of the house, and found one of the people.

CHAPTER TWENTY-NINE

MARLEY HIMSELF WAS SEATED IN a rustic armchair, burgundy leather and brass knobs on all the seams. He was wearing a robe, with a white t-shirt peering out from underneath it, and his feet were on the floor in front of him.

Everything in the room seemed picture-perfect, including the man himself, but that was the problem. Everything was still, *exactly* like a photograph. Even sleeping, Marley should have been moving a little. It was dark in the room, so I walked over and flicked on a light switch using my sleeve. The room flashed on in bright orange light, and I could tell immediately what was off.

Mr. Marley was sitting, his eyes were closed, and his chin was down. In the dark it had seemed as though the man was sleeping, just catching a nap after a nightcap or late-night snack before heading off to bed. But I knew the truth now.

The light had illuminated the horrible hole in Marley's head. The one that had splattered the inside of his head up onto the back of the tall chair and a little bit onto the wallpapered wall behind it. The hole I could see was small, nearly invisible in the dark, but there would be another one

— a much larger one — on the other side. I didn't need to see it, and I didn't want to.

I backed up, nearly tripping over the single step into the living room, and turned away. I didn't bother turning out the light — I'd already seen the dead guy. It was seared into the back of my eyes, forever stamped on my brain. I'd seen dead bodies before, and I would see them again, but every now and then there's one that takes you by surprise. You half-expect you might see them, then you do, and you realize you didn't expect it at all.

I sniffed, realizing the body hadn't begun to stink yet, and then walked back to the opposite corner of the room where the stairs came down. It hadn't been long since the man had been shot, probably only minutes. I had a feeling I wouldn't find Daniel Rayburn inside, but I needed to know. There were three options. He wouldn't have stayed here if someone had broken in to rob the place or just to shoot Marley. If it had been a breaking and entering, and they'd found Marley on the chair and just shot him to silence him, Daniel would have waited until they left and then ran to the police. Another option was he would have called the police from his room after hearing the shot, and this place would be swarming (with the two officers on night duty in Edisto). Or they were still on their way, Daniel was still in the room, which meant I needed to get up there, find him, and then get back out before they arrived.

All of those options were for events that hadn't transpired, however. I knew the truth: they hadn't come for Marley, and they hadn't come to rob him.

They'd come for Daniel.

I rushed up the stairs, two at a time, only then realizing that I *still* wasn't armed. I was asking to get shot, it seemed. I made a note to stop and grab a piece before I left for Hunting Island in a couple hours.

At the top of the stairs I was faced with the left-right decision the hallway offered. Since there were rooms all along the hallway around the second story, I wasn't sure which one would have been Daniel's and Hannah's, or if they would have slept in separate rooms. I also didn't remember how many rooms were up here. There were two small rooms downstairs, both off the main living room, which meant there should be space for at least six more up here.

I chose right. I carefully walked along the old wood floor, staying on the edge against the hallway wall to prevent any squeaking or creaking. The first room was to my left, and the door was hanging open a bit. I peered in, found it empty, and then continued along my journey around the top level.

The next two rooms were connected in the middle by a single door, and both were empty. Marley hadn't had a lot of business in the last year or so, and I wondered if his late wife had been the main driving force behind the bed and breakfast's existence. He might have kept the place running in honor of her, or because he didn't know anything better. This week, it seemed, he had only two guests.

The fourth room, on the opposite side of the house from the stairs I'd come up on, looked to be the same size as the first one I'd checked. I paused outside this room, as the door was shut. It wasn't locked. I turned it, slowly, the antique glass knob small and cold in my hand. I was afraid I would break it off if I gripped it any harder, but I finally got the knob turned enough to push the door open a crack without making a sound.

I gathered my confidence, feeling the adrenaline already beginning to rush in. There was a dead man sitting in a chair on the floor below me, I was tracking down a woman who had been kidnapped, and I was trying to do it before the cops got involved. I didn't need to be holding a gun to know that I'd be a substantial force to fight in this state.

I pushed the door a bit more and it creaked. Softly, but it was like a cannon firing in the still night air. I sucked in a breath, then waited. I pushed it all the way open, realizing that anyone still waiting inside the room would have spoken or shot at me by now.

The door was open, and I glanced from the left to the right. The left side of the room was clean, empty. So was the right, but it was another two-room space. The door connecting the rooms was standing open a crack. I walked in, past the huge bed that sat against the back window. As I came around to the door, I saw a suitcase lying on the floor on the side of the bed. I stopped, turning down to peer at it closer.

There was enough moonlight to see just a bit of the tag on it. H. Rayburn.

Hannah.

I'd found her suitcase, stored in what was apparently her room as well.

It meant her brother was probably staying in the next room, and I stepped toward the door connecting the two rooms to confirm it. On my way there I glanced around at Hannah's room once more. There wasn't much to see, as it appeared as though she really hadn't unpacked. She'd changed clothes at least once since I'd met her, but the suitcase sat unopened next to the bed. Probably had a bathroom bag sitting on the counter in the bathroom across the hall. I wondered if she'd taken some of her dresses or formalwear for the funeral and hung them up in the closet.

Aside from the suitcase, everything I could see in the room was not hers but part of the furniture of the place —

lamps, dresser, light fixture, rug at the foot of the bed. Then my eyes fell on the small tray sitting in front of the lamp on the left side of the bed.

I walked over. Two sets of earrings, both of them pairs I hadn't seen her wearing. One was a silvery leaf of some sort that hung down off of a group of three rings, and the other was a tiny, simpler gemstone.

But there was something else in the tray. My eye adhered to it like it had been trying to call my attention toward it since I'd walked into the room. I reached out for it and carefully poked the earrings out of the way.

The token.

A hefty, weighty object. Smaller than a silver dollar, larger than a quarter. Brown, from the tarnished remnants of what was once bronze. It had darkened and grown spotty in places, but there was a distinct impression of a man's bust on one side. No idea who the man was supposed to be, or what country's currency it was, if any. It was possible my father had made the token himself, stamping out the bronze in his shop years ago and using a template he'd found online.

Didn't matter where it came from originally. The point was that this token was absolutely unique. I knew its spots, stains, and tiny imperfections better than I knew anything. It was impossible to mistake for something else, and that was the point.

I flipped the coin around in my hand, feeling its weight. I would have known what it was just by the feel of it. The cold, dead metal feel in my palm represented so much to me. It represented the cold, dead feeling I had when the token was presented to me at the bar, just an unsuspecting schmuck hoping for a quick score, or a big score, or whatever else my father had persuaded them they would find. The cold, dead feeling of victory after they recognized what their score — their final score on this earth — would really be.

And then the cold, dead feeling I knew they felt after they were cold and dead.

I tossed the token in a pocket. I would need it later, to return to my boss. I usually needed it to get paid — I would stash the token in the box out in the woods and then check back the next day. It would be replaced by the money.

A simple system. One that had never failed.

A single token, and a single mark. Always.

Things had gotten complicated, and I didn't like that. I could handle the complications, and the pressure, but I didn't like the additional variables they brought into play.

I turned back around and set my sights on the door connecting the two rooms. The moment of truth.

I didn't hesitate this time. It was too late for hesitation. Too late for surprise. I shouldered the door open and barged through it.

And I nearly slipped on the blood.

CHAPTER THIRTY

THERE WAS BLOOD EVERYWHERE. THE floor seemed like a bottomless pit, the darkness and dim shadows combined with the crimson stuff completing the illusion. I gagged, choking on air. I could smell it, the thick coppery tinge of it.

I covered my mouth with my left hand and supported my weight with my right. I stood there, silent, appalled, until I was ready to truly *see* what was in front of me.

Daniel Rayburn was against the wall on the opposite side of the room, shirtless. He had long pants on, but they appeared to be pajama bottoms or something similar. He was barefoot. The bed in his room had been pushed toward the patio door, blocking the exit and clearing a space in the room. His head was down, but his arms were splayed out to his sides. I could see duct tape, it looked like, wrapped tightly around his wrists and smeared onto the wall. Enough of it to hold his weight on the wall and keep his arms stretched out.

The blood was pouring from his gut, a wide, jagged cut

open and leaking onto the floor. A little jostling around and I knew the insides would be on the outside, but at the moment everything appeared intact. There was a horrible mess of blood on the nightstand nearby, and I realized that it had been where they'd placed the tools.

The tools they'd used to torture the poor boy.

He was dead. It had taken some time for him to die, as well. The blood draining from his wound would have come out fast enough to kill him, but slowly enough to give him time to suffer. Had they gone a little deeper they might have punctured an organ and sped the process up, but I had a feeling they had done it this way on purpose. They had intended for him to die, and die slowly. They had done it right after they'd killed Marley, but thankfully the old man had gone much more quickly.

I stepped up closer anyway, to get a better look. I didn't want to turn the lights on, as that might offer too good a look, and I wasn't really ready for that. Instead, I needed to see something on him… something I'd noticed.

When I'd walked into the room I hadn't seen Daniel at first — he was nearly unrecognizable — but something else. Something on his body.

A number.

There, scrawled in his own blood on his chest, was a number. A string of numbers, ten altogether, that had been scratched onto his chest with a knife. Probably while he was still alive.

It was a message, and it was meant for me.

The audacity of it all was almost more appalling than the murder itself. They had actually left a *phone number* behind, something traceable and trackable, and something that would no doubt take this case from the status of small-town deranged psychopath murder to a state- or national-level alarm. Multiple precincts, multiple jurisdictions, possibly even Fed-level involvement.

They would have known that, and they would have continued along anyway. Without caring about the larger ramifications. It meant they were either too stupid to know, or they were too bold to care. I had a feeling their stupidity was not going to be an issue for them.

I needed to get out of here, before the cops arrived and the thing blew wide open.

I felt the rage building in my own chest as I committed the number to memory. I didn't dare take my phone out and call it from there, but I fingered the end of the antenna in my pocket as I stared daggers at the number.

They had Hannah, and now they want me.

They had used her brother as a tool. And they meant to use me, as well.

They knew I would want Hannah back — that I was invested enough in all of it to want her — and they probably thought I'd want revenge, too.

The thought of revenge didn't upset me.

There was nothing else of value in the room, and I'd almost incriminated myself by stepping in the pool of blood that had nearly reached the door, but I sidestepped it once again and walked out. I took the same path I'd entered, glancing at Hannah's suitcase on the floor. I thought about it a moment, then grabbed it.

It was heavy, an old-fashioned sort that had thick leather all around the single zipper and didn't roll. I hefted it with my right hand, feeling that it suited Hannah perfectly — a modern-day woman keeping up the impression of a classy, timeless dame.

The suitcase and I left the room, turned left, and reached the stairs on the opposite side of the hallway, the stairs on this side of the house that would take us down and out through the front door without having to see old man Marley and as little of the rest of the crime-scene house as possible.

The descent down the stairs was illuminated by the light spilling in through the still-open front door, the combination of moonlight and streetlight mixing into a wash of faint white-orange. I came to the bottom of the stairs, felt the urge to speed up, and walked over the threshold.

I was wondering if anyone had heard the gunshot, as that would have warranted a call to the police. Marley's was on a large lot, probably one that was the size of four of the surrounding ones, an old grandfather clause in the zoning. Still, a shot that had blown the brains out of an old man would have been *plenty* loud enough.

I looked left and right, both to check for flashing police lights and to see what sorts of establishments were closest to Marley's place. I already knew there was a corner store on the northern side of the lot, and I saw a small office building, like a dental practice or something similar on the southern side. Both would be closed at this hour, and it was likely no one would have been in the building.

For now, I was clear. If no one had called in the gunshot by now, no one would. And if the Rayburns really had been the only tenants in the bed and breakfast, it meant it would be days until anyone thought to check in with Marley.

Days for the trail to grow cold.

Then the cops would swoop in, shut the block down, and start the slow but menacing wheels turning in the direction of justice. They would follow protocol, allowing the guys who'd done it plenty of time to adapt, dodge, and stay one step ahead.

But I wasn't the cops, and I wasn't planning to follow any protocol but my own.

I had the number, and I planned on calling it as soon as I could.

CHAPTER THIRTY-ONE

I DROVE NORTH ON 174 once again, heading away from the coast, Edisto Beach, and everything I owned in this life. But I wasn't leaving this life behind — far from it. I needed to think, and I thought best out in the middle of nothing else but my own thoughts.

The road was harder to find at night, but not impossible if you knew what you were looking for. I'd made the trip plenty of times already, both at night and during daylight hours, so it was no trouble to pull off and drive along the shoulder, keeping a steady, slow speed until I found it.

There were some scuff marks in front of me from the battle I'd had against the other cars, and it helped give me a little idea of where I was. Some black tread marks, tracks in the sandy shoulder, and small pieces of car littered over the asphalt. Just past that mess I saw the turnoff for my sanctuary, and I took Joey's car down it a hundred feet or so.

I didn't want to get stuck, as even a five-minute drive back into town would become a twenty-five minute walk, and I didn't know if Joey's car could handle the terrain of the old beat-up path. I parked, shut the car off, and walked the rest of the way in the dark. A small moon offered more than enough light to bleed through the trees and illuminate the path in front of me just enough to get to the rock outcropping. I wasn't worried about wildlife, as there really wasn't anything out on the coast that I was concerned about, and I figured I'd scare off anything smaller than me well before I could hear it nearby.

The rocks were suddenly in front of me, looming, deep shadows of nothingness against a lighter blackness behind them. I dodged the two in my path and came around the last one, just as I had done earlier.

I didn't need to dig as far to find the box, which told me a couple of things: one, whoever had put it back in the ground had been a bit lazy, and two, that my father had been out here.

My father, my employer, was the only human on the planet besides me who knew about this location. It had been my idea, and because of that he'd always tried to make me feel like crap about it. 'What's wrong with a bank account?' he'd ask, like he thought tainted money from his sources would be safe to store with banks. Or 'why not a simple safe deposit box?' or something of that nature.

Truth was, I did it for two simple reasons. Probably weighted fifty-fifty. The first reason was that I didn't trust anyone but myself, and to a slightly lesser extent, Joey. He'd proven himself enough of a loyalist that I had started to no longer question him anymore. I didn't trust banks, or drop boxes, or any other 'regulated' sort of security exchange, including gym lockers (and there were no fancy gyms anywhere nearby). And I sure as hell didn't trust my boss.

The second reason was that I kind of liked the effect it had on him. He was constantly pissed at me for one thing or another, and more often than not it was simply because I wasn't exactly like him in that particular way. He hated that I had my opinion on things, and he *really* hated that I had training that had proven — time and time again — that my opinion, shaped and honed over years of experience, was often better than his. He hated that I felt a moderately-deep hole in the woods was by far a better place to hide money and other accoutrements than a bank or an old-school safe-deposit box somewhere.

We'd even gone over it more than once, since it took more than once for him to get the message. Worst case, the land it was on would be sold and developed, in which case I'd have to pay enough attention to get there before the inspectors, surveyor, and initial construction crew arrived. But that was a multi-month process, and if I wasn't out here more than once every few months to pick up my money, we had bigger problems.

Other cases that he'd argued, as implausible as they sounded, were things like if a hiker happened to stumble across the location and start digging in that exact one-foot square location for some odd reason, during the time between when he left the money for me and I came to get it. I explained that it was far more likely that a bank executive would receive a government-stamped mandate to open my box and snoop around. Or, in actuality, it would be far more likely that I just got struck by lightning on the way to the bank.

He dropped it after about three such scenarios, after I'd explained to him that I was contracted, not salaried. That meant a few things, but most importantly it meant that I could receive my money however I decided to receive it, and we promptly drew up and signed a contract stating that as soon as the money had hit the hole, as we called it, it was mine — if it got robbed before I got to it, that was on me.

That contract was the only document we'd signed, and we'd promptly thrown it into the bowl of our shared ashtray and lit it on fire. It was enough for both of us that we'd agreed to something, signed it, and then ceremoniously celebrated its brief existence over an illegal Cohibo. If my old man was anything, it was honest. He had never, to my knowledge, lied about anything. We weren't in a line of work that typically mandated pure honesty, but it was the sole source of pride I had in him that I could confidently say he was a man of his word.

That fact made our work even more impressive to me. He never told the marks what he had in store for them, but he somehow never lied, either. He would finally get in contact with the schmucks, hand them the token, and whisper something in their ear like, 'you need to see my pal down in Edisto when you pass through. He can get you what you deserve,' or 'take this. It's good for a two-for-one, if you know what I mean.'

Now, if you're a straight-laced, upstanding taxpaying citizen like the vast majority of us, we'd hear that as exactly what he said. But if you're anything else, including a scum-of-the-earth pornographer or a shitbag pedophile, you hear what you want to hear. You hear something *entirely* different than 'free drink' or 'deep discount for a hard-working grunt.' You hear something that sounds an awful lot like 'next score,' and 'this is what you've been waiting for.'

For those assholes, there's no better music to their ears. They're hearing it because they want to, and that's the genius of the company. That's the brilliance of the business model, because we don't have to lie, cheat, or steal.

We just have to kill.

But killing, to me, is an extension of living. And when

we forfeit our right to life, we forfeit our right to choose how and when we die.

And call it religion, belief construct, or simple blind ignorance, but one of the only things I've ever been one-hundred-percent sure about is the fact that if you decide to take someone else's right to life, or someone else's God-given right to *work* toward life, you abandon your own.

So I felt no remorse for the work I did.

Most of the time, really, I enjoyed it.

These folks come in with their swagger, confidence, and nonchalance, and I come in to remind them that their choices have a consequence. If I got to pour them a perfectly manicured drink beforehand, all the better. I call it foreshadowing.

I thought about all of this as I pulled the box out. There wouldn't be any reason for my boss to come by and dig it all up, then rebury it lazily unless he was going to pay me, and I knew by the weight of it that he had.

Thirty thousand dollars.

Not enough to carry me through the year, but not nothing, either.

I counted it out, in the darkness, feeling the Benjamins as much as seeing them. They felt dirty, but only in the physical, tired way. As I thought about the man I'd killed, and the reason I'd done it, they felt like the cleanest bills I'd ever put my hands on. I collected the edges and corners and placed them into their neat little stacks. Then I took the stacks and filled up my hands with them — one-hundred fifty bills in each hand, as it were — and set them aside for the moment. I placed the box back in the hole and filled it in, then picked up the stacks once again.

Thirty thousand dollars.

I usually got about a mark a quarter, once every few

months. Sometimes more. It took time for my old man to track them down, place them on a grid — a proprietary system he'd created that plotted their likelihood of being tracked by government agents against their probable net worth — and study their movements.

So thirty thousand was enough to carry me through the next six months, easily, including both property's rent and mortgage, Joey's salary, my overhead, and a few extra payments I intended to use to get the bar under my own name, and then some. It was enough that I knew I'd won with my boss — he wanted to make sure I had enough capital to get the job done, clean and done. No loose ends, no unknown variables, no questions. He wanted it as much as I did, and he knew there wasn't anyone else he could call.

We were in this together, and if he didn't fund it, no one would.

So I had thirty grand at my disposal, and I figured half would be a good stock for taking care of business — the other business — and the other half I'd split between fixing my ride and finding Hannah. I knew what they wanted, so I needed to also figure out how to get them off of it and get Hannah out alive, or else get Hannah away from it all and let the feds sort through the details.

I couldn't call my contact, that much was clear. My old friend was in over his head as much as I was, and he would be actively looking for a CYA-grade scapegoat. There was no way I was calling him and filling him in on details. I figured if he was good at his job he'd figure things out eventually and swoop in to save the day or blow it all up and we'd be no better or worse off for it.

Which meant I was pretty much on my own. Joey was good for some grunt work, but for that to be useful I had to have grunts for him to deal with and I had to know what I wanted him to do. I was flying blind, driving his car and heading into unknown territory.

But I was stubborn, and I was pissed. I had already decided what I would do, I just needed the catalyst. The moment of realization that came with a revelation. Something that would zap into my mind at exactly the right time until I knew what I was supposed to do.

Most people have no idea what to do in a situation like this, because they haven't been trained to deal with high pressure. They hesitate, they wait, they let others make the calls for them. They don't let their instincts drive them, and if they do their instincts lead them to try things they're not qualified to try.

But I *am* qualified. I've been trained, I've had practice, and I have that weird and unique combination of I-believe-I'm-right and I-don't-give-a-shit to make the practice stick. So being pissed, having a target, and knowing that I could do whatever the hell I wanted to do to them made me somewhat of a dangerous fool to mess with.

The problem, of course, was that I didn't know exactly where this target *was*. I could hit it, that was certain, but I needed to see it first.

CHAPTER THIRTY-TWO

I CALLED AS I DROVE. I headed up 174 to 17, planning on taking it across to 21, then down all the way to the end at Hunting Island. Hannah had mentioned her old place was right across the river from Harbor Island on the northern tip. I knew Harbor Island well, as I'd spent some time at the tavern there that supplied the work crews their booze. The northern tip of Harbor Island was mostly yacht owners and condominiums. The work crews were constantly busy tearing apart the old condos and redoing them for the new owners, in an endless and vicious cycle.

By my calculations, the house I was looking for would be visible just after the bridge over Johnson Creek. There was nothing else there, and the tip of the island wasn't very big.

I lifted the phone up in front of me and dialed the number I'd memorized as I drove. I picked up speed, feeling the intensity and adrenaline growing inside me.

It rang. Three times, and then it clicked onto a connection. The sound of static hit my ear, light, but I could tell there was a human on the other end.

I waited.

She started talking after a few more seconds. Scared, disturbed, losing her mind. Crying, of course. "Mason, is that — is that you?"

My nostrils flared, and I clenched the phone tighter in my hand. "Hannah," I said. "Are you —"

I could sense the phone on the other end being ripped away from her ear. She squealed, a quiet, compliant sound, not quite a scream. Then a grunt as something of force hit her.

"Listen up, you son of a —"

"I believe you are no longer in a position to negotiate," a new voice said, calmly, into my ear. "Wouldn't you agree?"

I seethed for a moment.

"Are you still there, Dixon? I hope so. We have been waiting, *impatiently*, for your call. I'm glad you found the number."

"What do you want?"

"We are a little bit past that, are we not? This is about business, plain and simple. Hannah's business, as she is now the sole living owner of the company."

Hannah wailed in the background, then she stopped suddenly. I winced, knowing why.

"Oh," the voice said. "I did forget to mention that to the lovely lady. Sorry. Mr. Dixon, why don't you fill her in on the details? One second."

I heard the clicking sound of the man fumbling with the phone, then the static increased and expanded — I was now on speakerphone on the other end, about to talk to the entire room.

"There. Hannah, can you let Mr. Dixon know you are able to hear him?"

She whimpered in the background.

"Hannah," I said. "Are you okay? Did they hurt you?"

"There will be time for catching up later. Soon, actually. For now, I need you to do what I've asked. Won't you tell Hannah how her brother is doing?"

I shook my head, not even caring that they couldn't see it.

"Be a good sport about it, my friend. There's really nothing you can do about him now. In fact, it will probably be, what, four or five days — *at least* — before anyone thinks to check for him? Wait, that's not right, is it? The funeral, of course, will happen Sunday. Today is, what, Thursday? So that narrows it down a bit. They'll be looking for him, starting rather soon. And we don't want to keep Hannah for that long. I'd feel much more comfortable to have this niggling little problem resolved, say, by Saturday evening."

"What do you *want*?" I asked again.

"I want you to tell Hannah how her brother is doing."

"She already knows you killed him."

I couldn't hear Hannah's response, but I could assume she was sitting there, wherever she was, shaking. With fury, with pain, with fear.

"Care to share the details?" the man asked.

"Not so much."

"Fine. We'll just have to share the pictures with her. Cell phones these days are quite miraculous, are they not? I can store *hundreds* of photos in here. I wonder how many more scenes need to be photographed before I'm out of memory?"

I clenched my teeth. Raged, internally, knowing that I couldn't do a damn thing from inside the car.

"What do you really want?"

"You really are dense, aren't you? I want the *business*. Plain and simple. That's what it was always about. Thanks to a competitor, I assume, the old man himself has been taken care of. No one believes it was a suicide. Either way, it made my job that much easier."

"You have the business. She's sitting right there. What's stopping you?"

"Yes, she is right here. Waiting patiently for your arrival, as am I. You see, I convinced her to sign her name on whatever documents I put in front of her within the first hour of her stay. It didn't take much negotiation, but then again I'm not surprised. I'm a *fantastic* negotiator."

I heard Hannah try to scream something in the background, but then she was quickly silenced to a whimper.

"So you have what you want now. Let her go."

I turned onto 17 and started the next leg of the journey. The road was silent, quiet except for a few trucks bundling through their route. I sped up, letting Joey's car shake a bit then settle in around ninety-five.

"Well, that's the thing. I *don't* have the business, actually. Something like this is a bit tricky, as I'm sure you know. This business is a little… *nuanced.* So a written document won't do much good getting me what I really want. I need the *transfer codes.*"

I had no idea what he was talking about, but I played along anyway.

"I have them. But they're not written down, obviously."

"Obviously."

"So I'm going to come to you in person, and give them to you. Then I'll take Hannah back, and then I'll kill you. See, win-win-win."

The voice laughed. "Well, that is some pun you've worked out. But I can't have loose ends in my business, you understand. You know all about that, don't you? Eliminating loose ends?"

"I do, actually. You're one of them."

"Well, the feeling is mutual. And I can't wait to discuss it with you in person."

The connection terminated, and I stared down at the phone for a few seconds.

A few thoughts raced through my mind. First, I needed to get to Hannah. I was terrified about what the man had said. If he'd just wanted to get the company, and he was telling the truth and Hannah had in fact signed it away, then why was she still there? Why didn't *she* have these 'transfer codes' this guy needed? And if she didn't, why was she still alive? The answers I could come up with were not something I wanted to ponder at the moment. Second, he was confident that I wouldn't bring the cops or anyone else into it. That meant Hannah had told him, at least a little bit, about who I was. Or — and I was hoping it was this — she'd told him I was the guy who could get him his transfer codes. She'd know I didn't have them, but it would bring me to her.

But there was another problem. One I hadn't expected. It hit me like a truck heading the opposite direction had just smashed into me head-on.

He had said that someone else had taken out her father. I knew that, and he knew that. But he'd said it had only helped things along. It had helped make the hostile takeover far more achievable.

My father had been the one to do it.

So it meant that he had inadvertently helped them get to Hannah.

CHAPTER THIRTY-THREE

I CALLED JOEY AS I got close to the bridge connecting St. Helena Island with Harbor Island. It was a longer bridge than the one between Harbor and Hunting, but more importantly it was still far enough away from my destination that I could take the time to talk for a bit before having to really put my guard up.

"How are things?" I asked.

"Good, nothing out of the ordinary. Why? You only ask me that when you're stressed."

"I'm a little stressed, yeah."

"Hannah?"

"They have her. Got to her brother, too. And Marley."

"Old man Marley?" he asked. "Why? He was a good guy."

"He was in their way. That's all it was to them, Joey. I'm on my way to Hannah's father's house, out on Hunting Island."

He sounded confused about it when he made me repeat it. I told him I'd been surprised also, but apparently the man was connected in high places and had been able to acquire some land out there. Only house on the island, I told him.

"What's the move? This ain't really our thing, boss."

I nodded, then confirmed. "Yeah, I know. It's not, and there's a reason for that. I'm no Rambo, and I don't want to be. But Hannah…"

I wasn't sure what it was about Hannah. I'm not even sure it was *about* Hannah. It was likely just the entire thing, the injustice of it all. I wasn't about to let them get away with it. They'd just gone the extra mile and *really* pissed me off by grabbing her.

"It's not about Hannah," Joey said, softly. "You know it's not."

The kid could read my mind. "No, Joey, it's not. But it certainly doesn't help that they have her."

"Okay, well, we're in it. You and me both, you hear? So don't go playing hero. I can help."

"It'll look more suspicious if we shut down the bar for no reason on a Friday night."

"I can come up with something. We have before."

I sniffed, thinking. "No, too risky. I'm just going out here to scope things out. I'm not prepared to get into any skirmishes. In and out, and I'll be back in three hours."

"I'll hold you to that."

"Please do," I said. "If I'm not back in three, let the cops know. It won't be a missing persons until tomorrow, but it'll help."

I knew he'd ignore the request and just come down here and try to find me himself, but I needed to at least pretend plausible deniability.

"You got it, boss," Joey said. "Take care of yourself."

I paused, thinking about the request. "You know, Joey, I'm not sure I've ever understood what that means."

I hung up, turning my focus again to the road. The bridge stretched out in front of me, and I could see the lights of the condominiums and their clubhouses far away to the north, out my driver's side window. There was a gas station just off the road, near the tavern, so I pulled off to fill up and plan my next move.

It was difficult not to just rush in, guns blazing, but it would be the wrong move. First, there was the simple fact that I didn't have *guns* to blaze. I had a small cache at my apartment, mostly collectible items but a few useful pieces of inventory, and I usually kept an extra 9mm at the bar. Joey didn't even know about it, or at least he hadn't told me yet that he knew about it.

Besides the issue of armament, I wasn't quite sure I wanted to rush in and start a fight with more than one bad guy while they had a hostage. It never seemed to be a smart move in the movies, so it sure as hell wasn't a smart move in real life. I'd been in a few scrapes and scuffles in my life, and I knew I could handle myself in a two- or three-on-one situation, but that was when it was a fair fight. No guns, no hostages, not many other unknowns.

I was heading into a place I didn't even know *existed*, and they would certainly be armed.

I filled the tank and took stock of my situation. Right now was not the time for a bold, careless attack. I needed to play defense first. They were ready for defense, which meant I had to figure out how to turn the tables on them. Only if I couldn't lure them out and fight them on my own terms would I even consider an offensive strategy.

Even before offense *or* defense, though, I knew I needed reconnaissance. I needed to know what I was up against, and how many. That was the purpose of my trip today. To explore and learn the territory. Find this mansion and determine the best way to proceed.

I was confident the mansion was where they were keeping Hannah. It had to be a place her father did his business, as they would want to have access to whatever files they needed, and it would be close to where they'd abducted her. Plus, there probably wouldn't be anyone —

Crap. I realized my mistake as soon as I'd started down that line of reasoning. I hung up the gas nozzle and hopped back into the car and fired it up. *Of* course *there would be people around,* I thought. *There's a funeral there on Sunday. Just over two days.* I had no idea if funerals required setup more than a day beforehand. If so, there would be people around, milling about and cleaning things, I was sure. A mansion isn't really worth showing off unless it's in order. And there would probably be family and friends and business acquaintances of the old man all there, ready and waiting to pay their respects.

Hannah had told me that they were heading to Hunting Island for a funeral — her father's. The only building I knew of on the island besides those of the park was his mansion. That meant the funeral would take place at or near the house itself, and that meant — I assumed — there would be people around today.

I slammed my hand against the steering wheel in frustration. There was no way Hannah's abductors would be stupid enough to take her to the house with all those people descending upon it soon. I had based the entire plan — the stakeout, the waiting, the careful maneuvering, the attack itself — on the fact that I *knew* she was somewhere on Hunting Island, inside her old house.

But if she wasn't in the mansion, I was screwed. I had no other ideas. The man whom I'm spoken to hadn't even cared to tell me where he would be waiting for me. He'd assumed

I'd already known. It had probably led to my subconscious assumption that she was, in fact, at the house.

I drove slower, winding around the area just past the bridge connecting St. Helena with the much smaller Harbor Island. The lights at the northern tip of the island from the Harbor Island Beach and Racquet Club twinkled in my peripheral vision, dancing left and right as the car swayed, beckoning me in. To relax, throw back a few drinks, and take it easy. It was a nice life if you could get it, and every now and then I got someone in my place who could get it. They would come in with a hesitant swagger, a confidence that they tried to hide with an air of curiosity. A physical manifestation of the thought, 'I wonder how the poor people live.'

I'd never had a huge desire to find out how anyone else's cards were stacked, as I was always so focused on improving my own deck. It wasn't a zero-sum game to me, and I could be just as happy with a half-paid-off bar and run-down apartment as a guy who owned a mansion on one island but a condo on the next one over.

Or so I thought.

Part of my outlook was based on the fact that I truly had never known what it was like to have the proverbial silver spoon in my mouth, so it was easy to rail against that vision and feign interest in reality. But a portion of my mind always wandered when I came around places like the one I was passing now. It nagged at me, pulling me in like the lights, gently nudging my psyche into wondering if there really was *more*.

I snapped back to the present and focused on the road. I drove for a minute and saw the tavern on my left, the restaurant and bar I'd spent some time in. The owner was a nice guy, a connoisseur of Irish whiskey, and we'd spent a few hours at the beginning of my career talking out what it was like to own a bar.

After the tavern there wasn't much left of the island except a low marshy area before the bridge started up again, this time connecting Harbor with Hunting. I saw the road narrow as it was squeezed between the grates of the bridge, but it wasn't the bridge or road I was focusing on. Instead, I noticed a flash of bright against the unnatural sheen of metal.

A car, parked just out of my sightline, hidden behind a large shrub. I wouldn't have seen it if its siding hadn't caught on the light and glanced off the bridge into my eyes. I noticed it as I drove by and started over the bridge.

Black, large SUV, simple stock tires with no embellishment whatsoever. A man sat in the driver's seat of the SUV, sunglasses and a dark suit.

There was nothing I'd seen in my life that screamed 'government issue' more than that guy and that car.

CHAPTER THIRTY-FOUR

ON ANY OTHER NIGHT I wouldn't have even blinked if I'd seen such a sight. I would have noticed it, I was sure, as I had been trained to notice things like that. But I wouldn't have *cared*. I would have driven past, maybe thinking it was an odd sight, but nothing really out of the ordinary. After all, the government types like this certainly *did* engage in waiting around and looking at the scenery, ostensibly on some sort of secret mission. It was only a matter of probability that I would eventually see one in action.

But this scene was different. The fact that there was a government-issued SUV driven by a government-issued driver, sitting in the most obvious spot on the most out-of-the-way road in the country, told me this scene was *very* different.

They were watching the road. They were watching me. And they weren't the people that took Hannah and murdered her brother. They were the people who were supposed to be on my side.

But I also knew these government types weren't wanting anyone else to be on *their* side. The man in the car had spotted me, and that meant I was now marked. No different than a mark, except that they weren't going to try to kill me. They'd try to pull me off, get me away from their territory. But if I refused, *then* they'd kill me.

FBI, DEA, possibly even CIA, depending on how big this Crimson Club business had gotten overseas. Didn't matter to me which one it was, as I didn't want *anything* to do with *any* of them. There wasn't a 'lesser of three evils' here, in this situation.

I needed to shake them. They'd pegged Joey's car and were probably pulling it up now in their database. They would know within an hour that I was friends with one of them, or at least a casual acquaintance. They would assume he had mentioned something to me and I was down here checking it out, a civilian taking on contractual duties for a federal agent. A huge no-no if it wasn't approved by the big boys.

So I had a new problem, and this one became more urgent. I passed the SUV but stared at it in my rearview mirror. It didn't move, but I could almost feel the guy's head inside swiveling slowly, keeping me in his sights all the way down the hill on the other side of the bridge. I sped up, taking the turn south a bit faster than I should have, and came upon the gate of Hannah's land.

It was massive, and it was immaculate.

The gate itself was like walking through an entrance to heaven itself, all weathered but in a perfectly acceptable way, the whitish stones peeking out from behind the gently manicured foliage of South Carolina coastline. Palms, brush, and other bright green vegetation, all blackened in the night light, culled back to form a natural opening to a large block of land just between the road and the ocean.

I'd been to Hunting Island State Park once before, but I

had never noticed the gate. I realized that it would be easy to miss even during the day if you weren't looking for it. It sat back a ways from the road, the thick forest filling in the gaps. I slowed the car and pulled off.

The gate was open, so I turned harder and pulled through, between the twin columns of stone. There was no moniker, no designation of any sort. I figured the Rayburns picked up their mail somewhere in town, or they just had a courier service deliver it personally. No reason to call undue attention by broadcasting the fact that this was the entrance to a fine residence.

The road turned to gravel, also white and perfectly placed in even spatterings of tiny rocks that stretched straight ahead for a hundred feet. There was grass on both sides of the road, and it was the lushest I'd seen in a long time. It wasn't the most difficult task in the world to keep grass green in South Carolina, but I had the feeling it would be from now on, after getting a look at Rayburn's work here. I wondered how many hired hands it required to keep the grass cut and fed.

After the white gravel road turned a bit it dumped into a much larger gravel parking lot, like a solid stream of tiny rocks that finally dumped out into a pristine, untouched lake of white rocks.

There were cars in the lot, which told me I had guessed correctly: people were here getting the estate ready for the funeral on Sunday. Probably not in the middle of the night, but they were at least inside.

And the estate.

My God, the house was amazing. I had seen mansions before, all gaudy and garish and poorly constructed, and usually designed to serve the singular, disgusting purpose of attracting attention from exactly the kinds of people who built mansions designed to attract attention. The vicious cycle of American prosperity.

But this house was different. It spoke to me the way the interior of poor Marley's had; it gave me that strange feeling of nostalgia I got when I thought about what I wanted my bar to become one day. This place had it in spades. It was absolutely gorgeous, in an understated way. In fact, it was the way it *was* all understated that made the point. There were no non-load-bearing decorative columns, no ridiculous fat-necked railing posts running around a monster patio on the fourth floor, and no oddly shaped windows. The lighting was perfect, as well. Flood lights from the ground illuminated the sides of the monstrous estate, while brighter spotlights from the areas where the roof met the sides of the house lit up the driveway and parking lot.

There was a symmetry to it, yet it pulled the eye to the north, to the left side of my field of view, toward the ocean. I could taste the salt air on my tongue and hear the waves crashing far in the distance, in what was this house's backyard, and I was in heaven.

I stopped the car, middle of the road, and got out. I took it in, breathed it in deep, ignoring the pressures and the situation that surrounded this house. Just for a moment. I needed this moment.

I loved this house, and I hadn't even stepped inside.

And I wouldn't.

I couldn't go into the house. Not yet. There were people there who would ask questions of me I couldn't answer, and I had no reason to be there now for a funeral that would happen in a couple days. Aside from that, the lookout SUV had clued me in to the fact that there were probably agents milling about the grounds, waiting for a 'suspicious fellow' like me to wander in, look around, and basically ask to be interrogated.

It was early enough in the game for me that I might not be apprehended if I just got back in and drove away. They might think I was just checking things out, surprised about the revelation I'd learned from the lady in the bar that there was a mansion on the state park island. That's what they might think, if they were already caught up in an investigation of the *other* people looking for me.

If the government folks were *also* early in the game, however, they might feel the need to grab me anyway, just to get the numbers up and start asking questions. They got a little fidgety if they didn't bring in some fresh meat every now and then to rough up a bit, and I was positive I looked pretty damn fresh. An older guy driving a beater up to a mansion for no good reason was more than a good enough reason for *them*.

So I wouldn't go in. Not yet. There had never been a plan I'd liked, but even if there had been one now it would have changed the moment I saw the SUV. I needed to regroup, to get back to Joey. I needed to think things through just a little more, figure out where they would have Hannah, and then move in without getting nabbed by the feds.

Instead of driving toward the mansion, then, I drove around it. I wanted to see the grounds, get a feel for the place, and the parking lot I was on seemed to go all the way around the house anyway. I took it south, around the front of the building, then turned left at the southern tip of the house and came around to the back of it.

There were more cars here, parked parallel to one another along the side of the gravel parking lot. I looked to the right and saw the ocean, suddenly there and suddenly massive. I never got fully used to seeing the ocean. The infiniteness of it, just a never-ending swath of blues and greens and browns, the same water connecting this foot of land with all the other coastlines of the world.

The wind had picked up a bit, and I could hear it whistling up and around the stripping in Joey's windows, and again I caught a whiff of the salty air. There was a strong part of me that just wanted to stop and live here forever, ignoring the fact that it wasn't my house and I was probably not invited. It was all so *perfect*. I couldn't understand how Hannah had ever left this place.

I drove north again on the backside of the house. I still hadn't seen anyone, but the cars told me there was activity inside the house, some sort of setup and preparation for the funeral. One car had the name of a local funeral service company on the side of it, another truck had a catering company's name wrapped around it.

I got to the north side of the house and noticed a smaller gravel trail split off from the parking lot. I slowed the car and followed it down with my eyes. It seemed to be a simple path cut through the brush, bending around a couple of trees and winding its way toward the beach. Another structure sat at the end of the path, and just on the other side of the building I saw the yacht. The path and the structure were lit with the same lights as the house, and it made for a miraculously appointed garden walkway.

The boat was massive, a size perfectly scaled to match the unbelievable house whose shadow I sat parked in now. I couldn't see the entire boat, but the stern of it stuck out twenty or so feet from the boathouse, allowing me an unobstructed view of the back side of it.

The *Wassamassaw*. I recognized the name and wondered if Rayburn had named his boat after the small town a few hours north. *An old American Indian tribe from around here*, I ɔd name for a boat, I figured, and the boat was ᴢnough to fit a name of that size. I knew nothing ᴜt I liked what I could see of this one. It was white ᴜ gravel paths and roads and the house itself, and the gate out front. All of it matched in a perfect symmetry of color harmony, the white a perfect base for a few splashes of carefully planned colors. From what I could tell, the yacht had some light blue on it as its accent color, including the *Wassamassaw* lettering. I could see a few deck chairs, and at least two stories spanning the entire length. The entirety of it was blown out in brilliant light from the deckhouse, and I wondered if it was bright enough to serve as a beacon for incoming ocean vessels.

I wanted to see more, but now was not the time. I pulled out again and turned around the northern side of the house, then headed back up the road toward the gate.

Hannah deserved a house like this, and I intended to get her back to it. I didn't yet know how, or when, but I was absolutely positive that I would succeed.

CHAPTER THIRTY-FIVE

"JOEY?"

"STILL HERE. EVERYTHING OKAY down there?" It had only been forty-five minutes since I'd last spoken to him, so he was probably wanting me to fill him on my progress. I wanted to, but that could come later. Right now, I needed to let him know about the *other* guys who had showed up.

I switched the phone to my other ear as I drove. I sped up, pushing the clunker to what had to be near its limit. The tiny sedan bucked and groaned in protest, but eventually obliged and hit 85. I was in a hurry, though I still didn't really have a great idea of what the hell I was going to do.

"Yeah. How's it going for you?" It was a stupid question — Thursday night (or Friday early morning) at my place was like a Monday lunchtime at a Chili's in a bigger city. The only difference was we were usually open a bit later.

"Stupid question. Pretty dead. McNaab and Pennington are here, complaining about the crappy fishing. Few others came and went, nothing special. How are you?"

"Been better. I'm on my way back. We can talk more in

person, about an hour until I'm in town. Can you meet me out back? I want to keep it under the radar as long as possible."

The car swung left in the lane, thanks to a strong gust of wind blowing in from the ocean. I felt the automobile lean into the opposite lane, urging me to give up and just let it happen, but I stubbornly yanked the wheel to the right and spun it straight again.

Two cars appeared behind me, one from the left side of the road, and another from the right, and took up position a few hundred feet behind me. I watched for a few seconds and realized that they had sped up. They were matching my speed, yet keeping a healthy distance.

More of these government types.

I couldn't tell if one of them was the grunt I'd seen posted up just before the bridge, but considering I hadn't seen him again when I'd left the Rayburn estate, I figured he was one of the two cars tailing me.

I had work to do, and these guys were getting in my way. As long as they tailed me and nothing else, we didn't have an issue. But I'd been tailed before, and I knew there was usually a reason for it. You didn't follow someone wherever they went if you were just curious about who their hairstylist was.

I smacked a palm against the steering wheel and focused again on the conversation at hand. "I got two bogeys behind me. Government types, and they're looking into the same crap we are."

"Think you can shake them?" Joey asked.

"Well sure, but that ain't going to get them off us forever," I replied. "I'm going to need help, Joey."

I said it in a way I knew he could interpret. I could almost hear the silent nod of his head on the other end of the line. "You got an ally here, boss. You know that. Don't even have to ask."

"I do," I said. "This time, especially. We're dealing with more than one mark, and now the feds are involved. I'm not sure how stinky of a dog turd it is we've dug up, but we can't just bury it again and call it a day."

"What do you need?"

"I'll need you, for one. Probably best if we closed up early tonight, and I wouldn't expect we'd be back and ready for action by tomorrow afternoon. Think you can make up a sign that says as much?"

"Sure thing, boss. I'll get the marker and whip up a 'gone killin'' sign."

I laughed. "Perfect. Might want to make up a 'got dead' one too, just in case."

Joey paused. "You really think we've got someone that serious we're dealing with?"

"They killed her brother, Joey. And they didn't do it in a way that seemed thoughtless, if you know what I mean."

"I'm with you. Still, what do they —"

"This isn't the type of group that's going to just put up a ransom note, wait for the money, and —"

This time I paused, even cutting myself off. I frowned, then glanced in the rearview once more to check the progress of the folks tailing me. Still a football field behind me, and so far staying put. They hadn't flashed their lights or anything, so I assumed they were tailing me, and not just wanting to eventually pass me. I breathed in a sharp breath, held it, then let it out.

"I just… I just thought of something," I said. "Hang on a sec."

"I've got a couple new arrivals who just walked in, actually," Joey said. "Call me back in a minute?"

"Sure, that's fine. I need to think about this. I think I figured something out. Let's just meet up behind the bar. Keep it subtle, Joey."

"You got it, boss."

The connection quit and I flipped the phone together again and tossed it onto the ripped, faded passenger seat. The ceiling fabric was hanging down, bubbling onto my head just enough to make it slightly annoying. I punched it, knowing it wouldn't do a damn thing, and found out I was correct.

The cars behind me sped up slightly, coming within fifty yards of my bumper.

"Getting a little too close for comfort, assholes," I whispered.

I focused on the road, wishing the car could handle another 15-20 MPH, if only so I could get into Edisto sooner. There wasn't a chance I'd be able to outrun the vehicles behind me unless they were four cylinder models made prior to 1991, and there wasn't a chance of that happening unless the government had suddenly and inexplicably gotten a lot more frugal lately with their print-on-demand money.

I had mentioned something to Joey that was now nagging at me. Something I'd thought about briefly earlier, but only for a flash of a moment. It wasn't even significant enough at the time to return to the thought, but when he'd brought it up it reminded me of my conversation with Hannah's captor.

'This isn't the type of group that's going to just put up a ransom note, wait for the money, and —'

I didn't think they were — this was an organized, planned, and well-executed mission undertaken by professionals. It was obvious they wanted control of

Rayburn's company, Crimson Club, or at least the piece of it that engaged in the unscrupulous activities that had initially caught my father's attention. And because of that, I had assumed they weren't interested in money in the form of a ransom.

But it had gotten me thinking a bit. What if they were, in fact, setting up a ransom? They still wanted *something,* or they wouldn't have captured Hannah.

I shuddered as I realized the truth of that statement. There was really no other use for her than as a bargaining chip. They *needed* her for something. If they hadn't had any use for her, she'd have ended up skewered to the wall in the same fashion as her brother.

So they'd taken her, and they'd meant to send a message using both her and her brother. The message was directed at *me.*

Which meant they wanted something from *me.*

I had written off this truth because, at the time, it hadn't seemed like the *simplest* explanation. The simplest reason I could come up with at the time they had taken Hannah was that they wanted me dead. A sort of payment for her life. I had meddled in their affairs, and they wanted their revenge for the mess of things I'd made for them.

Maybe it was a life-for-a-life arrangement. I'd taken out their young gun, back behind the bar, and they wanted revenge for him. All of those things made sense at the time. They still did, and I wasn't about to write off the idea that maybe they *did* want to get rid of me, just because they'd get their shits and giggles from it.

But that hypothetical solution was no longer the simplest.

What if they *had* wanted me for something other than

revenge? What if they thought I was far more involved in this whole thing, and Hannah was their bargaining chip for it?

Specifically, maybe they had no idea who had offed Hannah's father. They knew *they* hadn't done it. So perhaps they were thinking it was me? And in a way, it *was* me. It was my father's work, and as messy as it had been, it was still the company that employed me. If they thought I had done it, perhaps they thought I'd moved in to take over the company myself. I watched, waited, planned, and finally attacked, hoping to nab Hannah and Daniel — the other major shareholders — later.

The impact of it hit me all at once. I was tempted to pull over and get out of the car, take in some fresh, salty sea air, and just consider it for a moment. But I wasn't terribly excited about meeting my friends in the cars behind me, so I kept on heading north toward the turnoff for Edisto Beach.

They'd killed Daniel Rayburn, rendering his shares null and void, as far as I could tell. Maybe there was a clause that stuck his shares back into the pool upon his death, or even split it amongst the remaining shareholders. But they hadn't been the ones to kill his father, and they likely thought it had been me, which meant they assumed I was carrying around the bulk of the stock.

So they'd grabbed Hannah, knowing that if they wanted full control of Crimson Club, they needed full control of the stock package. Which meant they needed control of *me*. They wanted me in person because they needed my signature, my permission, my unequivocally positive statement, legally recorded, that *they*, and no one else, controlled the entity called Crimson Club.

It all came together like a perfectly orchestrated symphony. The initial threads of melody, hinting at and leaning into the harmonies that would be intertwined until they became one, a stronger version of the initial story, told over and over again until the inevitable fourth-movement conclusion.

Four movements of maneuvering, tweaking, planning, and leading, until the first strains were recapitulated into a finale. Hundreds of measures of notes, building toward a climax.

But where was I in the symphony? Was I the melody — the line that would continue onward until the bleeding end? Or was I some inverted counterpart, meant to contradict and surprise the melody?

Life was rarely as simple as music, after all. I enjoyed the moment of fleeting desire for everything to just fall into place, for it all to just simply make sense like Beethoven's Fifth or the Lacrimosa of Mozart's Requiem. There might be a 'grand composer' up there, putting all the pieces in place for a fantastic rendition of life's overture, but in my mind the maestro lacked a solid orchestrator.

I had no idea how these pieces would come together. It was equally likely I'd be able to grab Hannah and destroy everyone involved with taking her as it was likely that I'd end up splattered across the floor of her daddy's mansion. I'd helped write the opening movements, but I wasn't in full control of the ending.

I was still 45 minutes away, but I hoped Joey was already starting to mentally prepare himself for the challenge. The kid had done a lot for me, but this was something I'd never thought I'd have to ask. I wasn't ever a good mathematician, especially the statistics component of it, but I figured our odds of survival hovered around zero.

I gripped the wheel and twisted up and down with both

hands, turning the deep black rubber between my fingers and hands until tiny bits of old dirt rubbed off and fell to the floor. The car suddenly made me feel claustrophobic, as if all sides of the interior were pressing in and trying to squeeze the life out of me.

The cars behind me closed in, sealing the deal.

CHAPTER THIRTY-SIX

THE CARS FOLLOWED ME ALL the way into Edisto Beach, where just before entering the town proper one of them turned off and, I assume, went back to headquarters to debrief. The other car, a long black sedan that looked like a plain-vanilla Buick in black, kept on pursuing me. I could tell he wasn't interested in disguising the fact that he was tailing me, as he kept behind me far enough to adjust to my fluctuations in speed, but close enough that I could see him doing it.

The hell do these guys want? I thought. I considered just pulling over and asking him — in case things turned physical, taking on one of them would be at least twice as easy as taking on two of them — but thought better of it. They were sleuthing, albeit in a not-so-subtle way. They weren't interested in nabbing me and bringing me down for an interrogation, or they'd have already done it. Nor were they interested in eliminating me from the scene. There were a thousand rocks and trees to hide a sniper behind, and I would never have seen it coming.

So they didn't want to kill me — yet — and they didn't want to interrogate me — yet. That left one possibility: they didn't know what I was doing, but they knew I was involved. How much *they* knew about the situation with Hannah, her brother, and their father remained to be seen, but I was confident they knew about old man Rayburn's apparent suicide, and were snooping around his files to see if they could piece together the threads of evidence linking him to the darker sides of the Crimson Club business model.

I'd played the duck-duck-goose game with all the three-letter organizations before, so I knew how it played out. They'd poke around, looking for an obvious connection with their investigation that would provide a foray into my life and work, then they'd bring me down to their chamber for questioning. It was my policy to speak as little as possible, and only answer with single words when I could. I could play their psychological games better than they could most of the time, so I could see the bait-and-switches coming from a mile away.

It made me a bit salty during a questioning session, but I didn't care much about their hurt feelings.

I was innocent, as far as they were concerned, unless the kid I'd had Joey fishbait after our skirmish behind the bar happened to have been a high-profile suspect, but I doubted the United States government — whichever flavor of them it was keeping an eye on me — cared about a washed-up ex-military prick who'd gotten in with the wrong crowd. They might have been interested in seeing if he had any information about his bosses, but they wouldn't be bugging *me* for killing him.

So it had to be Crimson Club-related only. They thought I was involved in the big schtick, and they needed just a little bit of something or other to make it stick. Stick me to the schtick. A solid strategy, but considering I *hadn't* been involved with Hannah's father's company, I wasn't worried about it. Even still, I couldn't waste time proving all of that to them — I had Hannah to worry about.

If there was one thing these acronyms were good at, it was tailing people. I wasn't going to shake them, lose them, or discourage them, so I decided I'd do the next best thing: work with them. I grabbed the phone from my pocket and dialed the same number I'd committed to memory long ago.

"Truman," I said the second I heard the ringing stop and the connection begin.

"You'd better have a damn good way of convincing me you were just out for a little midnight tour of Hunting Island, and nothing more."

I chuckled. "Camping. That's all that's on the island anyway, I thought."

"I warned you, Mason. Out of your league, in every way. I —"

"So it's you? Your guys, I mean? Out here tailing me?"

"I… You know I can't…"

"You don't need to. No plausible deniability on this one, is there?"

"Mason, I like you better alive. But what you're messing with is a pretty great way to get yourself dead. And I'm not sure either of us would like you like that."

I sighed, looking out the windshield and watching the old stores and houses roll by. The beach in sight, just over the tops of the buildings on my left. I slowed down even more to let a group of seagulls fighting over some crumbs scramble to get out of my way.

"I told you before, I'm already in it. Can't help that, but I want out of it as much as you do. So tell me if it's your boys, and what they want with me."

"Mason, you know the answer to that question. I can't disclose that sort of information —"

"They think I did it? *You* think I did it?"

This time Truman sighed, a long, breathy release of air. I could almost feel the warm humidity through the tiny speaker hole on my flip phone.

"I'm not really sure *what* I think," he said.

"Fine. I'll tell you what to think. Bradley Rayburn's dead, and if you think I did it, you're insane. I didn't even know who the hell the old guy was until about a day ago. And his son's dead now, too. And they —"

"His son's dead?" Truman interrupted. "How? What do you know about it?"

"You'll know everything I know in a few hours, I'm sure, whenever he's found. I needed the head start, and I didn't want local authorities shutting me down prematurely. But if you want the same head start I had, have your grunts check out Marley's B&B here in town. Walked in on the bloodbath personally. That's when I found out they had Hannah."

"They have his *daughter* now?"

"Christ, Truman, what *do* you know?" I raised my voice a little. This surprised me. I would have figured they had been a few steps ahead of me the whole time, but it seemed as though I was the one breaking all the news. "She got taken by the group that wants to take over Crimson Club, I think. They need her to sign some sort of agreement. Not sure why they can't just forge it, or steal it anyway, but whatever. I'm not a lawyer."

I didn't state whether or not I thought there was a connection between Hannah's captors and her father's death. I figured Truman and his army already knew Bradley

Rayburn's 'suicide' was no suicide at all, but I didn't want Truman thinking there was a third party involved, or that that third party was my father. *Keep it simple*, I reminded myself.

"So they have Hannah. And where are they holding her?"

I froze. He had used the word 'and.'

CHAPTER THIRTY-SEVEN

IT WAS SUBTLE, BUT IT was there. The truth. Truman *did* know that Hannah had been taken. A gruff, to-the-point Truman would have simply run the two sentences together, excited and eager and not a little bit nervous all at the same time. It would have been an honest, truthful sentence, one that asked the question it was asking, and nothing more.

A more *elusive* Truman, the one I was friends with more often than not, would mask the insincere question with an attempt to pull out more information. He'd let the 'and' slip in there in a throwback to schoolyard accusatory insult-slinging. *'And who do you think you are?'* or something of that sort. I pictured my mother standing on the back porch, my friends and I racing back to beat the sunset, knowing we were already beyond late. *'And just where exactly were you?'* she would ask. Always the same lilt to the question, a half-veiled attempt to be angry at her cherished cherubim and his devious little friends.

I smiled at the memory, but I soured at the recognition that Truman *was* in fact a few steps ahead of me. And he had tried to hide it from me. He already knew the answer to the question he was overtly asking, but he had a deeper question he was trying to pose. He wanted to know my *true* involvement. Not necessarily how I'd met Hannah, and why we had started up a conversation in the first place, but how she had come to happen upon my little speakeasy in a tucked-away corner of South Carolina in the first place.

"I don't know where they're holding her," I said.

"Okay."

"Okay."

"Do you know what they want from her?" Truman asked.

"They want the company," I replied, bluntly. "Crimson Club, or at least the part of it that engages in the type of work that interests *you*."

"*Professionally* interests me, Mason."

"Fine. Why didn't you tell me you had guys on me?"

"Why didn't you tell me you were going to be snooping around the Rayburn estate?"

"Because it's me. You knew I'd come down here, but you told me to get lost. I didn't want to give you a play-by-play and have you ruin all the fun." I got serious, even sitting up straighter in my seat. "Truman. You know me better than this. I'm not going to be scared off by your Bureau grunts, even if they start getting real intimate with me. I've handled a few of your types before, and I'll do it again."

"I know you have, Mason, that's what worries me. We've got enough of an issue with this organization running around and murdering people without babysitting you."

"Then don't."

"I *have* to, Mason!" Truman was nearly shouting, and the poor phone speakers could only parse the distortion on the words. The volume was compressed and smashed back down to a reasonable level and passed through into my ear. "You are going to get yourself killed, or you're going to get *my* guys killed. I need you to *back off*, and I need you to do it yesterday."

"Where are they holding Hannah?"

"Mason, I —"

"You can't tell me, but you can also choose not to deny it if *I* tell *you*. I'm not backing off. You've got red tape and other government bullshit keeping you slow and useless, and you know it. I can be in and out of there in an *hour*, Truman. What can your guys do in an hour? Decide which of them is going to get coffee and doughnuts during the all-night stakeout of Rayburn's yacht?"

I was getting a little excited, but Truman needed to understand where I was coming from. "You can *use* me, Truman. Just give me something. Shit, give me *anything*."

"I'm giving you a chance," he said calmly. "A chance to get yourself far away from this mess of an investigation. You're going to incriminate yourself or get yourself eliminated entirely."

"Give me *something*. Please."

"No."

"Let me help you."

"No."

"I went to Rayburn's place. Scouted the entire facility by way of a perimeter march. Slow, steady, not focusing on anything in particular, but keeping my eyes and ears open, just like you taught me."

Silence.

I had him. Maybe. Just needed a little more pushing.

"It was just like Kuwait. You remember that? The oil magnate's place? I wanted to run in like an idiot, guns blazing, get it over with, all that? You made me stop and pay attention. The way those guards were keeping their distance from certain spots in the road. You remember that?"

"Of course I remember that, Mason."

"They were bombs. All over the damn road. This was the guy's *house*, for crying out loud. He had *kids*. They'd booby-trapped the house, for 'security.'"

"Get out of our way, Mason. I'm not going to tell you again."

"I did the same sort of thing at this house. Real slow, real easy, just a simple loop around the house. No bombs this time, which was lucky since I was in a car. I saw a lot of folks setting up for the funeral service. Did you know it was on Sunday? Is that a normal day for funerals? I think Gloria's was on a Sunday, wasn't it? What about your Debbie's? Do you even remember —"

"*Dammit*, Mason. Shut the hell up. You're about to get the entirety of the US Government's shit-stick shoved so far up your —"

"*Where are they keeping Hannah?*" I nearly screamed into the phone. I lifted it completely off the side of my face and yelled down into it.

"The house. You were there. That's why we were there."

I stopped. I breathed, once, then again. *The house?* The mansion I'd just visited? It had been swarming with people setting up for a massive funeral service and wake.

"The house? Rayburn's estate?"

"We believe, anyway. Haven't seen any suspicious activity in the last day."

I was still shocked. I didn't think he'd just come out and *say* it, even with all my pushing. And yet I *certainly* hadn't thought the answer was the mansion — the same place I just got back from There was a funeral scheduled to take place at that very location two days from now.

"I was just there, too. You know that. Truman, you're not a liar, so is that really the best place that you can come up with?"

"I'm telling the truth, Mason. You asked for it, I told you. That's where they're keeping her. We've had eyes on the place since Mr. Rayburn was found in his study."

"But how would they —"

"We don't know, but it's a big house. Plenty of rooms, plenty of doors. They could have snuck in any time."

"I thought you were watching the place."

"We *were* — we still are — but we don't even know what we're looking for. One of my agents saw a woman, about Hannah's size, walking into the house from the west side, followed by —"

"Wait, so you *don't* know if she's there?"

"Look," Truman said, clearly growing more and more agitated the longer he talked to me. "You wanted me to tell you what I knew, I'm telling you. We're *pretty sure* she's in the house. She's been in the house, and hasn't left the house."

I flicked the mouthpiece button on the tiny phone to put Truman on speakerphone and I tossed the phone onto the passenger seat. I squeezed my eyes shut and pushed at the skin between them with a few fingers. This had just gotten worse. Truman hadn't been withholding information from me just because he didn't want me involved — he had been withholding information from me because he wasn't even *sure of what he knew.*

"You've got to be kidding me."

"I'm sorry, Mason. That's what we know."

"Who took her? Any names? Identity? Hell, do you even know how many there are?"

"No."

"Dammit."

"We're struggling to play catch-up, here," Truman said. "We've been behind on everything so far, and we're not catching any breaks."

"Yeah, I'm picking up on that," I said. "Thanks for telling me what you know, though, I guess. Next time don't make me beg for it."

"Next time there won't be a next time."

"So what's your plan?" I asked. It was worth a shot, anyway. "You *do* have a plan, right?"

"We're already working the plan," he replied, sounding a bit short. "Follow you, watch the house, wait for more information."

"Wait for infor — what the hell is wrong with you?" I asked. "If she's in the house, go get her."

"We *can't*, Mason. It's not that simple. First, we never had the visual confirmation that she *is* in the house. She could have left again, somehow. Maybe an underground tunnel or something. Or she might not have even gone into the house in the first place. My guy could have seen a maid, or someone coming to help with the funeral, or something like that. Second, these things always take time. She's not just a hostage, Mason. She's part of a major international investigation involving more services than just mine. And she's either a major player in something much larger, or she's not a player at all."

"Which means *what*, exactly?" I asked.

"Which means she's not the target."

My mouth fell open. It was all clear to me, and I'd missed it. Of *course* they would wait. Of *course* they didn't care about Hannah's safe retrieval. She was a pawn in a larger game, or she was the queen herself. Either way, she was part of a game. Negotiating, espionage, maneuvering. It was all part of the game.

But she wasn't the final victory. She was the spoils of war.

Truman's job was to figure out who was *playing* the game, and take them down. His job was to disband the multi-whatever-illion-dollar gambit being played around all of us, stop Crimson Club's illegal activity, and bring the players to justice.

A tall order, but I'd seen him tackle taller things.

At the moment, however, I didn't give a shit about Truman. He was a big boy, and he had been one a lot longer than I had. I cared about Hannah, even more now that I understood what she had become a part of.

Everything was swirling around her, but I'm not sure there was a single soul involved outside of me who actually cared what happened to her by the end of it.

"You don't care if she lives or dies, do you?"

"I — no, Mason, don't put words in my mouth. *Of course* I want her to live, but —"

"There's nothing that comes after that 'but' that's going to convince me."

"Dammit, Mason, it's my *job*."

"And mine is to make drinks for people."

"What the hell is that supposed to mean?"

"It means exactly what it sounds like. I have a simple job: 'make drinks for people who come to my bar.' You have a simple job, too: 'do what your boss tells you.' At the end of the day, it's the same job. You mix up the drink that the big brass upstairs tells you to, and they drink it. But there's more to any job. You know that. You know *I* know that. There's nuance, and complexity. And you and I are cursed with a specific set of skills that makes it more than just simple oversight. We let people like Hannah die and it's on *us*, just because we *could have* stopped it. We're trained for this. Besides that —"

"I don't need a damn lecture from you, Mason."

I screamed again. "And I don't need you to feign ignorance to qualify your shitty justifications!"

"Jesus, Mason," Truman said, verbally distancing himself by dropping his voice to a near whisper and then pausing for a few seconds. "You care about this girl, I get that. But if you can tell me how to get her back without getting any of my guys killed, or me, you, or any of her captors — which we'll need to bring in for questioning — then I'm all ears."

I thought for a moment. I already had a plan, but I knew 'run in and shoot everything in sight until I had Hannah, and then shoot my way out' wasn't going to fly for Truman. I thought harder. "You don't need to bring in *all* of the guys."

"I need at least *one* of them," Truman admitted. "Preferably the ringleader, or one of the men in charge."

"And you don't need *all* of your agents to live," I added.

"Mason…"

"Kidding. But seriously, though. You guys have a real thing for paralysis by analysis, you know that? Obviously you've heard of collateral damage?"

"We have an entire department dedicated to cooking up reports about it," Truman said. I couldn't tell if he was joking. "They tell me it's statistically likely that I'll lose at least four percent of my agents on any live-fire mission."

"And how many do you have on this mission?" I asked.

"I can't tell you that."

"Let's say it's four. That's usually about what it is, right? In-the-field, buckled-down agents ready for anything, two hardened and two wet-behind-the-ears?"

No answer.

"Right. So four percent of four agents. That's what — losing an arm? Maybe a little leg?"

"This isn't a joke, Mason."

"I'm not the one sitting on my ass waiting for something to happen!" I shouted, even surprising myself at the volume. I instinctively ducked a little lower in the car and looked around outside. "You need to get those men into the mansion and have them look around. Shake it out a little bit. I'd bet they'll find *something* you can use, and if not — hell, you're the FBI, just say it was a training exercise."

I heard Truman trying to calm himself by breathing steadily. It didn't sound like it was working.

"I'm not going to waste any more of your time," I said. "I've got what I need, and —"

"You're not going to do anything rash," Truman said. It sounded like a question, as if he was trying to convince himself. I wasn't sure if I should let him believe it or let him think he shouldn't believe it. I said nothing. "You're not moving on this one, Mason."

I sat there, watching the empty streets roll slowly by until I saw the end of the road and just beyond that my tiny, lonely bar at the end of the strip. I turned the wheel to the left and pulled in to the access road toward the alleyway.

"Far as I'm concerned, Truman, we're on completely different cases. You've got your hands full with this Crimson Club crap. I couldn't care less about those jokers. I've got one job, and I'll be damned if you or anyone else is going to stop me from doing it."

I knew Truman long enough to know that a direct threat like that would severely piss him off.

But I also knew that his hands were tied, and I had a good feeling he wanted nothing more than to hear me speak those words.

CHAPTER THIRTY-EIGHT

I WAITED ON THE ACCESS street and watched out the rearview mirror. The headlights of Joey's car flooded the fence and section of alley road in front of me and bounced back to light part of the tiny strip of road the car was sitting in. For a minute I thought they'd already pulled off, but then I saw what I was looking for.

The car that had followed me all the way in had turned off its headlights and was cruising real slow, the way a man gets followed when he's on the wrong side of a city on the wrong side of the tracks with the wrong color of skin. Because they were in the dark and the only real light was from my own headlights, the angle made it impossible to see the person in the driver's seat. They knew it, too, because they stopped fully on the other side of the main road I'd just turned off of. They just sat there for a few seconds, and I could feel the agent's eyes on mine. He wouldn't be able to make out any details because of the light — I would just be a dark silhouette to him — but he would already know what I looked like.

He may even have had a dossier open on the seat next to

him, my glossy 8x10 face from fifteen years ago glaring up at him in two dimensions. More likely, Truman had force-fed him the information he'd needed to tail me, and the guy already had my face burned into his short-term memory the way only an FBI agent can do.

Whatever. The next few seconds were crucial, as it determined whether or not I'd gotten the nonverbal go-ahead from Truman. I watched the car, he watched me. A standoff. I knew Joey was waiting for me, probably already waiting out on the back steps. Maybe wondering why he saw the headlights but not the car.

Finally, just when I thought Truman might have smartened up in his old age and done something I wouldn't have expected, the car pulled away.

The agent drove off, accelerating naturally and easily, the least excited way to move a vehicle I had ever seen. He had simply fallen into motion, as if pulling away from a curb after picking up kids from soccer practice.

Truman had, with that order, given me the all-clear: he wanted me where he couldn't yet go. He wanted me to push on, to get Hannah, to cut loose and clear the way for his far more *civilized* experts to enter unobstructed to clean up the mess.

It was a good call, and it was what I had been hoping for. Truman was still the same grouchy old curmudgeon, but he was a grouchy old curmudgeon who was brutally efficient and tactically logical. He had a 'free play' card with me, and he'd decided to use it. I was a bit of a loose cannon to him, I figured, but a loose cannon that was at least facing the same enemy he was facing.

I figured his agents would still be paying attention to me, but they had been called off the all-night watch. I probably had a tracking beacon somewhere on my person or car, and they'd let that be enough for now.

I was fine with that, and I was fine with Truman's decision. As much as I wanted to believe it was out of loyalty or respect to me, or preferential treatment, I knew it was, in truth, a utilitarian decision. By sending me in first, he could not only claim plausible deniability — he would say he had no idea what my plan was, which was mostly true — and he would have much less of a chance to lose men.

The possibility of achieving what his bosses wanted him to achieve without having to do the bulk of the work himself or with his field agents would be a huge win for him.

And he had decided that knowingly allowing me to run headfirst into danger was a smaller price to pay.

And I was fine with that decision as well.

I pulled the car forward into the alley, turned left, then backed it up so I could get out right on the steps leading up into the kitchen and office area.

"Hey boss," I heard Joey say as I stepped out. He had been just out of the light of the steps.

"Joey," I replied. "Everything wrapped up tight here?"

"With a bow. You see the sign on the door?"

"No, sorry. You went with something other than 'gone killing,' right?"

"Yeah, sure." He winked at me.

"Well I'm glad you had fun. I'm afraid the fun's over. You ready?"

"Honestly?" he asked. "No. I have no idea what we're doing."

"You wrote the sign, Joey. What the hell do you think we're doing?"

He didn't answer.

I followed Joey up the steps into the darkened bar. Joey had shut down, cleaned up, and prepared the bar for the next opening day's service. A few emergency lights were on at all times, and it was enough to cast the entire place in an eerie, post-apocalyptic glow. Aside from making the labels on the bottles hard to read, I didn't hate it. It toned everything down a bit and made all the imperfections melt away into the soft glow of my imagination's perfection. I walked into the main room and took up a seat on the customer side of the bar.

"Pour you one?" Joey asked. He walked to the opposite side of the bar and raised an eyebrow, waiting for me to deliver my order.

"What are you drinking tonight?"

"Oh, I've had a daiquiri with a gal in from Charleston for the weekend, staying with her parents, and a Mai Tai with a middle-aged guy on his midlife crisis who thought South Carolina was the Bahamas and was pissed the surfing wasn't any good."

I smiled. "He's a surfer?"

Joey laughed. "Hardly. Weighed about three-hundred pounds, balding in all the wrong places and growing hair in all the worse ones. Couldn't barely stay balanced on the barstool. But he could've drank me under the table. Three Mai Tais and a Bahama Mama to finish it off."

I never prohibited Joey from drinking on the job, figuring it was better for business if he could throw a few back with the locals every now and then. Besides, I was usually liquored up quite a bit when I served, and I never wanted to be the type of boss that held a double standard.

The rule for me was that I condoned drinking, but not being drunk. Being drunk meant being unable to maintain the situational awareness required to serve well, and serve fast. It meant being unable to engage in the type of conversation I knew our customers came to us for — smart, quick, and witty. Drunkenness significantly diminished anyone's ability to engage in useful conversation.

Finally, I never wanted to be unfit for identifying and pressing a mark. And since Joey worked for me as an employee *and* a contracted laborer for our moonlighting gig, I needed him to be mostly sober as well.

We laughed about the midlife-crisis guy for a few minutes. We got that sort of thing in here every now and then, I told him. They'd come down from somewhere up north, sometimes even North Carolina or Virginia, hoping to find a Florida Keys-esque tiki bar dripping free rum and cokes and nubile women waltzing around seductively on wide-open white sand beaches. They ended up here, for whatever reason, and they could never hide their disappointment.

We always treated them nice, explaining that the sort of escape they were looking for was still a few hundred miles straight down the map, at least. But they should stay and enjoy a drink while they were here. They'd ask for something fruity, boozy, and sweet.

"So a tiki drink it is, then," I said. "Seems fitting."

"How's that?" he asked, turning to reach for two different kinds of rum.

"Sweetness for revenge, boozy for bold and rash decisions, and feeling like shit the next day for…"

"For hoping there *is* a next day," Joey said.

I smiled again. "I like that. A tiki drink it is."

"Perfect," he said. "I'll whip up two of this concoction I've been working on, but you start telling me this amazing plan *you've* been working on."

He grabbed another bottle — I couldn't read the label in the dark, but I knew it was Velvet Falernum. I watched him pour a jigger of it into a Boston shaker filled with ice, along with a few jiggers of the rums, then finally a half-jigger of pineapple juice. He shook it for a solid twenty seconds, just like I'd taught him, then strained out the fruity, foamy mixture into two copper mugs.

I thought he was done, but then he grabbed a bottle of one of our best bourbons and a bar spoon and poured a floater of whiskey on top of the drinks.

"Wow," I said. "That's a hell of a drink."

"For a hell of a plan," he said, not looking up from his work.

"In that case, you'd probably better pour another shot of bourbon on that."

CHAPTER THIRTY-NINE

JOEY AND I DRANK HIS creation, a delicious medley of a tiki drink with a boozy finish, and I asked for another. I didn't want him to think I was getting to be a lightweight, but I had to admit to myself that the drink was *very* boozy — I wasn't sure how many more of them I could handle. Thankfully, however, rather than mix up another round of tiki drinks he poured straight from the bourbon bottle this time, then asked about the plan again.

"'Plan' is really too strong a word," I said. "It's more like 'general idea.'"

"Okay, fair enough," Joey said. "What's the 'general idea' about what we're going to do?"

"Well, my first inclination is to go in Rambo style. Figure we find the bad guys right away because they'll be shooting back at us. Then we can pick up the pieces later, when it's all clear."

"But that won't work?"

I nodded, holding a sip of bourbon in my mouth for a few seconds until I felt it burn the edges of my gums where they met my teeth. I held it just another second, closing my eyes and breathing in through my nose, then swallowed. Corny, vanilla aromas transformed into beautiful oaky caramel flavors as the expensive bourbon fell through my senses.

I nodded again, this time for the whiskey. "Yeah," I said. "That won't work. They're holding her at the mansion, and there's a funeral there on Sunday."

"They gave you an ultimatum, though, right?" Joey asked. "Something about 'by Saturday?'"

"Yeah, they want this whole mess cleared up no later than Saturday. They think I offed her father, or something like that, because I wanted the company."

Joey's eyes widened. "Well *that's* a twist."

"Yeah," I said. "I guess it is. But it makes sense. They can't really ignore me, since they're not entirely sure of my involvement. I helped Hannah and her brother, and that makes me something to them."

"But a person interested in their company? Why?"

I thought for a minute, and recounted my reasoning on the way back to Edisto Beach. "Because I was in the right place at the right time — Bradley Rayburn ends up dead, likely not a suicide, and then I'm ready to go when a hitman comes in for her. Then, as if that wasn't enough, I get all bent out of shape and take it out on *another* one of their guys, after I killed one of them and injured two more."

"Don't forget about the fishbait you brought back in the trunk."

"Right, so I killed *two* of their guys. Whatever. Doesn't help my case any. From their perspective, I'm the silent partner — I'm the one who wants that piece of Crimson Club. They — whoever they are — have probably been working on this play for years. And I show up out of the blue and start messing around in Hannah's affairs, it's going to piss them off."

"Not to mention make you look like the culprit."

"Right," I said, nodding again. "Which *also* doesn't help me out with the government types."

Joey cocked an eyebrow. "You think they're on to you for Hannah's dad's assassination?"

"No, not necessarily for that. But they're definitely curious about the same things this other group is curious about. I've been in all the wrong places at all the wrong times, and it really does look like I'm involved."

"So Rayburn's funeral service is out on Hunting Island on Sunday, and we need to clean this mess up by tomorrow night."

"That's the gist of it, yeah."

"And the government is crawling all over you."

"Yeah." I didn't tell Joey it was the FBI, nor how I knew it was the FBI. I needed to keep a few cards close to my chest, and my relationship with Truman was one of them. If only for Joey's protection. He'd done me a lot of favors over the years, and I didn't need any of those 'favors' getting him in trouble with the feds.

"And we can't just walk in and start shooting the place up."

"Yeah, seems reckless."

"Yeah," Joey said, with a not-so-slight shade of sarcasm in his voice. "It does seem *a bit* reckless."

"So the general idea, at this point, is to sneak in. Somehow. They did it with Hannah, so we can do it, too. My — " I caught myself before I said 'my contact at the Bureau told me — "my gut tells me that if they snuck into the mansion with Hannah kicking and screaming, there's got to be some way to get through a cellar entrance, or a tunnel or something we could access."

"Or just pretend we're helping with the funeral."

I shot Joey a glance. "That's... that's not a bad idea."

"Beats digging around for a secret underground entrance that probably doesn't exist."

"True. Place is on the beach, I doubt there's a whole lot of underground anything."

I shifted in my old barstool, remembering how uncomfortable these chairs were. The leather had flattened down over the tops of the seats, the cushioning inside barely poofy enough to notice it was there. I made a mental note to shop for some better ones that hadn't been used in thousands of bars before they'd made their way to mine.

"How about we bring in a bunch of drink stuff? Pretend we're the bar?"

I shook my head. "No, place like that probably has a bar in every room already. There will be plenty of booze there."

"But they won't have a dedicated staff for pouring for large events like this."

"They usually do drinks at funerals?"

Joey shrugged. "Sure, why not? I mean, wouldn't you want a drink?"

"If I was dead, or if I was at a funeral for someone who was?"

He shrugged again.

"Fair enough," I said. "Seems a bit... I don't know, it seems a bit morbid, though."

"It'll work. If they have a drink service already, we'll just fake our way in as employees. No one's going to be guarding the door with a guest clipboard until Sunday. And if there's not supposed to be beverage service at funerals, they won't already have one. We'll say we're setting up for the wake.

Those are really just afterparties, anyway. Everyone wants to be drunk at those."

For a brief moment, my thoughts flashed back to the last funeral I'd been to.

Hers.

I clenched my jaw and forced another few sips of bourbon down. The memory came like a wave, crashing over me without a way to defend myself. The glass shook in my hand a bit, then steadied.

Joey looked at me, but I stared down the bar at the sign directing visitors to the restrooms, ignoring him.

This was another card I was playing close to my chest.

Finally, I looked up again.

"Yeah, Joey," I said. "That'll work. That'll definitely work."

CHAPTER FORTY

I RUBBED MY EYES AND walked into the back office area. *Go time.* I remembered my father saying that when I was a kid whenever it was time to leave somewhere earlier than I wanted to get up. I'd always been a night owl, but as the years went on I found my body requiring less and less sleep.

Or, more likely, there was just nothing my body would gain from more sleep. It had been beaten into submission over years of hard service to me, and the aches and pains that had been cloying and sporadic at first had become permanent fixtures. Sleep did nothing to help them along, so I didn't need as much of it.

Joey was already there, cooking up an unbelievably delightful-smelling concoction that included bacon, eggs, and what looked like hash browns.

"We had hash browns?" I had turned over the ordering to Joey a few months ago, as he was the master chef around here and knew when we were getting low better than I did. He also, somehow, had an uncanny way of knowing when there was going to be a run on something. The locals and oldies would come out and eat us clean out of catfish, or eggs, or something else, and Joey would surprise me by grabbing another stack of boxes full of the stuff from the tiny walk-in freezer, claiming he knew there would be a demand for it that week.

This time, too, he surprised me. "No," he said. "I used breadcrumbs from the way I do catfish and added some butter and paprika, made sort of a pan-fried egg and bacon thing."

I scrunched my nose. The delightful smell seemed to lessen when I thought of the smorgasbord he had whipped up.

"Don't knock it 'til you've tried it," he muttered.

I walked into the bar and flicked on the lights. The tables and chairs glistened, cleaned well from the early turndown service last night. I glanced around at the space with the same eyes I'd always looked through, seeing the same things as always and thinking the same things. The same upgrades, the same ideas, the same dreams.

After some time in the same space, there is a certain blindness that grows out of familiarity. It was no different here, and most days I came in I just stared, trying in vain to see the space through new, fresh eyes. I never wanted to see my bar as a paradigm, losing the ability to discern what my customers noticed. Did it smell? Was it outdated? Was there an obvious 800-pound gorilla in the room that turned people away?

Today was different. I had a brief flash of confusion, like my mind had finally pulled the blinders away and allowed me to see this space as if looking upon it for the first time. Only an instant, but it was enough. There was a smell to the place, but it wasn't bad. It was grainy, almost like baked bread without the freshness. Like beer, but not the spilled-on-the-floor-and-forgotten kind.

There was a dampness to the place, or something like it. I didn't really know how to describe it, but it wasn't good. I didn't like what I noticed with these new eyes in the moment I was allowed to use them, but I couldn't really pinpoint what it was. It was a certain funkiness, like an interior designer had started in on this place and then stopped halfway through. But instead of a line, a specific delineation point in the center of the room where the 'good' stopped and the 'bad' began, it was all mixed together, impossible to separate.

I frowned, blinked, and looked again. The old bar, the familiar territory I'd built and had been building for years, returned. The 'weirdness' of the place was gone, replaced by a calming sense of security.

Crap. I wanted to bring back the weirdness so I could study it a moment, but my mind had shifted back again and the moment was over.

The smell of eggs and bacon increased, and I heard a sizzling plate floating toward me.

"Here you go, boss," Joey's voice said from behind me. I whirled around and found a gigantic plate piled high with food. "Eat up."

"Go time," I said.

He looked at me funny.

"My dad used to say it all the time. "'Go time,' like 'ready or not,' or something like that."

"Got it," he said. He handed me the plate and then a fork, then headed back to the kitchen for his own plate. He returned and saw me glancing around. "What you looking at?"

I shrugged, then shook my head. "I don't know. I mean I don't know what I'm *trying* to look for. It's... something about this place."

I explained as best I could what I had been thinking about, and he started nodding. "The lights," he said, through a mouthful of eggs and bacon.

"What do you mean?"

I stuck my fork deep into the center of my egg-and-bacon mountain and took a bite. My mouth immediately began to water and my senses overloaded with the absolute amazement of it all. It was phenomenal, whatever it was. For the thousandth time I made myself a note to give Joey a raise.

"I'm saying the lighting is off in here," he said. "Always has been. Kind of a weird effect, actually. You'd think a place like this should be dimly lit, since it has a low ceiling and feels like a tiny speakeasy or something."

I looked over at him, but didn't stop eating.

"So you put up lights that aren't quite dim enough, but even then they're the wrong types."

"How are you a lighting expert now, too?" I asked.

"I'm not," he said. "Just been to a lot of places, and I was trying to figure out what was up with this place. I mean everything about it is great — best drinks in a 200-mile radius, good service, and — " he winked at me " — best damn catfish *anywhere*."

I laughed. "Okay, fine, Martha Stewart. What kind of lighting do we need in here?"

"Something a little smaller, and a little dimmer, and more of them. On a dimmer switch too, so you can really dial in the effect you want. You ever been to a fancy restaurant?"

"Like Red Lobster?"

He almost choked on an egg. "No… like… never mind. Yeah, like Red Lobster, I guess. They turn down the lights at certain times, to make it darker during dinner."

I thought about it as I ate my eggs. The idea had merit, and I had to admit I was the last person on Earth who should be deciding on things like interior design. Still, the lighting in here had cost a fortune. To think I'd have to redo it all. I grunted, a deep, angry thing that made Joey look up at me.

"You get any sleep last night?" he asked.

"Yeah, a bit. Doesn't seem to help anything these days, that's all."

"You mean you're still a pissed-off old dude?"

"A pissed-off old dude who can kick your ass," I replied.

"Yeah, challenge accepted. Anyway, we're here, we've eaten, what's the plan?"

I looked back at him, knowing what he was asking. "Same thing as yesterday. We need to get in and pretend we're working there. It's the only way."

"Yeah, I figured that. I'll give my buddy a call — he handles catering at that place in South Charleston, but he usually has a finger on the pulse of it all."

"The pulse of the *catering* market?" I asked, my voice betraying my attempt to not sound skeptical.

"Apparently there is a market, and apparently it's cutthroat out here," he said. "Whatever. He'll know."

"Okay," I said. "Great. Find out if there is anyone already providing beverage service for this thing, and what we need to bring either way. After that, we'll need to hustle. I want to get in there and get back out well before our deadline."

Joey took a bite and nodded. He chewed a moment. "Sounds good. Even though we're not going in 'Rambo style,' we'll still —"

"Don't worry about that," I said, cutting him off. "I've got that covered."

"Okay," Joey said. "Great. What else?"

"Your car."

He raised an eyebrow.

"It sucks."

"You're one to talk."

"Mine's going to still suck, even after Billy finishes with it, but next to yours it's a Rolls Royce."

"What's wrong with it?" he asked. I honestly couldn't tell if he was stringing me along or if he thought it was a decent enough ride.

"Joey, the thing's falling apart. You have three different tires —"

"They all went flat at different times. What, am I supposed to change all four at once?"

"— And the engine is starting to shake at 70."

"Hmm," he said. "Used to be 80."

Now I raised an eyebrow at him.

"Still, it's all we've got."

"No," I said. "This isn't the time to rely on something built last millennium. Let me make a call."

He nodded. "Okay, I've got that call to make myself. When are we shipping out?"

I looked at my watch, a cheap knockoff of a military issue. "Let's give it three hours to get ready. Go time is noon?"

"Go time is noon," he replied.

I reached out a hand. Joey looked at it for a moment, then grabbed it.

"I'm not trying to make this sentimental, but this is a big deal, Joey. I appreciate it."

He squeezed my hand tighter, as if challenging me. His eyes shone with the enthusiasm of a new recruit. "Don't mention it. Chances are I'll be the one saving your old ass, anyway."

CHAPTER FORTY-ONE

IT TOOK ME THE BETTER part of half an hour to walk to Marley's B&B, as I took a meandering route around the bend near the old corner of the beach, then back up along the coastline past the historic district. When I got there, the sun was shining fully and the sweat was starting to linger on the back of my neck.

There were tourists and a few locals out on the beach as I passed, the tourists standing out due to their brightly colored umbrellas and coolers strewn lazily around the park area. The locals always drove in, parking in one of the few spots that were open to the public yet hard to find, tucked away behind shops or houses yet still within walking distance to the water. They left their lunches and drinks in the vehicles instead.

I nodded to a few locals who recognized me as I passed, and hoped they didn't think it odd I was traipsing up and down the streets wearing jeans and black boots and a long-sleeved shirt. I was a businessman in their eyes, so I figured they just assumed I was on my way to business of some sort.

Standing at the front stoop of Marley's, it took me a moment to get my bearings. I had only been here once before, but it had been at night and I hadn't been standing still. I looked around and retraced my route up the steps, onto the porch, and then looked up at the back driveway and pictured the van rolling away with Hannah inside, screaming.

I recalled the man who'd chased me down, the idiot who hadn't known what he had signed up for trying to take me out. He was somewhere off the coast, strung up on paracord that had been tied around him and around a couple cinder blocks in some not-so-deep water. The next person he would be face-to-face with would be in for a disgusting, smelly shock.

The thought gave me little satisfaction, unfortunately. Hannah was still out there, still being terrorized by the assholes who thought I was involved in all of this. They wouldn't listen to logic or reason, and there was no way I could prove to them I had no interest in their shitty company. Hell, it would seem to them further proof that I *was* involved. Anyone taking part in an organization like that would have all kinds of loopholes and legal trapdoors in place to make their involvement invisible.

I turned around and looked out to the street. The streetlight that had provided me just a little help before was dark during the daylight hours, but it stuck out between two trees in my field of vision like a sore thumb. There was no one around, and there was certainly not anyone watching the house in the near vicinity. The local police had not yet been alerted to the fact that there were two gruesome murder scenes right inside, decomposing and beginning their short trip back to dust.

But I wasn't looking for a cop, or an innocent bystander. I was looking for something that would be a bit more subtle, not necessarily hidden but certainly not wanting to attract attention.

I saw it just past the streetlight, across the street from Marley's and down just a bit, almost to the gas station.

A black sedan that sat low to the ground, impossible to see unless you weren't blind. The gall of the government agencies to deploy their troops in the most obvious vehicles never ceased to amaze me. The tires had that oily look of having been changed out with brand new ones just a week ago, or even probably at the start of the mission, and the wheels themselves had that 'I'm nothing to look at' plainness to them that made me want to look at them. Cheap wheels on an expensive car only said one thing: government agent.

I started walking, hoping the guy or gal inside would see me coming and place a call to their boss. I imagined what the conversation would be like: 'sir/ma'am, I see that guy coming. The one we were supposed to be watching the other day.' 'Yeah? Are you still supposed to be watching them?' 'uh, no.' 'Okay… then stop watching them. Any action on the house?'

Unable to prevent a smile from forming on my lips, I laughed a bit and crossed the street. I would approach them on their passenger side, for two reasons. They had been directed to watch Marley's until the police investigation began, and I didn't want to obstruct their view. In addition, I believed it was a little less intimidating to approach on the opposite side as the driver. Something psychological maybe, but it seemed like it gave them more confidence in their ability to pull up a gun or a badge or whatever it was they were defending themselves with that day.

I came all the way up to the window and brought up a knuckle to start knocking before it rolled down. Dark bulletproof glass slid away to reveal a dark, not-bulletproof interior covered in leather.

"Wow," I said under my breath.

"Can I help you?" the agent — a guy who looked to be about half my age — said. His voice was more of an 'air,' the kind of voice reserved for kings who have been threatened by a field peasant.

"Uh, well, maybe," I said. "Just admiring your ride. Shame you can't ever let it up to speed, you know?"

The guy frowned. "Sir, I —"

I held up a hand. "I mean they got you watching Marley's place, but I'm telling you, the action's down south. Hunting Island."

There was just a hint of recognition in his eyes, but he redirected and hid it well. He knew what I was talking about, but he realized just a little bit too late that he wasn't supposed to *tell* me he knew what I was talking about.

A young gun. Even better.

"Listen," I said. "I get it. You're new on the job, but you're good. You'll go places. Won't take long. But you gotta put up with this bullshit for a few years, prove yourself. You know?"

"Again, sir, I —"

"Save it, pal. Get your fancy smartphone out and call your boss. Tell them I need a favor."

He looked at me blankly, not moving a muscle. I waited for it — the telltale sign of shifting around to grab a handgun, or a flicker to the rearview mirror to signal backup I hadn't seen coming — but nothing happened.

"Name's Mason Dixon," I said. "Funny name, not-so-funny guy. I'm going to tell you again. I need a favor."

"What — what can I help you with?"

I looked at him like he had just landed in the middle of a

street in a spaceship. "Shit, kid, you serious? You think I don't know who you are? I'm not buying whatever 'undercover cop here to help the citizens' crap you're dishing out. I. Need. A. Favor. Get that phone out, make it happen."

"Mr. Dixon, my orders — "

"Are to watch the house. Stupid, and a waste of my tax dollars. You know it, I know it. Nothing either of us can do about it, so I'd suggest you take a message and pass it up the chain for me."

"Or what?"

"Or I'll call Truman and tell him a toddler is throwing a tantrum. Won't do much, I admit, but come on, man, you really want that shit in your file?"

He stared me down from behind his stereotypical glasses, his jaw clenching and unclenching every few seconds. I smiled, throwing him my best I-don't-give-a-shit-about-your-excuses glance I could muster up. Finally, after a few more seconds of excruciating acting, I exhaled when I saw him relax.

"Okay, I'll pass it along," he said. "But no promises. I'm just the messenger."

I nodded, grinning.

"What's the favor?"

My grin turned back into a full-on smile, this time not trying to hide the excitement in my eyes.

"I need to borrow your car."

CHAPTER FORTY-TWO

"THEY JUST *GAVE* IT TO you?"

Joey was seated in the passenger seat of the Chrysler 300, admiring the interior. It was jet-black leather, and aside from a few scuff marks on the driver's seat and a worn smudge line on the drive knob, it looked brand new.

I knew better, but I was still impressed. The newer guys in the Bureau got the hand-me-downs from the seasoned veterans, and the guy I'd stumbled up to earlier today was most certainly a newer agent. If not for the way he handled me, I would have guessed it from the trumped-up surveillance mission he'd been assigned to.

I'd all but confirmed that there had been four field agents assigned to this mission, at least on the ground. There might be a surveillance and reconnaissance van or hotel room somewhere nearby, or even a safe house for the tactical outfitting, briefing/debriefing, and general hangout, staffed by one or two more agents, but there were about four of them providing the front-line support. The FBI didn't usually *tail* people the way they'd followed me, but typically *surrounded* people instead. They would use any number of agents depending on the location, level of surveillance needed, and density of population to keep a solid gaze on the mark.

Since I figured there were four, that meant three of them were off checking out the Rayburn estate, making plans, and generally staying busy with their assignments. The rube I had encountered had either pulled the short straw or was, in fact, a newbie. Judging by his age, I guessed it was the latter.

Which made his ride seem that much more impressive. It was outfitted with all the fancy upgrades the FBI liked to hide under the hood for their wheel artists, like the ability for the driver to flick off one or both headlights or brake lights at will, a built-in navigational computer, and heavy-duty bumpers for, I guess, heavy-duty bumping. I figured this had been commissioned as a serious follow vehicle at one time or another, so I assumed a closer inspection might even turn up aftermarket upgrades in the steering pump and radiator, and possibly brake lines.

Joey simply seemed to be wowed by the cleanliness and shine of it all.

"You know, if you just take care of your vehicle, it'll look this nice," I said.

He glanced over at me. "Says the guy who got his totaled."

"We don't know if it's totaled yet," I shot back. "Billy's still got it in the shop. Could just need a new fender or two."

"Right. Anyway, they just gave this thing to you? What'd you have to do for them?"

I shrugged. "Just called in a favor."

"You knew the guy? At the FBI? Or CIA?"

I held up a hand. I had played the cards close to my chest, and I wasn't trying to hide it from Joey that I knew someone at the Bureau, but I didn't need to be playing

227

twenty questions about it. I'd tell him, but on my time, not his.

"Knew the guy's boss, actually," I said. "No big deal."

"I bet it was no big deal. You know someone with the Feds?" he asked again.

I smirked. "Yeah, he was there a lifetime ago, but I know all the guys that used to work for him. One of them took his old position, and we're, you know, friends, I guess. And fine — he wasn't too happy about it."

"Him or his boss?"

"Yeah."

Joey laughed, then slid a finger across the oiled, supple glove box compartment. "Pretty nice upgrade from mine, still. Hope we get it back in one piece."

"Why? They didn't take a copy of my license and insurance."

"Yeah, that's true. So how's this work, then? We just… use it? And bring it back when we're done?"

"It's government, which means this whole deal's probably got a thousand strings attached to it that we'll never know about because all of them will be pulled opposite directions at the same time and the pullers will start fighting about it."

"So… you're going to keep it?"

I threw my head back and laughed. "No. I wish. They'll impound it for a year before they even start digging around the debrief files and try to figure out where to point the blame finger first. It'll be two years, minimum, before that kid we 'borrowed' it from gets it back. There's already civvy fingerprints all over the stupid thing, so they'll probably consider burning it out and leaving it in Southside Chicago as a more efficient option."

"Wow," Joey said. "Must have been a big favor you called in."

I threw the car into drive and pulled away from the curb. The kid who'd driven it across the street from Marley's was already long gone, heading south toward the rest of town to wait for a new ride.

"Just had to explain to him how much more use we'd get out of it than the guy driving it before."

I did a quick turnaround in front of Marley's and sped up, not wanting to linger any longer than necessary in front of the dead man's home and place of business. I shuddered, then sped up.

"Where we headed now?"

I was pointing south, the direction of our final destination on Hunting Island but opposite the highway that led out of Edisto Beach, but I had one more stop before we made our way to Rayburn's. We passed Joey's car in the lot of a gas station, where he'd dumped it after running a few errands himself. He'd met me at the FBI vehicle just as I had gotten the confirmation from the agent.

"My place."

Joey froze in his seat, and when I looked over at him I was surprised to see him staring back at me, wide-eyed.

"You… you really do have a place?"

I shook my head. "Why does everyone always do that? It's not like I live in the bar."

"Well I figured it was either there or your car."

"No, Joey, I have a place. It's an apartment."

"Where?"

"Near the bar. You'll see. Decent place actually, at least to me. Has everything I need, nothing more. But it's no looker, and we're only going in for a minute."

"Weapons?"

I nodded. "Any preferences?"

"Something that shoots straight."

229

I grinned. Joey had done some time in the Navy, but hadn't enjoyed the menial work during the months between deployments. He would have gone all the way to the top if he'd stuck it out, since he was a fantastic worker and had enough of a wit to stay sane, but I understood where he was coming from. My own father had instilled in me the nose-to-the-grindstone work ethic at a very young age, yet took every opportunity to remind me that the Army was for men who didn't know what they wanted in life. He had served a lifetime, but was mostly disappointed with the lackadaisical effort the brass put into the management and logistics of it all, and according to him, it had slid downhill the last couple of decades.

So it was even more of a surprise to me when he was livid about my decision to refuse to join up following high school and opt instead for a business degree and the much more exciting life of a bartender. About halfway through the degree and halfway toward bankruptcy I decided I needed some help paying for my education.

My father was nowhere to be found, so I joined the Army.

This, for some reason still unknown to me, pissed him off even more than when I told him after high school I *wouldn't* enlist. It wasn't the first schism we'd had in our relationship, but it seemed to be the final one before we'd simply stopped talking altogether for about ten years.

I looked over at Joey. I knew nothing of this kid's life, really, except that he was a veteran as much as I was, part of a system that carried with it more history and patriotism than reality and truth. He was Navy, I was Army, but we both had the same chips on our shoulders that had led us to chase a slower, more controlled life. I knew he had lived in Charleston for some time, doing sales at an Internet or marketing firm, or both — I didn't know anything about that crap — but he'd lost interest in the mundanity after a year. He visited my bar once or twice, then just kept coming back, claiming my Old Fashioned was the best in the state. I didn't believe him, because I didn't believe anyone under the age of forty would even know what a real Old Fashioned was, but he kept ordering them and I kept serving them, until the day I ran into him cooking at a stand on the beach.

I wondered about the kid's father — did he have one? Or did he have one like I had one, a guy milling about doing whatever the hell he wanted without a care in the world for the wife he left or the kids he'd estranged? I suddenly wanted to know.

We were driving to my house, a brief stopover before we started the battle in the war I'd signed us up for, two ex-military wash-ups who knew how to make a drink and flip a breaded fish fillet better than we knew how to plan an infiltration and take a target.

I had my skill set, and I knew it well. Joey had proven himself worthy time and again in specific, isolated circumstances, but this was another beast. We didn't know exactly what we were getting ourselves into, except that it required four on-the-ground agents of the United States government and countless others in bunkers spread out around the country keeping track remotely. We weren't sure if this was an easy smash-and-grab or a suicide mission.

"Joey," I said, my voice calm, nearly a whisper. "This might be… a tricky situation."

"Knock it off, Dixon," he said. "I've been in some sticky spots before."

"I know," I said, "it's just… this might be different. The rules of engagement are, uh, well they may not matter much."

"When have they ever mattered."

"You ever see live-fire action in the Navy?" I asked.

"I was mostly on bases, working remotely. Not too often was I on a ship, and no, I never saw anything nasty while I served."

"So this is going to be new for —"

"While I was *serving*, I said."

I looked over at him in the passenger seat and raised an eyebrow. "So you weren't always a goody-two-shoes, then? That what you're saying?"

"Something like that," he said.

I nodded, turning again to look out the windshield. I figured as much, honestly. Someone like Joey didn't just *happen* to be comfortable with the work we did. From day one he'd been at ease with the way I operated, and what I was doing. He didn't ask a lot of questions, and he certainly didn't try to justify anything one way or another, a sure sign of someone not quite ready.

He had always had a certain coolness about him, especially when things behind the bar got rough. During scuffles he was a good man to rely on, and I felt myself leaning more and more on his abilities lately.

But I had always assumed that whatever skills he had he'd earned in the Navy. It was an easy assumption, as most of the guys I knew who could act that way under pressure had a history in the military. After a few years of the disorganization they subjected you to, combined with the mindless drone of daily grunt work, you started to change your opinions about a lot of things, like what you cared about. They have a way of breaking you, and even if you don't stay there and end up a lifer, you leave changed. After enough jogging up and down a hill and pulling yourself on your elbows through miles of barb-wire infested mud, you feel pain differently.

For me, I started caring less about my own safety and more about the safety of the people around me, and I started looking at my own life as something temporary — because it was. I figured something similar had happened to Joey, but maybe that had all taken place at some point in his life *before* he'd joined up. Maybe it was a daddy-issue thing, even. I didn't know, and I wasn't going to ask.

"Well listen, Joey. I, uh, really appreciate your help. If you ever, you know, need anything…"

"You want to talk about our feelings now?"

"No," I said, "I just mean… I'm here. If — "

He laughed. "Thanks, boss. I got it. I'm good, and I'll be even better once we get those assholes who took your girl."

"My… okay, Joey, time to cut that out. She's not my —"

He was grinning from ear to ear, so I shut up and focused on the road.

"We're here," I said, probably a little too gruffly.

CHAPTER FORTY-THREE

I COULD SEE HIM CALCULATING, trying to price it out in his mind. It was a habit of gun people, and it was an easy way to tell if people knew their weaponry or not. Joey, it seemed, knew quite a bit.

He frowned, just as he should, when his eyes landed on my Colt Single Action Army, undoubtedly shocked and probably a bit impressed.

"That what I think it is?" he asked.

I nodded. "But it's a 2nd generation. If it were 1st, it'd be locked up tight somewhere, I wouldn't even show it to you.

He laughed.

"Wow," Joey said, looking at the other gear and weapons I had laid out on the table. "You've got all this just *sitting around* your house?"

"No," I said. "I'm not an idiot. I took it all out before I went out to find our ride. Can't help doing an inventory every now and then, and since we can't take them all, I figured it'd be nice to give the other ones some love."

"I'm fine with that," Joey said, already taking apart a Taurus 9mm on the edge of my coffee table.

I had a sparse setup in my apartment, out of both necessity and desire. Not much furniture, and what was there wasn't much to look at. I spent so much time in the bar, and when I wasn't down there I was sleeping. Didn't have a need for a television, as I hated watching or reading anything those idiots called 'news,' and my preferred method of entertainment was talking to the oldies and locals, and making up stories about the visitors and judging them on their drink selections.

So the gun-to-furniture ratio in my house was quite high, but I still had a lot of pieces. Joey was visibly impressed, and even more so after I'd dumped it all out on the coffee table. The table was about six feet long and two feet wide, and it was pretty much covered with weapons and ammunition. Loads of pistols — I tended to collect those, everything from antiques to conversation starters — but also an Uzi, a handful of working grenades, and two coveted rifles.

Joey put down the Taurus and picked up a Luger. He held it with the same care and attention to detail as I imagined the German soldier who'd originally held it did, and I watched him for a moment, like a father watching a son.

"Well," he said. "What are we going with?"

"This isn't a war," I said, "and we're looking at four, possibly five bogies. Bigger guns don't always mean bigger results."

"So keep it reasonable?"

I nodded. "Keep it reasonable. Handguns, maybe a rifle that we'll use for scoping out the mansion and seeing if there's an easy shot into the house. Might not even use that, but I'll pack it anyway."

"Will you recognize the guys that took Hannah?"

"Yeah," I said. "They'll be holding guns. Probably looking suspicious. Mustaches too. And frowning a lot."

Joey laughed. "We'd be so lucky."

"Yeah, I'm not counting on it either, but I've seen weirder stuff."

I poked around the items on the table until I found what I was looking for. A Sig Sauer P226, worn just the right way and engineered as if it was made for my own left hand. I hefted it, passing it back and forth in my hands a few times, then I loaded a magazine and pushed it into place. Joey followed suit with the Taurus, then we spent another few minutes filling extra magazines and shoving them into our pockets. When we finished that, I went into my bedroom closet and returned to the living room holding two leather chest holsters. Each had attached carrying cases for five or six more magazines, so I tossed one to Joey and we began filling those, too.

"Wow, you really do have an arsenal here."

"Yeah, it's a bit of a hobby at this point. My granddad and I used to camp all the time, and he would always be buying new gear. Tents, stoves, lanterns, knives, you name it. When I got old enough, we started buying guns together, and I guess I was never able to kick the habit."

"Did you hunt?" Joey asked.

I nodded. "A little. Not much, honestly. My mother never really liked us to do it, and my dad wasn't into it. My granddad really just liked to camp, so we'd go out for a weekend and shoot at logs and stuff, but not really much else."

"So your dead shot skills came from the Army?"

I laughed. "I wish I was half as good as my instructors, but yeah, I started putting things together during my stint. Never good enough to win any awards, but my skill set was in tactical movement and clearance. Back then I could sneak through a Chili's on Friday night with a 'free beer' sign without getting noticed."

"I take it we're not going to be doing much sneaking today," Joey said.

"Probably not, but that doesn't mean we need to start blowing shit up and screaming like banshees. We'll post up for a bit around the funeral setup, see what we see, then we'll move in. We've got the advantage that they don't know what we look like."

"Or that we're working together," Joey added.

"Or that."

We finished strapping up and getting set, then Joey turned to me, waiting. He still had his calm, collected look, but there was a certain look of questioning on his face. I wanted to tell him something, but I had no idea what I could come up with that I actually believed. I had no idea how this was going to go. It had been years since I'd done anything even *remotely* this bold and stupid.

"Ready?" I asked. I kicked myself for missing the moment to come up with an awesome speech.

He shrugged. "Gotta go out somehow, right?" He forced a laugh. "Might as well be like this."

CHAPTER FORTY-FOUR

IT HAD TAKEN THE BETTER part of two hours to get down the road and start in toward Hunting Island, mostly because I refused to push the car up over about 65. No sense going through all this trouble to stock up like we had just to get pulled over and arrested by some dipweed cop trying to earn a promotion.

Plus, I didn't want to rush in — I was anxious about Hannah's safety, of course, but I was also anxious for Joey's. Against my natural bent, I forced myself to not be rash, to think things through. A nice, meandering drive through the countryside was a perfect way to get my thoughts in order.

My first thought to get in order was about how to get into the house. We could likely get onto the grounds without being seen; the car we were in had darkened windows, not quite a full tint but enough that I was confident we'd be able to drive straight up to the house unseen.

Then we'd head around to the back, just as I had yesterday, and start unloading. Both of us were in black suits I'd pulled out of my closet — one a bit tighter and smaller from many years ago that Joey mostly fit into, and another one that I'd had tailored for my wife's funeral.

It felt odd to be wearing that suit once more, especially at another funeral, but then again I didn't have the opportunity to wear suits during my regular job, so it was weird just to wear one regardless.

We'd dressed according to Joey's Charleston friend; apparently there wasn't a dress code for most of the pouring services around here. Catering was another thing altogether, and he'd told Joey that they had uniforms, matching aprons, and sometimes little chef hats to really 'sell' it, but for pouring, even at a funeral, we'd fit right in with just black-tie formalwear.

I planned to pay off whoever was in charge of the drinks, telling them I was here undercover and needed to just walk around and get some information. Extra hundred bucks if they'd keep their mouth shut to the other service staff. We weren't going to be drinking anything, so I didn't see how it would be a problem. We were both trained bartenders so we should be able to stay incognito for the duration of our time there, mixing and fixing when we needed to.

If it *did* happen to be a problem, we'd maneuver and figure something out. We were already dressed like we belonged there, so it would only be a matter of fitting in with some of the other service staff or just scrapping the whole damn thing and running inside and hiding out.

I was leaning toward scrapping the whole damn thing, but just because I was comfortable flying blind didn't mean Joey was. He struck me as the type of guy who'd excel with a plan and make adjustments when necessary, so I wanted to stick to a plan, even if it wasn't fully fleshed out.

Once we were in the house, though, I had no plan whatsoever. I didn't know if any of the Rayburn extended family would be hanging around inside, or if they were still traveling and would arrive over the weekend. I didn't know if the house had a permanent staff that would be suspicious of us, or if the guys that nabbed Hannah would be posted up watching the interior.

I didn't really know *anything* about what we would do once we got there, except the two words I'd etched into the forefront of my mind and refused to let out of sight:

Get Hannah.

I would get her, I knew that much.

I would get her, and I would kill the bastards that took her.

"You okay?" Joey asked.

"Yeah," I said. "But I'll be better when we have Hannah back."

We drove on in silence for another few minutes, until the highway bent around a few times, signaling that we were about to reach the last bridge and start out toward the state park. I could see the expanse of ocean ahead and felt the urge to just toss in the towel and hit the beach. The weather was nice, warm for this time of year, and I knew the water would be refreshingly cold.

I shook my head, forcing the peaceful thoughts away and replacing them with the terrible reality of what I was here to do.

I went over the plan one final time, solidifying it into my psyche for Joey's sake, making sure I hadn't left anything out or forgotten something — any minor detail I would normally ignore and not try to control had a carefully assessed set of criteria for dealing with it.

We crossed the bridge and I subconsciously watched for any signs of FBI activity. Naturally they would make it difficult for their presence to be seen or felt, but I knew what I was looking for.

Broken branches and brush signaling a purposeful concealment of a path off the main road. Unmarked vehicles, of any shape and size, parked in places that were meant to look abandoned but had a certain in-use quality to them. People — literally any sort, from grandmas to teenagers — walking around carelessly, yet intently, as if on a secret mission to nowhere.

I didn't see any of these signs. In fact, there was next to nothing during the last stretch of drive that brought us over the bridge and onto Hunting Island. The land was quiet, and even the trees and grass seemed to know that something was coming. Everything was silently intense, a visible reminder of what I was feeling.

We pulled off the road and onto the same white, shining path I'd driven over last night, past the two sentinel-like towers marking the grounds and property of a man I had first heard of only days ago. In the sparkling daylight, the place had a miraculous sheen to it, like every stone in the long driveway had been daily polished and replaced. If the grass had been impressive by the light of the moon, today it was divine. I would have believed that it had been cut by hand, each blade painted a deep green.

Then the mansion — the place I'd been dreaming of ever since I'd seen it. It stood out from the rest of the scenery, dwarfing the beauty with its own regality that I did not know could exist in the United States. The windows glimmered and reflected the ground, and the perfect shade of pink-brown that was used on the entirety of the structure seemed to be alive, moving. The solid rock facade on the house was some sort of granite, and it was too far away to see individual characteristics of the stone, but the microscopic imperfections and pieces of embedded quartz danced and twinkled as we drove close.

I realized I had been ignoring Joey the entire time, and my eyes were hardly noticing the path and driveway. I didn't want to take my focus away from the absolute wonder of it all, but I yanked my gaze away and looked at Joey.

He, too, was beside himself in awe. His mouth was even open a little, and I'm sure if I looked closer I'd see a little bit of drool pooling on the inside of his lower lip.

He swallowed, looked up and down the beachside resort property, and then swallowed again.

"I — wow," he said.

"Yeah," I replied. "That was pretty much my reaction, too."

CHAPTER FORTY-FIVE

THE FRONT OF THE HOUSE was dead, but the back of the property was abuzz with activity. I wheeled the large sedan around the south corner of the lot, just as I'd done the night before in Joey's car, and as soon as we pulled back to the north to start along the backside of the house, people started appearing.

There were servers and workers in black suits just like ours, as well as white-clad servants busy with chores and typical household duties. One woman was emptying trash bins into a larger receptacle, while another man was raking small leaves out from between the pieces of gravel in the walkway. Farther along I could see a group of men and women gathered around in a circle, each of them holding a notebook and taking notes while one of them dictated orders of some sort.

We drove on, dodging a couple of cars that had been parked on the left side of the driveway closer to the house, but not veering too far to the right so as not to hit the cars parked diagonally there. There were probably twenty vehicles, and I suspected that at least some of the workers here had carpooled and that some of the servants and house staff lived inside.

That meant there were already at least thirty people milling about inside and in the backyard areas. How Hannah could have been held here against her will was beyond me, but we were here and we weren't going to leave until I'd had a good look around. Joey sat up straighter in the car, either trying to method act his way into his new persona or just steeling himself for the grueling work to come.

I kept on for another few hundred feet, finally coming to a stop at the end of the driveway in front of a stand of palm trees, right at the start of the gravel path that led down to the beach and the *Wassamassaw* docked there. In the daylight I could see that the beach on either side of the boathouse was pulled up farther inland a bit, and had been dug out and dredged to allow space for the boat to slip in and out. I was amazed at the engineering feat; the sheer cost would prohibit most people from accomplishing this, but the luxury of it alone — to want to be able to park your boat on the beach, closer to your house — was impressive.

Joey's eyes widened at the sight of it.

"You see that last night?" he asked.

I nodded. "Yeah, but I didn't take a close look at it. Wish we were here by invitation, we might be able to swing a tour."

He flashed me a grin. "Well, technically we *are* here by invitation."

I put the car in park and opened the door. "Come on," I said. "We've got some drinks to serve."

There was a large white tent erected on the north side of the property, and I could see ten or so people underneath, setting up tables and tablecloths and a few stacks of dinnerware. I pointed at it. "That's it, I think."

"Yeah, that'd be my guess."

"You ready?"

He nodded again. "Think so. Locked and loaded, if that's what you mean."

I walked to the back of the car and popped the trunk. No real easy way to do this if I was trying to keep my activity on the down-low, but I was still a bit leery about just swinging it wide open and letting anyone in the house see our little arsenal.

Joey seemed to anticipate this too, so he stepped up to my right side and glanced left and right, then at the house. "Seems clear," he said.

"Clear enough. Hurry up, and don't take too much. We don't want to be loaded down."

I had packed the rifle in the trunk along with another bucketful of ammunition, and though my belt and pockets were full, I grabbed two magazines and stuck them in my back pockets and considered slinging the rifle case over my shoulder. I wanted to have it in the trunk in case we had to post up in the woods, away from the house, and run surveillance. But getting inside the estate had proven to be a simple thing and the rifle was no longer needed. It wouldn't provide any more help inside the house than the Sig Sauer I already had.

No wallet, no keys, no phone. Nothing else to weigh me down. Joey followed suit, testing the weight and feel of his own holster. He put on his suit coat and double-checked that everything was in place, then jiggled around a bit to triple-check.

I grabbed one final object, slipping it under the strap of my suspenders on the opposite side of my chest, and put on my own coat. I slammed the trunk closed and whirled around to my left, just in time to be ambushed.

"Can I help you?"

The man strolled over, a concerned smile on his face. He looked us up and down for a moment, then stretched out a hand.

"I, uh —" I stuttered for a half-second and then remembered my manners. "Sorry. We're here with, the, uh,"

I looked at Joey.

"Rogers' Service."

The man frowned.

"The beverage and catering company? We're the bartenders. Did they not…"

Joey pasted on his own concerned citizen look.

The man stared again, then his face brightened a little. "Right, sorry. No, they must have booked that earlier this week. I just flew in, and I'm trying to help out where I'm needed. Trying to stay busy and all that…" his voice trailed off and he looked out to the water.

"Are you family, then?" I asked. The man wasn't harassing us about our employment, and he wasn't asking questions, so I figured he was here for the funeral.

He nodded once, still looking at the beach. "Yeah, my brother. Bradley was, I mean." He stuck out a hand. "Thanks for being here. Let me know when you get set up, I'll be your first customer."

"Thanks," I said. "And you got it."

"And it's on the house," Joey added.

I prepared to sidestep him and start walking toward the tent, but he grabbed my arm. "What — what was that I saw you take out of the trunk, if I may?"

I felt my face flush a little, but I reached into my coat anyway and pulled out the object I'd slid inside. I twisted my hand around it and let it fall out, rolling it in my palm.

His eyes narrowed, then widened.

The shaker had been a gift from many years ago, one of the first pieces of barware I'd acquired, long before I'd had my own place. The metallic sheen and luster had long since faded, but I knew its grooves and crevices so well it had become somewhat of a token for me. A good luck charm, even.

I handed it to Bradley Rayburn's brother and let him examine it. "They always have plenty of stuff like this already, but the company just buys the crappy gear in bulk. We like to carry our own ware sometimes, just to make sure we're doing it right."

He chuckled and handed it back to me. "I like that. You take pride in your work. Good man."

I smiled, stuck the shaker back under my suspender strap, and started toward the tent. I could nearly feel Joey's nervousness burning a hole through my back.

CHAPTER FORTY-SIX

"I GOT THIS PART," JOEY whispered as we stepped into the tent. My eyes adjusted and I saw that there was already a large amount of spirits spread out on the tables along one side of the white tent, and a few bartenders were working through and detailing — cleaning and prepping the bottles and getting them ready for service.

A woman, taller than me and rail-thin, beautiful but in a lived-a-hard-life sort of way, paced back-and-forth along the tent wall behind the tables. She held a clipboard, dragging the attached pen on its metal rope along the manicured grass floor.

I looked back at Joey. "You sure?" I asked, hinting at the sarcasm I was feeling. "Rogers' Service? Really?"

He shrugged. "What? Better than your 'uh, I, uh, well, uh —"

"Shut it," I said. "What if they ask who we are? They'll know there's no such thing as Rogers' Service. What kind of name is that anyway?"

"All the fancy catering companies use a personal name like that. Makes it sound distinguished."

"Yeah, but 'Roger' sounds like a guy who just got fired from a bank teller job but decided he was entrepreneurial enough to put out his own shingle."

Joey shook his head. "No, see, that's why I put the apostrophe *after* Rogers. There are more than one Rogers, because it's a family name. Not 'Roger' like one guy."

"You think he got all that from your apostrophe placement?"

Joey whipped his head around and stared me down. "Again, way better than your answer."

"Fine. Still, what are we going to —"

"*You're* not going to anything. I said I got this."

Before I could grab him he ducked away and started toward the lady behind the longest of the tables, set perpendicular to the rest against one side of the closed-walled tent. He raised a hand in greeting as he drew near.

I had to hand it to him, the kid was confident.

I strolled up just as they started their conversation.

"— just got here, and wanted to make sure you were set," Joey said.

"I, uh, where did you say you —"

"Looks like you're fully stocked," Joey said, "so I'll check the wells. You have an ice machine around here?"

She frowned, then turned and pointed. "Over there, behind that truck. It's portable, so we had to hook it into the hose. It's going, but won't be full until tomorrow morning. First drink service is right after a small get-together on the lawn, tomorrow afternoon. Then Sunday's showtime."

Joey made a face. "You're making ice out of..." he stopped himself, then smiled. "Okay, I'll check out the stations and jump in. Just holler if you need anything."

Before the woman could argue he was off again, and she seemed suddenly conflicted about tracking him and realizing that he hadn't come alone. She pulled her eyes away from Joey and saw me. Her head tilted sideways just a bit and I smiled, the biggest fakest smile I could muster.

"I'm… with him," I said.

"Right," she said. "Got it."

She turned the other direction and started hollering at a few workers standing around. Something about making sure she had the list of help for the weekend on the clipboard and checked for accuracy.

Good, I thought. *We're walking into a maelstrom of chaos, just as we had hoped.* I knew we wouldn't be around for the get-together tomorrow or the drink service after, but it was good to get some details about the plans. She was probably not frustrated that she didn't know who we were, but frustrated at her team for scheduling two extra grunts for today's setup when they could have gotten by with fewer.

I wasn't a caterer, and I'd never poured for large corporate events like this, but I knew that scheduling and payroll were two of the most niggling annoyances any professional firm faced. I'd kept things dead simple from the beginning, only hiring Joey after he'd proven to me that my life was far easier with him around. So this woman, no doubt in charge of some aspect of the catering or beverage service, was frustrated that she now had to worry about another few hours of minimum wage expenses.

Joey was already close to the far end of the tent, working his way down the tables and glancing at the assortment of liquors and liqueurs on display. Some of the tops had been replaced with QuickPour spouts. They helped with neither pouring easier or quicker, but were nice for measuring proper amounts of liquor in mixed drinks, a necessity for an event as large as this.

He was hustling, obviously trying to look busy for the gal

in charge without actually taking up too much of our precious time. I caught up to him in a few seconds and copied his actions, glancing down at bottles, spinning some of them around so the labels faced us, and checking the QuickPours for a tight seal.

"What are we doing?" I asked through the side of my mouth.

"Looking busy," he said.

"No, I got that. I mean *after* this. Are we safe?"

He shook his head. "Not yet. I want to make sure the others see us working, just so we'll have an alibi later."

"Joey, I don't plan on getting arrested today."

"Neither do I. Just due diligence."

"Well *my* due diligence is done. I'm ready to start shooting some bad guys."

"Me too, boss. Just a few more minutes of faking it and we'll make a move. you go back out the way we came in, and I'll head around the outside of the tent. Meet somewhere near the rear exit."

"What if she —"

Joey cut me off. "She'll probably ask you *something.* Just say you're hitting the restroom."

I nodded, feeling for the first time in a long time that I had a teammate I could trust with my life.

Except that he wanted *me* to get confronted with the lady again. I didn't like the lady. She gave me the creeps.

CHAPTER FORTY-SEVEN

WE MET BY THE LARGE double doors that led from the house to the driveway, then down to the path toward the beach. Seeing the massive doors gave the house some directional organization. There was a similar set a little to the south, and I figured there was one set of main doors for both the north and south wings of the mansion, with one huge entrance on the front side of the estate.

There were other doors, scattered around and in small nooks that led into the house, but we weren't sure if they led straight in or were like patio doors that led into bedrooms and sitting rooms. I figured we'd be safest just walking in through the main doors and seeing what we could see.

We were armed, and while I was positive Hannah's crew would be at least equally armed, I counted on the fact that they weren't just waiting inside pointing guns at the main entrances. There were too many entrances to guard, and it was a good bet the funeral staff and guests wouldn't take too kindly to a contingent of mercenaries walking around.

No one knew what we looked like, and no one knew I had a companion with me. To anyone we ran into, including the thugs, we would seem like just a couple of servants or staffers. I was suddenly glad I'd left the rifle in the trunk. Having the black leather tube hanging on my shoulder would cause no alarm for a civilian, but anyone who had ever served or spent any time with firearms would know exactly what I was carrying. I looked at Joey and knew there was nothing about us that could give us away.

We walked through the back foyer of the great house, into a large hallway that stretched to the left. To our right was the northern wing of the house, but it was mostly filled by the single massive room at the end of the hallway. A fireplace sat at the end of the room, glass walls on either side of the rock structure, and I could see the waves a few hundred feet beyond crashing up onto the beach. The ocean met with the inlet here, the bay that separated this island from Edisto Beach to the north. There were no boats on the water at the moment, but I could almost picture the view from inside the house during a lazy summer day, watching the yachts and sailboats maneuvering around the bay, the larger rigs far out on the horizon line heading south for their offshore dropoffs.

I shook my head, taking it all in. The scale and scope of the house was appalling, but every detail seemed to be in place.

I looked up at the lights. I could see clearly inside, yet the hallway seemed to be dimly lit. Far above our heads a double set of chandeliers twinkled with their artificial candle light, casting small shadows on the intricate crown molding covering the edges of the walls and ceiling. About five feet from the top of the walls a ridge jutted out a few inches and ran horizontally the length of the hallway. More light washed out from the small shelf, providing a beautiful ambient glow that mixed perfectly with the chandelier light.

"That's the kind of interior lighting I was talking about," Joey said. "For the bar. Use the right lights and you can make it dim enough to feel nice, but still let people see."

"Yeah, well, I don't think I'll be putting any chandeliers up anytime soon." I looked back down the hall, then up again at Joey. "Which way should we start?"

"Well," Joey said, "assuming we're sticking together, let's just make our way down the hall, north to south, checking every room. Then we can go upstairs and start over."

I shook my head. "I'd bet all the downstairs rooms are larger meeting spaces, living areas, and kitchens. Too open to hide anyone, and with the funeral going on they would have been spotted."

Just as I said it, a pair of workers, dressed in the whites of a catering company, entered, turned left in front of us, and started down the hall. They nodded at us as they passed, then disappeared into a large space through a set of wood and glass double doors.

"Let's just walk down to the stairs at the middle of the house," I said. "We can peek into the rooms on the way and see if there's anything we'd want to check out more closely."

"How do you know the stairs are in the center?" Joey asked.

I flashed him a grin. "Haven't you seen any movies? The stairs are always at the center. Big, elaborate, grand staircases, spiraling down along the huge curved walls."

He laughed, and we started down the hall. I felt the weight of the pistol under my coat giving me strength, encouraging me to continue on. I wasn't one to place my trust in the tool but instead in the wielder of the tool, yet today I felt like I needed the weapon more than it needed me.

The hall barely echoed our footsteps. Rugs and tables on

the floor dampened and broke up the sounds, and large framed landscape paintings covered the walls, acting like acoustic paneling. Beneath the rugs a dark, deeply stained and worn wood floor cracked at us while we walked. I knew this place hadn't been here forever, but it seemed as though the wood I was walking over had been. I pictured it being pulled from the sides of a massive pirate ship, bent straight and cut into sections, then sanded down and finished.

My imagination was acting up again, a sign that I was feeling the stress of a situation I wasn't entirely comfortable with. The stress would eventually give way to adrenaline, but until then I had the built-in response of over-analyzing every minute detail and bringing it to life in my mind.

"There," Joey said.

I followed his finger and saw the staircase I had pictured. It was actually two staircases, one close to us and one farther down, both twisting downstairs into a large, round atrium. I couldn't see the front door, but I knew it would be just opposite the bottoms of the stairs.

We turned and walked upstairs without seeing anyone else. At the top of the flight another hallway, this one narrower and darker, stretched all along the same north-south route of its first-floor counterpart.

"Looks like all the bedrooms and bathrooms," Joey said. "Start on one side, or right here in the middle?"

"Middle," I said. "I don't want to waste any more time. Whatever this guy wants, I don't have it, so I want to get in there and let him know as soon as we can."

"Then he'll just say, 'okay, no problem, sorry for the inconvenience' and let Hannah go?"

"Yeah," I said. "Something like that."

CHAPTER FORTY-EIGHT

MOST OF THE ROOMS WERE locked, but we did get a glance into one of the bedrooms we passed. It was lavish, a purplish hue to the whole thing caused by the natural light from the glass balcony doors spilling in through a light lavender curtain. The bed was a perfect fit for the vague-Southern style of the rest of the house, a vertically massive king with bedposts that stretched to the ceiling, all strung up with more linens and frills than I had ever owned in my entire life.

A vanity, large plush chair, dresser, and full-size standing mirror completed the furniture assortment, and a closet lined one wall while a doorway into a bathroom stood on the other. It wasn't a particularly large room, but it was well-appointed enough to fit into any of Charleston's top hotels.

"Nice place," Joey said.

"Yeah, wish we could stay awhile," I said. "Maybe when this is all over…"

He winked at me. "We get Hannah back, I have no doubt she'll invite you to a sleepover."

I pushed him down the hall away from the room,

ignoring the comment. Deep beneath the feelings of anger and building adrenaline and the longing to bring Hannah's captors to justice, I felt a smaller, yet growing, desire. I wanted Joey to be right, and I had been secretly wishing for the same thing.

"How do we know these guys won't be behind a locked door?" Joey asked. "Shouldn't we try to at least pick the locks and look inside?"

"First, *they* invited *me* here, remember? They'll be waiting impatiently for me, so I doubt they'll make me pick a lock or break in to get to them. This is a negotiation, not hide-and-seek. Second, they're confident. They wouldn't bring her here during a time when the house is going to be busy with visitors unless they knew they had the situation under control."

"What about the Feds?" Joey asked. "Don't they know about them?"

I shook my head. "Unlikely, or they'd have already bailed and taken Hannah somewhere they can't get to her. Plus, the suits are slow. They'll be scheming for days and waiting for every piece to fall into place. We're sort of their advance team."

Joey shot me a look that said, 'you mean we're the infantry.' I shot him a glance that said, 'yeah.'

"Right," he said. "So the door will be unlocked and they'll be waiting for us. Should we have our weapons out?"

I thought about this for a moment, recalling the plan I'd made.

"No, not yet. I want to be checking the rooms myself first, while you wait in the hall. You'll know when we have the right one, so when I go in I need you to duck out of the way for a bit, while they check the hall. When it's clear again, come back and post up nearby, preferably within earshot. If you hear gunshots, come on in."

Joey stared at me. "*That's* your plan? You've got to be kidding me."

I sneered at him. "You have a better one?"

"Yeah," he said. "Literally *anything* else would be better than that. What if they just shoot you in the head when you open the door? What if there's nowhere to hide and they shoot *me* in the head after you go in? What if they —"

"Joey. Listen. I don't usually make plans for this sort of thing."

"You don't usually *do* this sort of thing."

We were whispering, but our voices were growing louder and louder the more heated we became. I held up a hand, waited for Joey to cool off, and started talking again.

"What I was going to say was that I don't usually make a plan for this sort of thing. I *don't* do this often, but that doesn't mean I never have. You don't always get a nice, clean mark. But I can't risk your life, or Hannah's, so I couldn't just do it the old way and run in shooting."

"Still," Joey said. "That plan is nuts. You're going to get all of us killed."

I shrugged. "Best I had at the time."

"Okay, you wanted me to wait in the hall. For what? Gunshots? Arguing? A thumbs-up sign?"

"Something like that, I guess. You're a smart guy, and you've been in some sticky situations. I guess I figured you'd just know when to come save the day. If I needed you to."

Joey's eyes widened. "*There* it is," he said. "That's what you've been worried about. You think that I'm your responsibility or something, like you've got to protect me. You think I don't really understand what we're into here and you've got to keep me out of harm's way."

I stared at him.

"Well?"

I shrugged.

"Jesus, Dixon. I'm not a kid. Get over yourself. If I wanted to stay out of harm's way, I *would have stayed out of harm's way.* I didn't follow you down here because I'm just so completely wooed by your heroism."

"I know that."

"Okay, then bring me *in*, man. Let me *help* you."

"Then how do you suggest we —"

Two gunshots cracked through the hallway, one of them landing with a deep thud into the hardwood paneling that covered the lower half of the wall just behind me.

I reached out to push Joey out of the way, but he was already in motion, diving for the floor. I repeated the motion, landing hard on the thin rug and smashing my knee against the foot of a side table. I gritted my teeth and looked up, trying to place where the shots had come from.

My instinct was that they had been shooting from the northern side, the wing of the house we were currently in, but I realized I was facing the wrong direction.

I looked up and my suspicions were confirmed. There was nobody in front of us — the hallway was empty.

Shit. I knew I wouldn't be able to swivel around and get my pistol out quick enough to get a shot off before the opposing shooter —

Crack!

Another round burst into my eardrums, and I flinched. This shot was louder, closer.

I opened my eyes as I finished my rotation on the floor, coming to a prone position next to the wall and the legs of the side table jutting out a foot from it. Another blast echoed into my ears, momentarily deafening me.

I looked up and saw the shooter, stopped in the middle of the floor. He was on one knee, but holding a handgun in one hand and a walkie-talkie in the other.

Joey was also on one knee, aiming down the hallway toward the enemy with both hands on a pistol that had the telltale smoke of a round freshly fired steaming off the back of it.

He watched the man, and I saw out of the corner of my eye him fall to his other knee, then finally backwards onto the hallway floor. Joey had fallen facing the other direction — the *right* direction — and had gotten off the two shots quickly enough to take the man down.

The guy was on the floor now, but he was trying to talk into his radio. The pistol had fallen away, resting a few feet away on another rug.

We waited, silent, until the man lay still.

"Uh, thanks," I said. My knee was going to swell up, and some of the pain had already set in, but I forced it to the side of my conscious mind and let the adrenaline pool in to take its place.

Joey lowered his weapon and looked over at me. There was a mischievous look of rage mixed with excitement in his eye, but he still seemed calm and collected.

He nodded, then stood. "I think it's time I earned that raise."

CHAPTER FORTY-NINE

"OKAY, WISE GUY," I WHISPERED. "What's the play?"

"Work our way down the hall, saving your ass the entire way."

I nodded and smiled, my pistol still up and ready. "Sounds good to me. Lead the way, Rambo."

Joey stepped out and poked each door on his side of the hall with the end of his pistol. I did the same on my side, and each of us took turns glancing down the way we'd come from to make sure we weren't being ambushed from behind.

"They're going to know we're here," he said.

"They're going to know *I'm* here. And they're going to know one of their own is down, since they heard his shots and the return fire, then nothing else."

"So they'll be expecting you," he said.

"They already were. Same plan, okay? I want them to think it's just me as long as possible. That has to be better than letting them know you're here."

"Yes, that part makes sense," Joey said. "I'm just a pawn — they don't want anything from me, so they'll probably try to get rid of me right away. But once you're in, I'm not sitting quiet while you try to talk your way out of this."

"I'm not following," I whispered.

"I'm going to give you five minutes in there," he said, holding up his wristwatch so I could see it. "That's it. Five minutes, then it's party time."

I thought about it and nodded. "Fine. Not much I can do to stop you, so if you think that's best. Just…"

"Dixon, I'm not going to put Hannah in any more danger than she's already in."

I half-smiled, then continued on. I pushed a third door and felt it give a little.

I let it fall open about six inches, warily eyeing the interior of the room. About six more inches passed and I found myself staring at the business end of a steel barrel.

Joey had been watching from the opposite side of the hall and I saw his eyes widen when he realized we had found the room. He shuffled down to the end of the hall and stepped into a reading room that made up the northern end of the second floor.

Satisfied he was well-hidden, I pushed the door open more with my foot and looked inside.

Two men with pistols, one without. Two of them were large, beefy men, the type that used to be in great shape but had let a little time and a lot of tacos get the best of them. They both had shaved heads and wore earpieces I assumed were connected to the radio band they were all on.

The man not holding a weapon was standing in front of the bed, another monstrous period piece like the one we'd seen in the room down the hall. He had a mustache that placed him somewhere between 1970's B-list actor and Saddam Hussein, and he was lacking the thickset structure that really would have sold it. He motioned me inside with a crooked smile on his face.

"Hello," he said. His voice was deep and cool, and if it wasn't for the situation we were in where I was going to kill him in a minute, I would have been inclined to ask him a question, just to keep listening to his voice.

I nodded at each of the men, buying some time, then stepped inside.

"Are you armed?" he asked.

I had put the pistol back inside my coat, but I looked at him like he was insane.

"Of course I'm armed. Where's Hannah?"

The man's head raised a bit, an intrigued look on his face.

"Ms. Rayburn is safe, for the moment. She has been reluctant to speak, but we've been getting acquainted with one another."

I *loved* this guy's voice. It was so assertive, so distinct. I would have recognized it anywhere. But I also knew in that moment, because of that voice, that he was not the man I'd spoken with on the phone. I squinted one eye, trying to figure out what pieces were now in play and how they were all related to one another.

This guy wasn't the ultimate guy in charge, or he was and the guy I'd spoken to on the phone wasn't.

"Where is Hannah?" I asked again.

The man ignored me and ducked his head to the side. The two gunmen, the fat ones with no hair, rushed over and started searching me. I knew I could have taken them out right then, stealing one of their weapons or grabbing my own when they took them out of my pockets, then shooting the third guy before he knew what the hell was happening.

I figured the Tom Sellick of the group, the man I was

talking to now, was also armed, but playing the 'I'm your friend' card with me. And somewhere in the room or nearby was the man I'd spoken to on the phone. He might have a few other grunts with him, too, like the dead one out in the hall.

So I let them search me, knowing that I still had a Joey-sized card up my sleeve, as well. They took my pistol, seemed disappointed that it was all I had on me, and threw it on the bed.

My main man walked over, a quick two-step and he was right in my face. I was taller than him, which I liked, but not by much. We stared at one another for a moment, then he spoke again.

"Do you have what Mr. Rayburn wants?" He asked.

I stared at him. I refused to let him know that I had no idea what he was talking about, and I had no idea why he thought it was something Mr. Rayburn would want.

And that Mr. Rayburn wasn't dead.

He asked me again, this time a bit more tension in his voice. "Do you or do you not have what Mr. Rayburn wants?"

I shook my head. "Nah, I'm afraid I don't. And Mr. Rayburn's dead."

At this, he laughed. "Good one."

Okay, I was thoroughly and utterly confused now, but I was playing a role. Cat-and-mouse, and the mouse had been caught by the cat but the cat was an idiot and the mouse had a friend waiting in the hall.

"Mr Rayburn will be here in one minute," he said. "And he is going to be ready to make the transaction. Did you bring the transfer information?"

I turned my brain on overdrive and began crunching through the information that had been stirring there for the last few days. Hannah's father had owned an organization that was taking part in some sketchy activities, likely overseas, and he had been killed for it. My own father had done the deed, trying to take out a mark on his own. That had started a ball rolling and had pushed Hannah and her brother into the crosshairs next, and started a mad grab for the reigns of the company.

This group, whoever they were, wanted control, and they almost had it. They didn't know my father had killed Rayburn — they just figured it was me. No one thought it was a suicide, so the puzzle pieces could easily be arranged that way and it would make sense.

Hannah was still alive because she had convinced them — or they had assumed — that I had some interest in the company as well, as a shareholder. Maybe they thought I'd bought it from Hannah or her brother, or that I had been a silent partner all along. I was brought in because they simply couldn't move forward without my shares.

But I had no shares to give. I didn't have a clue what transfer codes they were after, and if it was some offshore bank's routing and account numbers, I certainly didn't have those. My bluff was about to be called, so I needed a plan.

I thought for a moment, but everyone in the room was staring at me. I could feel the tension. They knew I was bluffing, and I knew I was bluffing.

"Can I use the restroom?" I asked.

The man frowned.

"I have to piss."

He glanced at the other men. Apparently this was not a scenario they had planned for. I marked that down as a little victory and had a smug little moment.

"No," he said.

"Okay," I replied. "Worth a shot."

Come on, Joey, I thought. *Any minute now.*

I was running out of ideas, even though I wasn't sure the 'I have to pee' idea counted as an idea in the first place. I needed something concrete.

I assessed the room, trying to figure out if I could manage an attack if their eyes flicked to the doorway to see if Joey was coming in. He would be ready to shoot, but he had the disadvantage of knowing I was in the room somewhere, so he couldn't — I hoped — just start shooting things that looked alive.

On the other hand, the men knew that their own leader — apparently Mr. Rayburn — was coming in as well, so they couldn't exactly start shooting the second a man rounded the corner, either.

That gave *me* the only attacking advantage. I didn't have a weapon, but I didn't have to hesitate for anything, either. I could start running at the nearest guy with a pistol, get it out of his hand, and start in on someone else before everybody realized what was going on.

Unfortunately it all relied on Joey actually walking *into* the the room. I wasn't about to start a fight against four armed men, three of whom were standing at-the-ready, without knowing Joey was there to back me up.

I didn't have a believable way to stall, so that left me with only one option.

I decided to tell the truth.

"Look," I said. "I'm just a bartender. I met Hannah when she came in to my place. We had a moment, you know? Nice girl. I'd really like to not see her harmed."

"You killed two of our men, and put two more in the hospital."

"*Those* guys are in the hospital? Come on — I barely touched them." I paused, then looked at all three of my captors in turn. "And by the way, it was *three*. Homeboy out in the hall, your idiot grunt over at Marley's B&B, and that sad little frat boy you tried to throw in to keep things interesting."

It seemed like Mustache was actually doing the math in his head. I waited, politely, for him to finish.

"You're not a bartender," he said. "Why would you kill those guys if you had no interest in Mr. Rayburn's affairs?"

"You damn well better believe I am. And I killed those assholes because they were *assholes*. You don't come marching into my bar with a gun looking for a fight without getting one."

"You're not *just* a bartender."

"Let me make you a drink, prove it to you. You got a minibar in here?"

I thought I saw one of the fat guys laugh, just a quick little snap of a smile. That was enough. I needed it. I decided I'd try to kill him last.

"You're wasting time, Mr. Dixon."

I raised an eyebrow. "You know my name already. That's impressive."

"As I told you, Ms. Rayburn and I have been growing close. And I'm sure Mr. Rayburn told you how *persuasive* he can be."

I felt a wave of revulsion. *How could a man treat his daughter that way?* I didn't understand — I didn't *believe* it. Bradley Rayburn had kidnapped his own daughter? And tortured her? And…

I didn't take the next step in my mind. It was already enough that *anyone* would dare to touch her, and I'd already decided I'd kill whoever did that. It made it more difficult that he was already dead.

I was confused, and I was no longer trying to hide it.

"Let me have Hannah," I said. "And I'll give you your company."

The man stepped back, then smiled. His mustache barely moved, just a caterpillar of hair sitting on his thick upper lip. "That is *much* more amenable, Mr. Dixon. And that is precisely the arrangement Mr. Rayburn was hoping for."

I nodded, then turned around when I heard footsteps in the doorway. If it was Joey, he'd probably just killed us both by loudly announcing stomping his arrival and ruining the surprise.

It *was* Joey, but he wasn't alone.

Instead, the man we had run into outside after we'd parked came into the room, pushing Joey into the room with the barrel of a nasty-looking pistol.

"Good afternoon again, Mr. Dixon. I'm glad you made it to my brother's funeral."

CHAPTER FIFTY

"YOU'RE EARLIER THAN I EXPECTED," Rayburn — the *other* Rayburn — said.

"Who the hell are you, anyway?" I asked.

I sensed the two fat guys move in toward me. I waited, trying to anticipate their next move. They'd try to squeeze my arms at the bicep, forcing me to stand between them, and they'd guide me to wherever Hannah was being held.

Or they'd knock me out, kill Joey, then take me to Hannah.

Or they'd torture all of us, kill Joey, and then —

I forced my mind back to the present. This was exactly why I didn't make plans. There are too many variables, too many options, too many possible outcomes.

As much as I was pained to admit it, Joey and I were *both* collateral here. If we made it out alive, great. But my only goal today was getting Hannah to safety. Nothing else mattered.

So the fat guys came forward and grabbed my arms, just as I'd suspected. But instead of moving me toward the door, they just turned me. A little bit, so I was *facing* the door.

And Joey.

He had a half-smirk, half-frown on his face, a weird contortion that told me he was sorry yet pissed they'd gotten him in the first place.

"How'd he find you, Joey?" I asked.

He shrugged. "Right place, right time."

"Yeah," I said. "I guess so."

Rayburn nudged Joey farther into the room so we were almost face-to-face. He sniffed, then looked at me.

"We are close," he said. "Do you have what I need?"

"I — I do," I lied.

"Why the stutter?"

"I just… just — j — just do that, every — every now and then."

I'm not sure it worked. Rayburn shook his head like he was about to scold a toddler.

"Seriously?" he asked. "Has that bullshit ever worked?"

"Every now and then. Mostly —"

"Stop!" he yelled. "Do you have what I need?"

"Your company? Yeah. In my head. But I need to know you've got what *I* need."

"The girl?"

I shook my head. "Nope, sorry. Plan's changed. I need the girl… and I need him." I nodded toward Joey.

Joey gave me a small nod in return.

"Unacceptable," the man said. "That wasn't our arrangement. You were to —"

"We *had* no arrangement, asshole. You told me to come visit you, I'm here."

"I told *you* to come visit. Not *him*."

"He was just along for the ride. Not his fault."

The man scowled. "I never said it *was* his fault. It's *your* fault. And I'm going to make you pay for it by forcing you to watch."

"Watch wh —"

Joey howled in pain and dropped to one knee. He screamed again when his knee hit the carpeted floor and I saw that the man, Rayburn, had Joey's hand in his.

Specifically, he had one *finger* in his hand.

Joey blew air out his mouth, trying to fight off the pain of the broken index finger.

"I discovered long ago that I didn't really need to take the weapons away, I just needed to ensure that they couldn't be *fired* by anyone I didn't trust.

I nodded. Seemed like a pretty effective strategy, I had to admit.

The man continued. "And did you know that most small pistols can be fired with just a *pinky*? Not even on the dominant hand. Accuracy decreases wildly, it seems, but sometimes when you're desperate…"

"Listen up, asshole. I've got what you want. Just —"

The man tensed up and I could see the pain in Joey's eyes even before I heard the telltale muffled *crack* of another finger. He whimpered once, then raised his head up and stared straight ahead. He was still on one knee, so he was staring into the buckle of my belt.

"Sometimes when you're desperate," the man continued, "you'll do *anything*. Like attempt to fire a weapon with nothing but a pinky finger. So we have eight tries left, don't we? I trust that you will not interrupt me again, Dixon. Is that clear?"

I waited a few extra beats to make sure he wasn't going to talk again and I'd inadvertently interrupt him. "Yeah. Sure. Whatever you say."

"Good. Now, let's get to business. You've got the transfer codes. I've got the girl. Hannah Rayburn."

"Show me."

"All in good time," he said.

I shook my head. "No, now. Show her to me, and you get the codes immediately. No more games."

I watched his beady eyes thinking through the possibilities. I'd already done my best to think through them, and all I'd come up with was that if he had intended to turn over Hannah once he received the company shares, he would honor my request to see her.

If he *didn't* intend to release Hannah, he would force me to reveal what I knew right now, right here. Then he would kill us both. And then Hannah.

So this was sort of a turning point. This Rayburn asshole would reveal a little bit of his character to me, right now. I was already going to kill him, of that much I was certain. But how I did it might — *maybe* — just change a bit if he stuck to his guns and gave me Hannah.

And if he took me to her right now, so I could verify that *his* bargaining chip was intact and safe, and relatively unharmed, I might believe that he'd give her up once he had what he wanted.

I ignored the fact that *I* didn't have what I'd promised him. It was all a matter of buying time.

"Fine," he said. "That's a fair arrangement."

He started to turn around, and I felt the fat guys' vice grips on my arms tighten some more, then Rayburn stopped. He turned back to me, frowning.

"But I forgot."

I frowned.

"Your partner here. We don't need him."

He lifted his arm, the one holding the pistol, letting his other arm drop a bit and loosen its grip on Joey's broken hand.

Then he fired.

CHAPTER FIFTY-ONE

I WAS MOVING EVEN BEFORE my mind had fully accepted what was happening. When I get real motivated, I'm pretty damn fast.

But I'm not near as fast as a bullet, so I must have already sensed it, already intuited that it was going to happen. The handgun came up, I sensed the squeeze and tension there right before the pistol fired, and I was already moving.

I didn't have much else to aim for, so Joey got it.

The two fatties still had my arms in their grip, and I knew they'd instinctively tighten up with both hands to make sure I didn't slip away, meaning they'd also have no free hands to draw their weapons.

I was counting on all of that. I used their rock-solid grip as a fulcrum and swung my legs up and out as hard as I could, planting my feet right smack in the center of Joey's chest. I'm sure it could have cracked a rib or three, but there was no other option.

The pistol fired, but Joey and Rayburn were already flying backwards toward the door. Rayburn hit the edge of the doorframe, smacking like a dead fish as he fumbled back into the hallway, but Joey fell clean through.

The force of my double-footed kick on Joey's chest pushed me and the two guys holding me backwards a few feet. I hoped it would be enough to get out of their grip.

The two guys on me and Mr. Mustache were shocked, a little dazed, and probably deafened by the explosive noise of it. I felt the guys' grips wrenching my arms off their mounts, but I twisted sideways as my feet started falling back toward the floor. I twisted, hard, feeling the pressure build in my shoulders, but it worked.

My left arm fell free from the man's hands and I lifted it up just as my feet hit the floor. I caught my balance, stood up, and smashed my closed fist into the face of the other fat guy — the one who'd laughed earlier.

"Sorry," I mumbled. "Wanted to wait until last with you, but…"

He stumbled a bit, somehow still holding onto my arm, so I hit him again. And again.

Finally my right arm popped free, and just in time.

Mustache and the first fat guy had pretty much recovered and seemed to have gotten their wits about them once again, and I could see both of them reaching for their weapons.

I was closest to the guy I'd just punched three times, so I reached into his belt and felt around for the weapon, keeping his girth in front of me. He was easy to maneuver, as he was all but knocked out — still wobbling, but on his feet, trying to steady himself.

I got the pistol, tipped it back, and fired a quick shot, not even lifting the weapon out from under the guy's coat. It was an odd dance, me grasping the man's belt with one hand, holding a pistol and aiming out the back of his coat with the other, and kneeling on the floor.

But it worked. The other guy went down, and Mustache couldn't get a shot off without hitting his own —

Mustache aimed and let off three rounds in quick succession, completely blowing up my theory. The man I was using as cover starting falling forward, toward me, just a huge, soft dead weight that would surely trap me beneath.

Unacceptable. I lunged sideways and got to the side of the bed just as the man fell with a heavy thud onto a beautiful old rug that lay at the foot of the massive bed.

Mustache had calculated the same way I had, decided it was far more worth it to kill me than to protect his own guy, and started shooting. I was in some deep shit, and now that shit had gained a new facet: they were going to kill us *no matter the cost.*

Great.

I was prone between the wall and the bed with enough room to roll over but not enough to actually *hide*. Mustache would be on me in seconds, and I would be toast.

I looked out the door to see if Joey was around. He hadn't hit anything on his path out of the room, but I had really kicked the crap out of him. Two boots to the chest from a guy dead-set on kicking you as hard as he could really could do a number on you, so I wouldn't have been surprised if Joey was just out cold for a spell. I wouldn't have faulted him for it, but it would be really convenient if —

Joey was, in fact, awake. He entered the room again surprisingly similar to how he'd done it the first time, with a pistol at his back.

Rayburn was bleeding from the side of his head, but he otherwise seemed fine. Pissed, snarling, and ready to do some damage, but fine. He had a smattering of Joey's hair in his hand, and Joey was holding his broken, mangled fingers delicately with his other hand.

Christ, I thought. *This really can't get any worse.*

I sat up next to the bed, noticing that Mustache was tracking me with his eyes *and* his weapon, and stuck my hands up. I carefully dropped the weapon to the floor and kicked it over to Rayburn.

My hands went up again, this time resting behind my head. I shook my head slowly, trying to piece together some way out of this mess.

I was at a loss.

Joey's face was contorted in pain, but he seemed to share my assessment of the situation. He shook his head slowly, in reply.

"I've changed my mind," Rayburn said. "I'm not going to kill your friend here. Yet."

He pushed Joey's head down and then smacked him on the side of it, just above his ear, with the butt of his pistol. Joey fell, gasping in pain. He forced Joey to his feet once again, the entire time staring directly at me.

"I am going to take both of you to where I am keeping Hannah. There we can discuss the rest of our time together. If it goes smoothly, I kill your friends quickly. If not…"

He reached in front of Joey and grabbed at his wrist. Joey's eyes widened and he pulled away.

Rayburn smiled. "Such a simple procedure, but severely effective. No one wants to know what ten broken fingers looks like, do they? And certainly not ten broken fingers that have had a little time to *heal*."

Mustache had walked over to the foot of the bed and motioned at me to start walking. I walked toward Joey and Rayburn and Mustache took a position behind me. Rayburn swung Joey around and marched him out the door.

"Thing is," Rayburn said as we entered the hall, "I'm not going to give your friend the *opportunity* to let those fingers heal, because you can't heal when you're dead, can you? You ruined that, didn't you, Mr. Dixon?"

CHAPTER FIFTY-TWO

THE MAN JOEY HAD SHOT in the hall was still there, staring up at me with his big, dead eyes and open mouth as we passed by. Rayburn didn't even turn his head, and from what I could tell hardly seemed to notice. I couldn't see Mustache's reaction, but I figured it would be equally cold, especially after watching him shoot his own buddy to get to me.

Whatever these guys are after, it's serious business, I thought.

Rayburn had told me he wanted the parts of Crimson Club that had *true* value. I knew it was really a way of saying he wanted the *sleazy* parts of the company, but I did believe those were the parts of the business that made the most money.

He thought I wanted the same thing, too, since I had been meddling with his team for a couple of days now, and he had reason to believe I was the one who'd started the ball rolling in the first place, by taking out his brother.

And yet I still had no idea what to tell him. I'd bought time, taken out two more of his men, and had gotten the odds shaved down considerably to 2-on-2, assuming it was just Mustache and Rayburn himself left.

But I realized too that there might be someone else guarding Hannah, and Joey was probably out of commission with his hand in the shape it was in. So back to 2- or 3-on-1.

Not as good, but still better.

But I didn't have a *play*. I didn't know what I would do to make sure I could get both men down before one of them took out me, Hannah, or Joey, or all three. I was unarmed again, and the cards were continuing to stack against me.

"Where are we going?" I asked.

Rayburn turned right at the large staircase and started pushing Joey down.

"Outside."

I nodded. *Okay, fair enough.* He wanted to keep us in the dark. Another card in the deck stacked against me.

We made it through the foyer and into the downstairs hallway without being spotted, then into a large open room at the back of the house on the east side. It was dark and seemed to be unused, but there was a door leading outside at the rear end of the space.

Rayburn pushed Joey toward it and told him to pull the door open. Up close I could tell it was one of the small, 'normal looking' doors I'd seen from outside, one that led into some room of the lower level.

The daylight was blinding compared to the dark room, and we all took a second for our eyes to adjust. The gravel driveway and parking strip was directly in front of us, the grass of the lawn just beyond, and even farther away the beach began and met with the waves of the Atlantic.

There were still people around, but everyone seemed to be busy with something only they knew about. Heads were down and the only people walking around looked to be headed for a specific destination. No one was strolling casually through the grounds, no one was enjoying the scenery, and no one saw us.

I realized in that moment the genius of Rayburn's plan. He was now one of the patriarchs of this family, if not *the* patriarch. I had no idea if he would come to own the mansion in light of his brother's passing, but he certainly wouldn't warrant any strange looks from anyone else around the estate — he would fit in as well as Hannah herself would.

Rayburn could move throughout the premises without being accosted, questioned, or even wondered about, and that meant no one would care about the four of us walking somewhere in broad daylight.

He pushed Joey outside and into the sun, and Mustache pushed me. There were three steps to descend before my feet hit the white gravel lot and the salty air hit my nose. I walked to the row of cars, turning to the left only when I saw Rayburn lead Joey in that direction.

We stopped again at a pair of large golf carts, the gas-powered kinds you find at theme parks, chauffeuring people around who would rather burn money than calories. Rayburn shoved Joey into the driver's seat, Mustache shoved me into ours, and then they both fell into the passenger's seats.

"Head down the path over there," Rayburn said as he pointed to our left, northeast.

It was the same winding path that I had seen earlier, the one that led down to the boathouse and dock, with the *Wassamassaw* waiting behind it.

Joey fidgeted a bit as he tried to place his hands on the steering wheel without stressing his broken fingers, but he eventually gave up and decided to one-hand it. I nodded once at him as they passed, and I took up the back of the line.

Mustache's pistol jabbed hard into my side, bruising a rib. I jumped a bit and scowled. "Listen, asshole, if we're going to be this close, maybe you can tell me your name?"

He sniffed, looked out at the beach, then pressed the handgun harder into my side.

I slammed the wheel to the left and smashed the gas pedal, whipping Mustache around and almost out of the vehicle. He caught his balance as I righted the wheel and slowed back down, finding a bit of pleasure in his momentarily terrified face.

"Sorry," I said. "Thought I saw a squirrel."

"Do that shit again and I put one through your side."

"Where you've got that stick aiming, it'll be just a flesh wound," I retorted as I turned onto the path and headed down to the beach. "And that would *really* not make me happy."

He seemed put off by this, but I found a little more pleasure once again as he tried to slide the pistol around my side, finally landing on a spot he apparently thought would be a good location for a kill shot.

We drove on for a few hundred feet, reaching the boathouse without passing anyone else. No one even looked in our direction. I watched the back of Joey's head as he parked and got out. Rayburn had his weapon trained on Joey, but he was watching me. I got out of the golf cart, not bothering to park it nicely up against Joey's, and walked toward Rayburn. Mustache tracked me the whole time.

I kept my gaze steady, my nerves calm, and my steps even, but I suddenly felt weary. Old age or hard life, or a combination of both, but I was starting to feel like I was going to crack.

CHAPTER FIFTY-THREE

THE BOATHOUSE WAS MADE OF slatted wood paneling, interspersed with vertical strips of white painted metal. It didn't match the house, but it wasn't too far off. The designer had obviously chosen modern simplicity over trying to congeal the mansion and boathouse together into one unified look.

Rayburn saw me eyeing the house. "My brother designed it. This yacht was his little pet project. Started getting real interested in boats about ten or so years ago, but he rarely actually went out on the water. Just liked working from inside it." He paused, as if realizing that he was shooting the breeze with the enemy, but then his face relaxed a bit and he continued. "It's damn impressive, too. Wait until you see the office workspace he set up inside. You'd never guess you were floating."

I remembered Hannah saying much the same back at the bar. Her father had a massive office in the house, she'd said, but he hardly ever worked from there later in his life. He'd preferred the calm rocking of the boat in the dredged spot on the water apparently, where he could be alone with his thoughts. Or away from the house. I wasn't sure about the man's motive, but if *I* had a yacht, I'd want to be working there a lot, too.

I got it. If you have a multimillion dollar yacht, you want to use it. Didn't matter if he wasn't much of a 'boat guy,' at least he was in there doing something.

We started walking toward the door on the side of the small boathouse, and I could see the *Wassamassaw* sticking out from behind it as we drew nearer. It was even more spectacular up close. I reveled in every detail of it, from the hand-carved solid wood railings to the single, large ocean kayak hanging on a mount just off the starboard side of the yacht.

The stern dipped down a steep vertical and jutted out again to form an entry deck on the back of the boat. A watertight door on that deck led somewhere into the bowels of the engine room. Just to the side of the deck on the long, shining starboard wall, was the single-word moniker.

Wassamassaw.

I stared at the word and the ship it had been inscribed upon for as long as our captors would allow. I took it in, breathing in the ocean spray and dreaming of a different life, one where I owned this thing and there was no one trying to kill me.

After a few seconds I felt Mustache's pistol nudge me forward. We were standing just outside of a door into the boathouse, and I started walking toward it. Joey was there in front of me, and I let him and Rayburn pass and move inside.

The interior of the boathouse was sparse, but still held the same delicately planned, purposeful design. The slats of wood and metal shone and reflected the light bouncing off the water. The 'house' was actually a roof with three walls — the wall facing the ocean was completely missing, a widened and expanded dock in its place. A ramp rose from the dock to the starboard gate on the *Wassamassaw.*

Near the ramp a few plastic crates were stored, and on the opposite wall was a shelf, full of well-organized tools and supplies. A small chest freezer and a refrigerator sat on the wall opposite the *Wassamassaw*, and I could see a trash can full of empty beer boxes next to it.

At the very least they might offer me a beer, I thought.

Mustache and Rayburn pushed us up the ramp. Rayburn led, Joey just behind him, and I followed. Mustache waited on the dock with his handgun pointed at my ass the whole time. Again, nothing more than a flesh wound, but one that would really piss me off.

Stepping onto the deck was a surreal experience. I didn't come from money, so this was the first time I'd been on a boat this size, and certainly the first time I'd been on one this *nice.* Everything was fancy — the handrail felt so smooth and polished, as if it had never seen a day of saltwater or sunshine. The windows were clean and set into the hull a bit, a line of matching wood stripping running the length and height of each to frame them out. And the deck itself was waxed and spotless, yet it still held the perfect amount of stick so I didn't slip.

We were on the main deck, and from what I could tell there were three decks, not including a top-level, smaller sun deck.

"Damn," Joey whispered, "this thing must be over a hundred feet long."

"131 feet, actually," Rayburn said. "A Pichiotti, built in

the early nineties. Bought it brand-new through the company for about eight million, probably put another million into it. Twin Caterpillars, 650 horsepower."

"So she's fast?" I asked. I knew nothing about yachts. I didn't even know if 'fast' was considered a selling point. Far as I was concerned, just sitting on this thing and not moving at all would be just fine.

"No idea," Rayburn said. "Like I said, he rarely took it out. And I had never been on it."

"Before just now?"

"Before…" Rayburn caught himself.

I got the message. I cocked an eyebrow, even though he couldn't see my face. "So you brought her here," I said. "She's on the boat, now?"

"She's… yes."

"Let's go. Now."

All the fury of the past two days suddenly returned, and I no longer cared about the yacht. I no longer cared about the amazing view, the immaculate scenery surrounding me, and I no longer cared about trying to make small talk with these assholes to loosen them up.

"Rest assured, Hannah is fine," Rayburn said. He walked beside me and started toward the front of the yacht. I could see a doorway leading to the interior and assumed it was going to be where the bridge and captain's cabin was.

"My brother wouldn't have allowed us on in these shoes," Rayburn said, somewhat under his breath. "But that doesn't matter anymore, does it?"

He asked this in an accusatory way, and I began to respond. "I didn't —"

I caught myself before I finished the sentence, not wanting to open a line of questioning that would get us in trouble. He didn't need to know I hadn't killed his brother, and he certainly didn't need to know my father *had*.

As far as I could tell, he thought I had staged his brother's suicide to get to his company, and that was the only card I had in my favor at this point. I didn't want to reveal my hand and make this situation any worse than it already was.

We walked along the side of the massive yacht and finally into the doorway I'd seen before. Like the windows, the doorframe was lined with the dark mahogany trim, and the threshold was a polished brass-colored metal. It was made to be watertight, yet starkly beautiful. A line of cabinets stretched both directions from one corner of the long room, and a beautifully appointed full bar and counter had been set onto the wall just beneath the cabinets. The cabinets themselves were glass-front, offering a clear view at the gems within.

And gems they were. 15- and 18-year scotches, one Laphroag 25, even a fancy single-barrel Irish whiskey I'd never seen outside of specialized conventions. I probably focused on the cabinet a bit too long, but I couldn't help myself. Rayburn — Hannah's father — must have had a fantastic taste for fine whiskeys, something we would have shared had I known him.

I let my gaze drift all the way across the cabinets, allowing myself a final indulgence before I snapped back to reality. The bourbon selection in particular was quite nice, including a few Michter's options, the obligatory Angel's Envy Cask Strength, and a Booker's overproof label I hadn't tried yet but had heard was fantastic.

I pulled my eyes away from the elaborate bar setup, stepped inside, and felt the calm plush of the carpet subtly give way under my feet. White, to match the white-rock walkways and paths surrounding the mansion. The furniture was made of the same wood that trimmed out the boat, and it was all spaced perfectly in the room. Large, rounded leather chairs that looked like they belonged in an old-fashioned men's smoking room provided the seating, and a matching couch sat along the opposite wall.

And there, on the couch, was Hannah.

CHAPTER FIFTY-FOUR

I RUSHED OVER TO HER. She was sleeping, stretched out on the couch, her arms raised above her head, her hands cuffed and secured to a support pole that ran floor-to-ceiling against the wall.

My fury and impatience grew. "Listen, you bastard, there's no reason —"

I stopped.

Hannah wasn't sleeping. One of her eyes had been plastered shut, a purplish bruise forming around it. Her other eye was open, but barely. She was staring at me. I stared back, watching her pained expression as her breasts rose and fell with each breath. She was wearing the same thing she'd been wearing when they'd grabbed her — the skirt and blouse, but she was missing her burlap shoes. Her blouse was up a bit, revealing her stomach, and the skirt looked wrinkled and worn, as if she'd slept there for some time. Those same perfect legs, now pointed toward one another at the knees, lay still on the couch.

"As I told you," Rayburn said softly, "she is fine."

"Fine?" I swung around to face him, seething. "Are you insane? She is *not* fine. She's —"

I turned back to Hannah and noticed that she had turned her head and was looking at me. I walked back over, knelt down, and placed my hand on her forehead. She was warm, but not feverish. Or she was, and my own heat was radiating back to me and canceling out hers. I was never any good at being able to tell. She seemed younger somehow, yet her eyes — or at least the one that was partly open — told me otherwise.

"Dammit," I whispered. My eyes welled up a bit. "I'm sorry, Hannah. I'm going to get you out of here."

She swallowed, a motion that appeared to be extremely painful, and nodded once, just a slight tilt of her head. "I know," she whispered. Even at that volume I could hear the cracking dryness of her voice.

"I promise you, I'm going to get you out," I said again. "And then I'm going to kill the sons of b —"

I didn't really feel the hit on the back of my skull, but I heard it, internally, bouncing around in my head for a second.

And then I blacked out.

CHAPTER FIFTY-FIVE

I SAW THE LED DISPLAY of a clock on a panel of instruments across from me.

2:43.

I must have been out the entire time, and yet my head was begging me to go out again. A splitting headache was bursting through my brain, and a dagger-like prick of pain lanced into the center of it from where the handgun had struck me.

But I'm still alive, I thought, *which means I'm still going to kill them.*

I realized I had been moved into another room. Hannah was still back in the parlor, or saloon, or sitting room, or whatever 'luxurious living rooms' are called on yachts. But I had been moved to much more sparse accommodations. The instrument panel was on the back wall, and I was facing a plain, white door with a simple circular window on it. Opposite the instrument panel on the right side of the door was a closed cabinet, stretching the height of the room.

I carefully moved my head so as not to upset my headache and took stock of my surroundings. A table to the left jutted out from the wall, just below a long, curved window. I couldn't see what was on it, and I realized why.

I was sitting down on the floor of the room, and my hands had been handcuffed above my head to a steering wheel.

The bridge.

I moved my arms left and right, but the wheel was locked and only offered a few inches of give in either direction. I knew it was hopeless to try to break out, and that my wrists would be destroyed long before the steering mount would.

I looked to my right. Another table, another window. More instruments and communication gear would be piled on these tables, possibly maps as well. Certainly not a weapon, unless I was the luckiest man alive.

I tried to move again and realized that if there *was* some sort of weapon on the table, it would be a cruel joke. I couldn't even get close to the table.

I grunted through a few more exercises, testing my captivity and aging body. I was in pretty good shape for a near-fifty-year-old, but at the end of the day I was still closing in on fifty. I wasn't going to perform some feat of contortionism and pretzel my way out of the steering wheel.

I heard footsteps.

"Good afternoon again, Mr. Dixon," Rayburn's voice said. I looked up and saw him in the porthole. The door unlocked, then swung open. I wanted it to hit my feet so I could kick the shit out of it and get him in the nose, but I was too far away. The room was narrow, but not small.

"I brought us something to ease us through the transaction," Rayburn said. He had two cigars in a pocket of his shirt, and I could see the bulge of a lighter hidden in there as well. He stepped fully into the room and I could see a cart sitting in the hallway behind him. "I'm not much into torturing, my friend, regardless of what you've been led to believe."

He pulled the cart farther inside and I couldn't help sitting up straighter, trying to get a good look at what was on it.

Bottles of liquor, judging from the differing shapes and sizes. A couple glasses, a metal bucket with a lid. Probably full of ice. He continued sliding the cart on its casters into the bridge and let it stop in front of him.

"But you understand," he continued, "I'm not *above* torture. It's just such a dirty way to conduct business. Your friend, Joey? How do you know each other?"

Rayburn reached for one of the bottles, a scotch. One I had poured a thousand shots of before. Decent, for a fifty dollar bottle.

I heard a scream, something brutal and sharp. A man's scream, echoing around in the room and open hallway.

Rayburn frowned and smiled at the same time. "It really is a brutal way to conduct ourselves, wouldn't you say?"

I gritted my teeth.

"My associate is with your friend right now, actually. And from the sound of it, you got a little too long of a nap. That leaves, what? Six tries?"

I didn't understand at first, but then it hit me.

Joey's fingers.

"Shit," I said. "Shit."

Rayburn shook his head and brought the scotch up to his mouth. "No, it really isn't *shit*. This is an *opportunity*. Certainly an opportunity for me, but really an opportunity for you. To not die. Might not be too late for your pal, either, if you can come up with those transfer codes, Dixon."

My nostrils flared, and I yanked hard against the steering wheel and handcuffs connecting them. It hurt like hell, and nothing budged. I felt one of the cuffs wrench against my skin, drawing blood. I knew it was there, but my anger masked the pain.

"Give me the transfer codes and I'll head down to my brother's computer and get them entered. That's it. Plain and simple, and we're done here. You saw the girl, and you know I've held up my end of the bargain."

He stepped over to the cabinet to my right and pulled the handle. When he opened it, I saw a spiraling set of stairs that shot straight down.

"We're right above the office, and the computer is ready to go. We've already got the login, we just need the transfer codes."

I frowned. "You had to hack your brother's computer?"

He laughed, then took a sip of scotch. "Hardly," he said. "Would you believe the password to his computer — everything he had been working on, everything he had been trying to *hide* from me — was just a single word? A single, plain, word. Nothing more, nothing less."

In that moment I knew. Of *course* I knew. It was so obvious. It had been staring me in the face the entire time.

"Hannah."

He nodded. "No one would think it would be that simple. No capital letters, no numbers. Just six letters. Hannah." He laughed again and sipped again. Then his demeanor changed. "So we're close, Dixon. The transfer codes?"

"Your own niece," I said. I thought about spitting to really underline my pissed-off-ness.

"My own niece," he said. "Not surprising, when you think about it. Bradley, my brother, always seemed to have more of an interest in his boy. They were inseparable. But there's always a special place in Daddy's heart for his little girl, no? So I knew she was the one, even before he told the rest of us."

I was actually interested now, so I tried to tell him that with my expression. I wanted him to talk, to keep things moving, but I knew Joey — and Hannah — were in the boat as well, and we were running out of time for at least one of them.

"Bradley had all of us — the business partners — over for dinner a few years ago, and he told us the succession plan. I don't know that I'd expected it to be Hannah, and I certainly didn't expect it to be me."

"You were chosen?" I asked.

He laughed. "No, unfortunately. As I said, I never expected it *would* be me. But I did think he would keep things simple. I thought it would be Daniel, or one of the more senior partners. But I didn't think he would split it up completely."

I got it. Rayburn had told his team about what would happen if and when he died — part of the company would go to Daniel, part of it to Hannah, and the rest of it would be split up evenly amongst the other owners. The estate of Bradley Rayburn would not have an ownership interest any longer.

"Why? Why split it up at all?" I asked. I knew I was buying time, and I knew the other Rayburn knew it as well. But get someone talking about themselves, or about something they care about, and you might as well grab a beer and a chair and get comfortable.

"To keep his name clean, and to protect his children," Rayburn said. "As you know, Crimson Club engaged in some extracurricular affairs that weren't part of the original company's manifest. My brother thought it put a bit of a smudge on the family name, so he wanted to make sure that the pieces of the company that his children received were clean."

"But you want the stuff that *isn't* clean, don't you?"

He looked at me with a wry smile. "As do you, correct? The portion of the business that *truly* has value."

He still didn't know who I was, even though I'd tried to tell his boys that I was just a lowly bartender, and none of them believed me. Maybe it was time to try convincing Rayburn.

"I'm just a bartender," I said. "Nothing more."

He cocked an eyebrow. "I see. A bartender with a flair for, what? What's your flavor, Dixon?"

I stared at him, not wanting to try to understand what he was talking about.

"Oh, come on, it's just us here — two men wanting the same thing. We're both in it for the financial upside, but let's be honest. We have our *preferences* about it, as well. Mine's girls, actually. Younger than Hannah, though she's quite tempting, even for family."

This time I didn't even want to spit. I decided to up the stakes a bit. I never was great with negotiations like this, but then again I never had been handcuffed to the wheel of a multimillion-dollar yacht with a psychopathic pervert threatening me and my friends.

He had swayed over my way just a bit, probably reacting subconsciously to the gentle movement of the floating yacht. He still wasn't quite close enough to do anything substantial, but I wasn't going for substantial. I was going for annoying.

I lashed out with my left foot, catching the bottom of his glass of scotch, still nearly full with two fingers of sharp liquor, sending it pummeling toward his face.

It connected with a satisfying crunch with his nose, and the scotch splashed down his chin, over his neckline, and soaked the shirt he was wearing almost to the breasts. He sprang backward in surprise, even eliciting a small cry of pain as the blow to his nose reached his brain, but then he stood still again — this time out of my foot's reach.

I settled back down, working on an Eastwood-level frown with my eyes and a James Dean-esque wry grin with my mouth. He didn't seem impressed, and for a second I thought he was going to simply put me out of my misery and be done with it.

But he must have *really* wanted this company. Crimson Club was certainly worth something to this guy, and even though I had absolutely no interest in the smut they were dealing in, I could understand how a man would be so drawn to a cash cow that dealt in international currency.

He wiped his mouth and chin with a shoulder, taking the time to make sure there was nothing left of the mid-shelf scotch on his face. We waited there, staring each other down, for a few seconds, neither of us speaking.

The scotch was soaked through his shirt, the alcohol stuck in liquid form in the material. I knew from experience that it would evaporate, the alcohol eventually vaporizing and drifting away, leaving his shirt with a minor stain and a great smell.

My mind raced, suddenly getting an idea.

"I'm terribly sorry about that," I said. "I'm not sure what came over me. I — I have a bit of an epileptic leg, sometimes it gets out of hand."

"Similar to your stutter?"

"No, that… that was just bullshitting. Trying to buy time."

"And what would you call this?" he asked. "Mr. Dixon, I don't think I need to remind you the state your friend is in. And I know I don't need to remind you about Hannah."

He paused, his demeanor changing. He shifted, widening his legs a bit and adjusting. "You know," he continued, "I am feeling a little… *anxious*. Hannah might be a relation, but she is, still, a beautiful woman."

"You son of a —"

"Besides, we never really saw much of each other. It's not like most families — my brother's family was actually pretty reclusive, and we didn't get invited over for holidays. After his wife died, it was even more…"

He drifted off, his eyes looking somewhere out in the distance.

"Dixon, we're done screwing around. I'm getting restless, and I've got business to attend to. Hannah is part of that business, and if you don't cough up those transfer codes in the next thirty seconds, I'm going to make you watch."

My face melted into the best 'I give up' expression it could generate, and I widened my eyes just a bit to really sell it.

"I — I'm sorry," I whispered.

He waited.

"I'm so sorry. I was told never to —"

"Just *tell* me, ass—"

"LC9545MD —"

"Hold on," Rayburn said. He scrambled, pacing around the narrow room as he looked for something to write with. "Start over," he said.

Mustache was suddenly there, his face appearing in the open doorway. He stepped in, grinning, a stupid-looking victorious thing that made his face even more detestable. I almost told him he had a face for radio — and the voice for it, too. He must have heard the noise from my perfectly aimed kick to Rayburn's glass, as he walked over and pulled out a second pair of cuffs from his back pocket. He then laid on my legs, as if they were snakes with a life of their own and he felt the need to corral them, and pulled them together and toward a pipe in the corner of the room.

He cuffed one of my ankles, still laying across the tops of my shins, and then brought the cuffs around the pipe and onto my right ankle. I heard the clicking sound of the cuff latching back to itself. Mustache stood up, looked down at me for a moment as I tried in vain to get more comfortable, then smiled.

"That ought to keep you in one place," he growled.

I nodded. "Yep, it ought to." I wriggled my feet a bit and was surprised at just how sturdy everything felt. I was now stretched out between the bridge's steering wheel and a pipe, and my back was at a diagonal. If I pulled tight, I could even get my ass lifted off the floor.

"Ready," Rayburn said, turning back to me. He had a pad of paper and a tiny pencil, the kind I've used at golf courses and literally nowhere else. I wondered if they sold them like that to normal people or if you had to be a golf course owner to get them.

I started again, bullshitting a string of numbers that sounded like a fancy transfer code a bank might use. "LC9545" — for my first address growing up, 9545 Lancer Court — "MD" — my initials — "2358" — part of the Fibonacci sequence. No idea why I remembered what the hell that was, but I guessed it was from a Kevin Tumlinson book or something.

Rayburn wrote, Mustache ugly-grinned down at me. I waited for Rayburn to finish, then he looked up. "The second code?"

I looked up at the ceiling of the bridge, feigning a deep-in-thought recall of a memory I didn't have. I waited, milking it, then shot my eyes back to Rayburn.

"Okay, here it is. 8532EN5459DM." I waited for them to call my bluff. Rayburn was writing, not thinking, and Mustache was just... not thinking. It was the same sequence of alphanumeric characters in reverse, and to mask it a little without forgetting what was next I just substituted the *next* letter in the English alphabet for the actual letter I was intending. Instead of 'D,' 'E.' Instead of 'M,' 'N.'

It appeared they were none the wiser.

The first part of my plan — to give them two strings of numbers that I could actually recall at will without messing up — had worked. The second part? Well, that really depended on how 'ready' they were to get the transfer codes. Like all negotiations, time was of the essence. In my case, as the hostage, I needed more of it.

So it really depended on how ready they were to type in the transfer codes — was the computer already booted up? Was the 'hannah' password typed in and the transfer code entry site loaded?

These questions were all stressing me out. One of the many reasons I don't like making plans. If I don't have a plan, the plan can't fail.

But I had a plan, so I knew there were about a thousand ways it could fail. Whatever. Hannah and Joey were worth the risk.

Mustache took the small piece of paper from Rayburn and began heading toward the stairs.

This was my shot.

CHAPTER FIFTY-SIX

"YOU SMOKING THOSE WITH MUSTACHE after you close this deal?" I asked, genuinely curious. "Seems like you can find a better smoking buddy than that loser."

Rayburn scoffed. "Oh, you mean Riley? He's good for a few things, but 'smoking buddy' isn't one of them."

"So what do you say, then? Considering our business is about to be complete."

Rayburn looked at me like I was somehow conning him. I could literally see him working through the scenarios, the possibilities, trying to figure out my game.

"I've figured it out already, Rayburn," I said, keeping with the calm, quiet voice of a man who'd lost. "You're not letting me go. Or Hannah, or Joey. We're dead. It's fine, I get it. I gave you what you want, so there's no more negotiating power for me."

His head turned sideways a bit, still trying to figure me out.

"Maybe you will let me go. I'd prefer that, obviously. But I get it if not. Really. So… maybe we have a quick cigar?"

He laughed, a genuine laugh, too. A quick snort and a couple chuckles. "No such thing as a 'quick cigar.'"

I smiled. "Fair enough. Maybe I'm just trying to postpone the inevitable. And while we're at it, I could go for a drink, too."

At this he seemed to loosen up a bit, still swaying slightly with the boat's rocking. He looked at me for a minute, then turned and walked out of the room and past the bar cart. I could hear him messing around at the bar just through the hallway, which meant the bridge — where I was now — was on the same level and just forward of the main hall where they were keeping Hannah. I also couldn't hear her, which meant she was sleeping...

Or otherwise incapacitated.

The thought caused a minor panic in me, and I raced through the feeble idea I'd been working on. It wasn't much, but it was better than nothing. Maybe.

"What's your drink?"

Rayburn's voice carried through the tiny hallway and into the bridge, and I thought for a moment. "Well, considering," I said, "how's that bottle of Booker's looking?"

He didn't respond, but I heard him rummaging around the cabinets, the clinking of the bottles as he retrieved one, and then the distinct sound of amber liquor pouring into a rocks glass. He repeated the sound — pouring one for himself, I assumed — and then more clinking, and then footsteps.

"You'd better not waste my time *and* my cigar," he said.

"Noted. This bourbon isn't yours, though. So we wouldn't be wasting that, at least. Let's just enjoy that, yeah?"

He sneered, but set the glass down next to me. I was still stretched between the wheel and the pipe, so the best I could do was stare at the glass from above it. The smell of it wafted upward into my nostrils. Heavy on the oak and caramel, lighter on the vanilla, and that bang of 130-proof liquor. 65 percent pure ethanol, cut with water. I sniffed a bit deeper, trying to force more of the vapor into my nose, but the glass was too far away.

He reached into his pocket, grabbing the two cigars. I couldn't tell what they were, but I was far from a connoisseur so that didn't surprise me. I owned a pipe and used it on occasion, and preferred it to the nasty smell and taste in my mouth of most cigars I'd had, but I wasn't about to be picky.

They were already clipped and ready to go, and he took a deep sniff. "Not Cubans," he said, "but basically the same thing. When the embargo began many of the producers went to nearby nations — Honduras, Nicaragua, Dominican Republic — with their crop. They started growing wherever they ended up, and I'm not sure I can tell the difference. Legal to import, smokes great, and might as well be the best on the planet."

I nodded along, pretending to care. "Sounds good to me. I'm not picky." And in my head, *hurry the hell up, Rayburn.*

Mustache was still downstairs working with the computer, and I knew it was only minutes before he'd return and complain that I'd lied to them. Possibly less. *Not much time.*

He nodded, offered me one of the robustos, and waited. Then he saw my handcuffs, as if remembering that he still had me in captivity.

"Sorry," I said, "you'll have to do most of the work. Or I guess we can just forget it."

"You trying something? What's your game?"

I shook my head. "No, honestly. I was trying to figure out a way out of these cuffs, but I'm definitely no Robert Houdin."

Rayburn stared at me like I'd just spoken to him in Japanese.

"I prefer Houdin to Houdini. Houdin was the original — Houdini based his name on ol' Robert's. Anyway, where am I going to go?" I made a point of making a bunch of noise with the cuffs around my ankles and the pipe, trying to show him that I was pretty well locked up.

"Okay," he said. "Fine." He set the cigars down on the table near my pipe, then pulled out a long, shiny pistol from a hidden holster behind his back. He flipped it over a few times and checked the magazine, then loaded it again. "Here's the thing. I might need you later, so I won't kill you. But rest assured — you make a move I don't like, I blow your kneecaps out, one at a time. After that, an elbow, or a shoulder, or maybe I do like your friend in there and take your fingers. But with this thing, there won't be anything left of them to heal. Got it?"

I nodded. It was a legitimate nod — I wasn't about to test him.

I opened my palms, showing five fingers on each handcuffed hand, the only possible thing I could do to show him I was physically unable to retaliate. He reached into another pocket and pulled out a handcuff key, still holding the pistol. When he had the key ready to go, he turned the pistol and stuck it on the top side of my kneecap, feeling around with it a bit to make sure it was on the plated boney part — no chance for anything other than a massacred leg if he took the shot.

This was it. The moment, the chance, all I had. I didn't need my hands for anything, really, but they would help later, after it all went down.

CHAPTER FIFTY-SEVEN

"STICK IT ON YOUR OTHER hand," Rayburn said.

I knew what he meant. I was supposed to put the handcuffs on my left hand, securing my left hand and arm to the steering wheel with my right.

I did it, even giving him a ceremonial flourish of my left arm, tightly cuffed to the wheel and unable to move more than an inch or so. My right hand was free, and I held it open to show him how vulnerable and victimized I still was.

He grabbed the cigars from the table and walked over, handing me one of them. I placed it in my mouth, feeling the sharp sting of the spicy tobacco almost immediately as it hit my lips. I gently chewed on the cut end of it for a few seconds, trying to summon all of the knowledge and etiquette I had about cigar smoking for this crucial moment of my life.

I had to hand it to him, the tobacco was tasty. A high-quality blend, from a well-maintained estate. I wouldn't have been able to tell him where it had originated, but I could definitely appreciate a good toke on this thing. I nodded my approval.

He was copying my actions, chewing and salivating on the end of his own cigar. We looked each other down for a minute, chewing and thinking and wetting the tobacco, until it was time.

He pulled the lighter out of his shirt pocket, the same place the cigars had been hidden. A quick flick and the flame came out, dancing and dodging for a few seconds until the fuel source kicked in fully and he brought it up to examine it.

Satisfied, he blew out the flame with a quick exhale and offered to light my cigar first.

I nodded, then leaned forward, all the while trying not to move my right hand too quickly. Mustache was still — thankfully — down in the computer room, trying to get everything booted up and logged in.

Rayburn lit my cigar, and I did the puffy breathing thing until mine was lit — another minor annoyance that made me prefer pipes to cigars — and I took in a small, testing breath.

The cigar was good. *Very* good, in fact. Deep, dark, and mysterious, but in a familiar way. I wasn't sure how to describe it other than that. It was something I could appreciate more than enjoy, and yet I knew it was a high-dollar piece.

At the same time, I reached down for my glass of whiskey. He'd set it down on my left side, but my left hand was still cuffed to the wheel. I left the cigar in my mouth — this was going to be a tricky thing to pull off with just one hand — but I reached over my body and held the glass up to my mouth as well. The smoke from the cigar caught and tangled with the open hole of the top of the glass and fell in, and I finagled the grip I had on the glass until I felt confident enough.

"Be careful," he said. "That high-proof stuff is highly flammable."

I shot my eyes up to his. I could see it in his face, testing. Questioning.

This was it. My chance.

I waved away the comment with a quick flip of my hand, then set the glass back down, between my legs. I figured that would add a layer of intrigue to the whole affair. I could feel Rayburn's eyes watching me. Burning into me.

I grabbed the lit cigar from my mouth and twirled it around a bit for some flourish. "Nah," I said. "That's a hoax. It's how they get you. Because the water percentage is high enough, it doesn't matter how strong the alcohol is. Almost as soon as the whiskey leaves the bottle, the alcohol burns off. Watch."

I wasn't sure if he was buying my line of bullshit, but I was committed now. Plus, I didn't have anything else to try. I was all-in.

I held the cigar up and let him see the glowing orange cake on the end of it. Then I twirled it back around and shoved it straight down into the top of the glass. It hit the surface of the liquor with an abrupt hissing sound and…

Nothing happened. The ember died, nothing more than a blackened chunk of ash floating around in the bottom of my glass.

Perfect.

"See?" I said. "I've even seen a guy put out a lit cigarette by tossing into the full gas tank of a car. Crazy." I laughed to underline my point.

He frowned, thinking about it.

"Science, right? Gets me every time."

He straightened up a bit, then nodded. "Yeah, okay. Whatever. Let's see where Riley is. It's already been —"

I heard footsteps.

Shit. Come on, man. Light that thing up.

Rayburn smiled, an evil thing like he already knew what Riley was going to say. But then he lifted the lighter up, preparing to light his own cigar.

I watched it in slow-motion. His hand turned, opening the business end of the lighter to the end of the cigar, and his thumb tensed and started the downward motion of rotating the striking flint.

A tiny spark screamed out of the lighter and went out immediately.

More footsteps, I could see Riley's shadow on the narrow stairwell now.

Rayburn tried again. Flick, twist, spark.

This time it caught, and the yellow and blue flame flickered once again to life.

I took a deep sip of the whiskey, trying as hard as I could to ignore the carbonized tobacco ball still soaking in the bottom of the glass. It burned, but I forced more of the Booker's into my mouth. I let it fall behind my tongue, almost down my throat, but refused to let it choke me. My cheeks blew outward as I accepted another few ounces into each of them, nearly emptying the glass.

I had lied to Rayburn.

It was a great line, invoking the science and mystique of whiskey distilling and all that, but it was bullshit, through-and-through.

It was true that a lit cigarette or cigar wouldn't ignite alcohol, but it had nothing to do with the lies of evil corporations trying to get one over on us normal folk.

I couldn't stand it any longer. My mouth was twice the size it should have been, and there was whiskey juice trickling down my chin through my tightly pursed lips. I wasn't going to be able to hold it in.

I looked at Rayburn. He was still twisting, rotating the cigar in his mouth, trying to get a good solid light going. The pistol dangled at his side in his other hand. His eyes were crossed, intently focusing on the end of his cigar and the flame.

The flame.

The *open* flame.

That was the difference — my old man had showed me that trick long ago. A lighted cigarette in a gas tank doesn't cause an explosion. Even though the ethanol in gasoline is nearly pure, there's not an open flame to ignite the vapors.

More footsteps. Out of the corner of my eye Mustache — Riley — jumped off the top stair. He was in the room. He must have sped up.

I aimed, tilting my chin back a bit.

With all the contained energy I had in my mouth, neck, and cheeks, I let out a small pencil-thin stream of the high-proof spirit, directly at Rayburn's face. The line hit the flame of the lighter.

It was enough.

CHAPTER FIFTY-EIGHT

FROM MY PERSPECTIVE, RAYBURN'S FACE simply exploded. All I could see was the flame, now increased in size a thousand-fold, blasting and cooking his skin. The ignition had been even larger than I'd anticipated, startling me almost enough to choke on the fluid still in my mouth.

I kept up with the steady stream though, really making sure I was giving him a good braise. He had dropped the handgun and the lighter, but I could see the end of the cigar still poking out of the corner of his crisping mouth.

A beautiful sight, I had to admit. It was jarring and somewhat of a juxtaposition, his body standing there, in shock, unmoving, all the while the licking flames blasting around his head and face with a rapidity and fury I hadn't imagined in my wildest dreams.

Mustache was there too, frozen on the spot. He'd figure it out in a second, and I would need to react to his next attack at some point. But I really wanted to do the job well with Rayburn. The bastard needed to die, and I figured it was better late than never. Hell, if I was lucky, he might even live through this flaming and choke on his own blood or vomit, or — still better — just sit there gasping and weeping and begging for mercy.

I'd be able to have a bit of fun with the rest of his uncooked body then. Again, I wasn't much for torture, but… the guy really did deserve *something* shitty.

I finished the stream, and to my delight and surprise his shirt, still soaked with the rest of the scotch I'd kicked all over him earlier, caught fire as well.

He started moving then, flailing with his arms but stumbling slowly with his legs. I imagine he couldn't see anything, at least not well, even if his eyes hadn't been boiled yet. He hit the doorframe, bouncing back and then down to a knee. He actually tried to stand back up then, but fell backwards onto the bar cart, then into the small hallway separating the bridge from the larger living area behind it.

I heard a groan from Rayburn, then a roar from Mustache, and we all snapped back to reality. Rayburn started rolling wildly on the floor, trying desperately to put out the flames around his neck. Mustache ran toward me — two complete lunges and he was on me.

I hadn't prepared for the attack, but I'd anticipated it. I swung a fist out and caught him just off the groin. Not enough to incapacitate him but apparently enough to piss him off more. He lifted a knee and caught me under the chin.

I cried out in pain, feeling my senses wane and my mind going dizzy. He hit me again, this time glancing a fist off the side of my head and scraping my ear. It didn't do much damage, but it did give me enough time to recover from his *first* attack.

There was nothing I could do to move around, as I was

still levered up against the wheel and strung across to the pipe, and I already knew the pipe wouldn't budge. With one free hand to swing, I wasn't going to offer much of a challenge to even the weakest competitor, so I did the only thing I could.

I hit him again in the groin, this time taking the time as he wound up again to really land it well. I was at eye-level with it sitting on the floor, so it didn't prove to be much of an issue to really get in there and squash it. I absolutely crushed him, and he doubled over immediately, sinking to the floor next to me.

His head fell close to my legs, and I took advantage of the momentary victory by stretching out more to give my legs some additional slack, then lifted my right knee and placed it over his head. As he tried to push himself off the floor, still woozy from my blow, I squeezed my leg back down, trapping his neck between my knees.

The pipe I was handcuffed too still didn't budge, and for the first time that day I was glad for it. I used it as leverage, pulling as hard as I could in and together with my legs, toward the rest of my body. It caused a clamp-like hold on his neck, and my own strength combined with the pulling against the pipe started to do the trick.

It's a nasty thing to choke someone out, and still trickier to do it long enough to kill them. Usually a writhing, flapping-like-a-fish head is what you want, as it allows you to use the person's momentum and leverage against themselves to snap their neck, making it take a lot less time.

But Riley was a solid contender, and he didn't give me that option. He lay still, wiggling around a bit with his torso and legs, but his hands came up around his own neck to try and squeeze them around it, to put a brace between his neck and my knees.

I buckled my knees and then shot them straight again, forcing his hands away again and his head down. His forehead smacked against my shin. It hurt like hell, but I knew the only option was to keep my hold on him. I started to sweat, my ankles were begging to be released, and my single wrist on the wheel handcuffs was beginning to bleed. A line of red trickled down my forearm, but still I held on.

I was gasping for breath, but at least the air was there. Mustache was gasping, but he just looked like a dying fish. There was nothing for him, and as long as I could hold on for the minute or so it would take, I'd have him beat.

He retrieved one of his hands from next to his face and reached down for something shoved into his belt.

The pistol.

Shit. I had forgotten about the weapon. Luckily he hadn't had it drawn when he'd come up the stairs or I would have gotten a quick one to the temple.

His palm opened and his fingers clasped around it, and I saw the pistol moving slowly out of his belt. It was an awkward position for him, not something that would have been comfortable at all, but if I let him get it all the way out of his pants he would be able to bring up underneath his torso and then out. Either all the way out and pointed toward my chest or face, or partly out and just resting on the underside of my leg.

Both would be unfortunate for me.

I reached as far as I could with my free hand and realized I was still a good foot away from his arm and the weapon. My bloody wrist was about to wrench free of my arm for good, and I didn't want that either, so I let up and just redoubled my efforts on my legs and his neck.

I buckled down again, twice, trying to dislodge the gun from his fingers or at least dislodge his focus from the pistol.

Neither happened, and the cold steel of the end of the barrel came up against my calf.

Not good.

He'd deafen himself, probably permanently, discharging a pistol that close to his head, but the effect would be exactly what he —

The muffled *blam* of the pistol took me by surprise, and I blinked a few times. My legs were still stiff, still holding tightly to their prize, and I knew it would be only a few more seconds before Riley lost his grip and the rest of his air.

And then the most godawful pain I'd ever experienced only twice before in my life hit me. My calf exploded in fury, my brain screaming obscenities at the rest of my body and my mouth about to follow suit.

Blood spattered along the bottom of the table and below it on the bridge wall to my left, and I could already see daylight from the tiny bullet hole that had pierced the thin wall.

I screamed in rage and might have even whimpered just a bit from the pain of it all, and yet somehow it still increased. More. And more. And dammit — still more.

I sat there for probably 8-tenths of a second, but it seemed like eight days. Just sitting, gasping now in pain from every limb — somehow my free hand hurt as well, which really frustrated and confused me — but especially in the back of my right leg.

And then, as if the Universe was just having a bad day and I was an itch it needed to scratch away, Riley got up. Simply, easily, like I wasn't even there. He just lifted his head and pushed against my injured leg, and sat up.

Holding the pistol.

Pointing it at my face.

I closed my eyes, screaming internally and angry at the world for being defeated.

I heard the shots, two of them, and still my eyes were closed.

CHAPTER FIFTY-NINE

I OPENED ONE EYE, THEN the other.

Smoke rose from Rayburn's crispy body, and in front of that, between Rayburn and where I still sat hunched over between the wheel and the pipe in the bridge, Riley lay lifeless.

Blood seemed to be everywhere. Pooling around his facedown body, around the pistol laying next to him, on the wall and table on the more unfortunate side of my calf, and — somehow, miraculously — a few drips on the ceiling.

I stared up at these little bloody constellations and just breathed. Rayburn was either dead or severely wounded, and Riley was absolutely dead. Hannah and Joey were somewhere nearby, hopefully alive, and I was alive and wishing I wasn't.

A silhouette appeared in the doorway, a suppressed pistol in his right hand. He came forward, stepping over Rayburn and entering the doorway to the bridge. He looked around, looked up, and then looked at me.

"Dixon," he said. "Glad you're okay."

"You've got to be shitting me," I said. My voice was barely my own. It felt froggy, like I'd barely recovered from a month-long cold. But it also added authority, meanness. "Bout time you showed up, Truman. How's the family?"

"Need some help with those cuffs?" Truman asked.

I nodded, sniffed, then spit out a giant wad of whatever post-fight monstrosity my saliva glands had cooked up. "Yeah, sure. And I could really use a drink, too."

CHAPTER SIXTY

TRUMAN AND I SAT IN the main room, across from each other. Truman had pulled over one of the huge chairs near the door, and I sat sideways on the same couch we'd found Hannah on. I had opted for one of the chairs, but some of his team had ordered me to stretch my leg out on the couch so they could — poorly, I might add — work on my leg.

'Just a flesh wound,' they'd said, but it had torn through muscle and fat and an inconceivable amount of nerves, and only a few of the little bastards had let up. The pain was excruciating, but I was already hard at work dulling it all away with some of my own medical experience.

Truman had poured the rest of the Booker's overproof into two more glasses and handed me one. I took about three sips and coughed, but the strong elixir began to work its magic immediately. I kept at it, committed, and before Truman had even finished two sips I'd made my way through half of the four fingers.

"Tell me what happened," Truman said. "After you gave Riley the codes. They weren't the right codes, were they?"

"Why are you still caught up in the codes? The bad guys are dead. What else do you need?"

Truman shifted in his seat, trying to make himself look more comfortable but failing. "I told you on the phone this is a *big* project for us," he said. "It's cross-departmental, and it's international. We've been working on it for months."

"So?" I asked. "What's that got to do with this stuff today?"

"Well," he said. "You showed up. You got involved, I got suspicious."

"Of *me*?"

He shifted again. "Well, no, not you necessarily… Look, Mason. It just seemed odd that you — someone who's got absolutely no ties to this family or this business — would show up, claiming to have just met this girl and wanting to help out, and suddenly take a *serious* interest in it all."

"Well… that's exactly what happened."

"I know," he said. "That's what my guys have been figuring out. You were in the right place at the right —" he stopped, looked at my leg — "sorry, *wrong* place at the wrong time. Hannah walked into your life, not the other way around. That matters to us. For the record."

"For the record."

"And we've been watching the house and the yacht for days. Trying to get a plan for making a move."

At this I raised an eyebrow. "So… you could have stormed in here and stopped all of this? Even after you knew Hannah was inside?"

I started breathing faster, unable to control my anger. The pain didn't help.

Truman held up a palm. "Calm down, Mason. You have to understand the pressure and details of it all, from my perspective. Hannah was certainly a top priority, but at the end of the day, there was a much larger mission."

"A much more *important* one."

He didn't acknowledge that, but he didn't need to.

"We need those codes, Mason. All of this hinges on the *correct* transfer codes. I was ordered to stand down until we were *positive* they were here. I was almost positive you didn't know them, but I had to wait and see for sure. You told them you knew them, so I was forced to wait it out. We've been listening in."

"You bugged the yacht?"

"We bugged *everything*. Sorry. You weren't supposed to be anywhere near this, Mason. But rest assured, no one touched Hannah — scuffed her up a bit, scared the shit out of her, but they didn't want to risk losing her as a bargaining chip."

The anger was still there, burning, like Rayburn's face, but at least now I was able to redirect it from Truman. I looked over at the blackened stain on the carpet. Rayburn's body had been removed, minutes after I'd been taken from the bridge. I'd heard Riley was still in the bridge, apparently still posing for the final photographing session of his shitty life.

Rayburn hadn't been dead when they'd carried me over him. I could see his nostrils, burned down to open holes in his face — still working, trying to breathe through all the blood. I took great satisfaction in that little moment as I floated over him.

He'd died on the way to the ambulance.

Truman started up again. "So you would have no way of knowing the codes. Right?"

I nodded, squinting a bit. I was trying to figure out his game. There was always a game with these government types. Something bigger they were working toward. Even for

Truman, a man I could consider a friend and an ally. "You still need the codes, don't you?"

This time he didn't even try to look comfortable. "My ass is on the line for this one, Dixon. The guys upstairs have been listening in to everything happening, reading all the reports, trying to get the codes. That's what this all comes down to. Even with the tech we've got access to, we can't hack into an international banking system to bring down a corporate entity. It'd work in the States, but overseas is a different story."

"You can't serve them a warrant? Get access to the server, something like that?"

Truman shook his head. "No. We might be able to work a deal, but…"

He pushed his tongue around inside his mouth, working through it. Wanting *me* to work through it.

"Oh," I said quickly. "You don't *know* which bank it is."

He nodded. "Sort of. These transfer codes aren't just simple bank routing numbers and accounts. They're cyber-encrypted information repositories. Basically, the program that Riley pulled up on Bradley Rayburn's computer was a decryptor. Type in the right string of codes, and the program spits out a list of the banks and the information for each account."

"You need that to prosecute the business, right?" I asked.

"Sort of. We need it to prosecute anyone we find involved with it all, but the codes, we believe, *also* give us a list of the people *actually* involved."

"Because those people alone would have access to those banks."

"Correct. It's always the last layer of security at multinational banks. Having a password is nothing if you're not who you say you are," Truman said.

"So you'll be able to get the people involved, with absolute proof that they're the culprits, because their names alone will be associated with the bank accounts."

"Exactly. And it will save us years in prosecution time, since Crimson Club dealt in legal and aboveboard wares as well. Those account numbers and people associated will be in the system, and the transactions will line up with legitimate transactions on the other end. But the ones that *aren't* legitimate — the ones we need to bust — will be in there as well, and a quick search as the buyer and seller on the other end of those transactions will disprove their innocence."

"I see," I said. I winced as I accidentally shifted my leg. "Well I might be able to help you out."

Truman's eyes widened. "Wh — what do you mean?" I didn't expect him to be so surprised, but I sort of wanted to revel in it a bit.

"I want to see Hannah, make sure she's okay. She's the key to all of this anyway."

Truman frowned. "Well, okay, sure. She's in the ambulance out in the parking lot right now. Joey's there, too. They're both going to be fine. But what does she have to do with it all? From what we could tell, she wasn't involved —"

"She's not involved," I said. "Don't let anyone think that. But her father — Bradley Rayburn — seemed to have trouble connecting with his daughter growing up. But he certainly had an affinity for her. Named her 'Hannah,' after all."

"Right, the key to his computer," Truman said. "We already know that. All lowercase."

"No," I said. "She's the key to *everything*."

CHAPTER SIXTY-ONE

"WELL HEY THERE," I SAID. It was jovial, lighthearted. I had said it like that on purpose, but I immediately second-guessed my decision as the words slipped out of my mouth. For one, my voice still carried the heavily strained smoker's accent of overexertion. And I didn't know how Hannah would react. Was I diminishing the situation? Was I being ignorant?

She smiled. "Hi," she said. "How are you doing?"

She and Joey had been filled in to my escapades shortly after they'd been rescued by Truman's team, and both had wanted to come in and welcome me back to the real world as soon as possible.

I wanted a reunion more than anything, but there was still work to do. Truman and one of his men stood by in the room, each so eager I was worried they'd pounce on me if I didn't get to the point.

"You're the key to it all, my Hannah."

She frowned, and her eyes welled up with tears. I suddenly regretted saying it. "Why — how do you know that?" she asked.

"You told me, back at the bar. Remember? You said your dad always used to tell you that."

She sniffed, wiped her eye, and straightened up. "Yeah," she said, "sorry. I do remember that now. It's been... it's been a —"

"I know, it's okay. I shouldn't have reminded you of him. But I think he was trying to tell you something. Give you a way to fight all of this."

"But... why not just *tell* me?"

"Because it was too dangerous." I turned to Truman, but kept speaking to Hannah. "I don't believe your father had anything to do with the more sinister parts of the Crimson Club organization, the one the Feds are after."

"You don't?"

I shook my head. "No, and I think we can prove it and clean his slate. Daniel's, too."

Her lip quivered, and I thought I'd lost her once again. But she took a step forward into the room, sat in one of the chairs across from me and my bum leg, and waited for me to continue.

"I think they're both innocent, just like you, and your father was trying to protect you. By giving you a stake in the company, he was telling everyone you had a role to play. But I'd bet my life your stake is somehow protected from the larger organization, legally. Meaning he wanted you to have part of his legacy without the crap of the fallout he knew was coming."

Truman spoke up. "He's right, Hannah. Your father wanted you to be secure, to take care of you. Even..."

"Even after he died," Hannah said. "He must have known that he would become a target. My uncle wanted to take over, and Dad thought he would be coming for him."

I almost cringed, but I held it together. I still couldn't tell

Hannah that her father had been murdered by *my* father, but that wasn't her cross to bear. It was mine.

They both looked at me.

"Right. So, I think your old man left you a legacy, but he also wanted to protect his family's name. As well as his business. He always told you 'you're the key, my Hannah.' He liked puzzles, word games, right?"

She nodded.

"So I think he's been trying to tell you — and us — something this whole time. Your name, lowercase, was his computer password. The computer he did just about *all* of his work on, here on the yacht. His yacht, the *Wassamassaw*."

I waited.

"So…"

"Hannah. H-A-N-N-A-H. A palindrome, remember?"

"Of course."

"*Wassamassaw.* Same thing. Spelled the same backward and forward."

Truman took another sip of bourbon and clicked it in his mouth. I couldn't tell if that was validation or he thought I was an idiot.

"I guess… he liked palindromes, but isn't it named for one of the local American Indian tribes that was in this region?"

I shrugged. "No idea. Did your dad have any ties to American Indians? Any reason to name it that?"

"No… I don't think so."

"So it's not about American Indians. It's a *clue*."

"Mason…" Truman was trying to reign me in, but I wasn't about to let up.

"Your father was trying to tell you that's it's all a puzzle. He couldn't realistically write any of this stuff down, at least not in a secret file, or password-protected database, or anything else. Not without fear of it getting compromised. And he couldn't just memorize it — what if he died without passing it on?"

"So he bought a *yacht* to hide it on? Is that really what you're saying?"

I nodded. "Yeah, that's exactly what I'm saying. He didn't even take this thing out on the water, did he? How often did you get to ride around on it?"

"Well, never, I guess."

"So it's a piece of the puzzle. How to hide something massive, something big enough to kill for, in plain sight? Something only someone he *deeply* trusted would be able to find?"

"Mason," Truman started again, "*Wassamassaw* is certainly convenient, but that's not the transfer code. Hell, it's not even *one* of the transfer codes. There will be more than one, and it's going to be a long string of alphanumeric characters. Possibly even special characters as well."

"I know," I said. "That's where I'm stuck. 'Hannah' was his computer password, hidden on the *Wassamassaw*, but I can't figure out —"

I stopped.

Tried to stand up, fell back down as my leg screamed at me.

"It's…"

I couldn't even speak, I was so excited.

"What? Mason, what is it?" Hannah asked.

I stared at Hannah. *This had to be it. The answer.*

"Hannah, was your father into kayaking?"

CHAPTER SIXTY-TWO

"IT WORKS!"

I HEARD THE woman's voice shout up from the office belowdecks, and Truman broke into a wide grin.

"Son of a bitch," he said, looking at me. "You did it."

He stood up and came over to shake my hand, and the woman yelled again. "Everything's here. Records, transaction, banks and account numbers, all of it."

"Wow," I said. "I almost didn't think that would work."

Hannah was smiling as well. "Why *did* you think it would work?" she asked.

"Well your dad's boat was brand new, right? Built in the nineties, probably sold without a lot of extra features, no bells and whistles or anything, since he put another million into it after."

"Right," she said.

"So it wouldn't have come with a kayak."

She laughed. "No, and I can't imagine him ever getting into one."

"And yet the *Wassamassaw* has a huge kayak mounted up just above the rail. K-A-Y-A-K kayak. Another palindrome."

Truman spoke up. "It was on the kayak's interior wall, just below the serial number. A tiny piece of paper taped to the panel. It had all three of the transfer codes we needed."

"Well," Hannah said. "I guess I *was* the key to everything."

She walked over as Truman returned to the bar to refill our drinks. I saw her sidling up to me, her curves, her tousled hair, her bandages, and I tried to sit up straighter.

She leaned in, grabbing my chin, and kissed me.

I kissed her back, a deep, well-meaning thing I hadn't done in over ten years. I suddenly wished even harder that I hadn't been shot through the leg, but I didn't want to take this kiss away, either. I sat back, drained, drowning in Hannah's affection.

She pulled back and Truman was there, smiling. He had two glasses in tow, darker colored than the Booker's.

"Well," he said. "I would offer to leave you two here, but I think my team has a bit more to clear up. Hate to ask you, but…"

"No," Hannah said, "it's fine. I can thank Mason a little later."

I couldn't help but grin a stupid, idiot-looking grin.

She smacked my shoulder as she stood up. "Stop it. Don't get any fancy ideas. I told you I would pay you. With *money.*"

She left the yacht and I waited around for someone to bring me a set of crutches. My leg had been wrapped and tightly bound, but the pain of moving it was still intense. I wanted to get out of there, to get back to my place and the bar, and to debrief with Joey.

He came in next.

"Hey boss," he said. "How you feeling?"

Joey had his hand wrapped in a sling, four of his fingers bound in gauze and set in temporary casts.

"Better than you, I'd guess," I said.

"Really?" Joey asked. "With your leg, I think I got the better end of the deal."

"Well, at least I had the satisfaction of taking care of things myself. You decided to stay back in the other room."

"You'd better watch your mouth, Dixon, or I'll shoot your other leg."

I laughed. "Right, with your aim? You'd be lucky to make another hole in this boat."

"Well, at least I can walk."

I chuckled. "We need to work on your comebacks, kid. But, I do think you earned that raise."

Joey walked over to the bar and grabbed at an 18-year scotch on the top shelf. He had to fight with it a bit to get it open with one hand, but he poured himself a drink and came over to sit where Hannah had been sitting earlier.

We looked each other over, not speaking, and Joey lifted his glass.

I nodded, smiling. Then I lifted my glass and clinked it on the side of his.

"Cheers," he said.

"Cheers."

CHAPTER SIXTY-THREE

HANNAH WAS THERE. JOEY WAS there. The locals and oldies were all there, too. We drank, talked, and generally had a great time. I looked around at all of it and felt, once again, the feeling of intense satisfaction I'd felt the day I opened.

It was the same place, and yet it had changed over the years. The clientele had grown, but some had died off and some had moved away. The oldies were still their curmudgeonly selves, ready to pounce on me for pouring too little into a double on the rocks, or for garnishing a drink with anything more robust than a lemon twist.

Joey flipped the catfish and served them up, and poured his share of drinks. To the visitors it all seemed to be a normal service. A normal day, in the normal lives of the normal bartenders. No one knew what had transpired just a day before, and no one asked.

They'd assumed we'd been fishing. It wasn't common for my place to shut down on a Friday night, but it wasn't exactly unheard of, either. News about Marley would reach the local paper late tonight, and everyone in town would know about it by tomorrow morning.

But tonight, everything was normal. Great, even.

I was happy, Hannah was trying her best to stop thinking about her father and her brother — Truman had offered to send one of his team to Daniel's wife, to tell her the news. She'd figured that would seem better somehow, more official. Maybe even more respectable. So she allowed it, and vowed to give her a call tomorrow or Monday.

Joey was happy, too. He was usually happy, in a satisfied way, not a happy-go-lucky way. He was a good man to have around, and I had been reminded of that a thousand times this week. When we arrived at the bar this morning, he didn't even ask about the raise.

So it was with great pleasure that I surprised him with something even better: I offered him a small stake in ownership of the company. I wanted to expand one day, I told him, and I would need someone to do the lighting in the new place. If he was really lucky I might even let him flip catfish.

He was ecstatic, blown away that I'd even offer. After we joked around about it, I confided in him that I wanted him to take on a bigger managerial role around here, if he wanted it, and that of course would come with more money. Again, he accepted.

We were all at the bar, Joey and me on one side and Hannah on the other, and we laughed and talked for a few hours while the guests milled about and played their cards around us.

We were in the middle of hearing one of Joey's terrible Navy stories (from my perspective, *all* Navy stories are terrible), when Truman walked in.

He was wearing blue jeans and a weird tight sweater, but

I figured this was the only attempt his wardrobe could provide at 'casual dress.' He walked up to the counter.

"What can I get you?" I asked.

"What's good?"

"I hate that question. What do you like?"

"What are you drinking?"

"Rum. Real gamey stuff Joey brought back from a vacation to Jamaica a couple years ago."

"Sounds… terrible. Will I like it?"

"If you like the taste of sour meat and shitty molasses, sure."

Joey smiled.

"Sounds good," Truman said. "Give me one of those. On the rocks."

I nodded and readied a glass to pour him a drink, but Joey was already there. "Don't listen to a word he says," Joey said. "It's amazing. Overproof, so go slow."

He passed the glass over to Truman. Truman took a long pull on it, thinking and tasting, contemplating the beverage. He swirled it around in his mouth and chortled it over his tongue a few times like an old pro.

"It's… horrendous."

Joey and I laughed, and this time Hannah joined in from next to Truman.

"No, really," Truman said between coughs. "It's absolutely disgusting. You really drink this stuff?"

Joey smiled wider. "No, we use it for mixers only. It's pretty rough. We're drinking some of that Booker's Overproof you guys had on Rayburn's yacht." He explained it as he took Truman's glass of rum away and replaced it with a finger of Booker's, on the rocks.

"You're a bastard, you know that?" Truman said, still

licking the inside of his mouth to remove the taste. "You are too, you little shit," he said to Joey.

He sipped the Booker's for a moment, clearly enjoying the glass a lot more, then looked up at me. "About that yacht…"

I cocked an eyebrow and looked at Hannah. She grinned.

"Ms. Rayburn here gave me a call this morning," he said. "We finished with our work on the boat, so it was all clear pretty early today. Since she's the next heir in the company — the *legitimate* portions of the company — and the heir to Rayburn himself, the yacht technically belongs to her."

"Wow," I said. "What about the mansion?"

"The estate will be a bit more difficult," Truman explained, "as it was built on land that's state-owned. It'll probably fall to Hannah as well, but it's going to be a bit of a legal battle for a year or so until we clear it up. But my team's already on it, and if they can find any workarounds or loopholes, they'll let her know."

I turned to Hannah. "Sorry about all this, Hannah. It's going to be a nightmare."

"I know," she said. "But it's nothing compared to what happened. I'm just glad it's all over."

Truman spoke again. "Hannah and I talked about it, and it turns out that she had a verbal arrangement with you regarding payment for services rendered?"

I waved Truman off. "Please," I said. "Don't even bring that up. Hannah, you know I did this to help you, and that's it. I didn't want your money even before I knew —"

"Shut up, Dixon," she said. "I'm going to pay you. So that's that. I know you did it to help me out, but you have to understand how I feel about all of it. You're not turning me down. Just hear him out."

I turned back to Truman. Joey had finished making a drink for an oldie and he slipped in next to me as well.

"And my legal team informed us that since Mr. Dixon has so far helped Ms. Rayburn out of the kindness of his heart, it would seem that someone could claim Mr. Dixon did, in fact, have another motive in mind."

"What *motive* are you talking about?" I asked. I started to grip the bar top harder.

"Nothing serious. But it would require some court visits, debriefing summaries, a bunch of paperwork and crap none of us want to do."

"So... what?"

"So," Truman said, "if you were to accept an offering from Ms. Rayburn, my legal team would be formally required to accept the truth that you worked for Ms. Rayburn in expectation of a payment, and nothing more."

"So she *has* to pay me, or I'll be annoyed by you for another few months."

"Possibly years."

"Wonderful."

Hannah leaned in. "It's what I want, Dixon. I'm never going to use it. After... after everything, especially. I want you to have it."

I looked down at the empty glass in my hand and then back up at her. "Wait. Are you serious? You want me to have the *yacht?*"

Joey and Truman smiled, and Hannah nodded. "Yes, I do. It would be perfect. I'm going to go away for awhile, maybe stay with some cousins overseas, but I want someone to take care of it while I'm gone. It's sort of the last piece of my father I have left, and I don't like the idea of selling it. Plus it'll need a new name and a few coats of paint. I was thinking the 'Mason-Dixon' would be a *perfect* name for it."

Joey laughed. "That *is* a perfect name for a big-ass, lumbering boat."

"No," I said. "There's no *way* I'm naming a boat after myself."

"Well," Hannah said, "we can discuss it further tonight. Drinks, on the yacht? Maybe a little deck-sitting? My dad never used it, but I think there's even a master bedroom with a giant whirlpool tub inside."

I had to admit, that sounded like a great idea.

"On one condition," Truman added.

Great. "What is that?"

"Guy on my team says he used to have a small yacht. He knows his way around boats, and was *dying* to take the *Wassamassaw* out for a spin. How about after you two, uh, *break it in*, we have a little party for my team on board? They need a vacation, and a little one-night stint might be the perfect thing. Monday or Tuesday night should be fine — most of them are not expected back in the office until Wednesday afternoon anyway."

"I —"

He held up a hand. "Plus, he tells me you owe him a big favor for — how did he put it — 'jacking his car from him.'"

I hung my head and smiled. "Yeah, Truman. That sounds fine with me. I'll play bartender, too."

CHAPTER SIXTY-FOUR

I WAS STIFF AND SORE, and not just because my leg still had a bleeding bullet wound in it.

Hannah and I had a phenomenal night together, hanging out on the sun deck to watch the sunset, testing out the hot tub and whirlpool, and basking in the moonlight with a couple bottles of wine on the deck chairs. The kayak had been removed and brought to some storage facility somewhere, probably never to be seen again, and some of the carpeting had been cut and pulled up in the bridge and hallway.

The bridge had been cleaned by a professional service Truman's team had brought in, and they'd taken only about three hours to get the space looking brand-new. The carpet would be replaced if Hannah could get in touch with the company that had done the interior, otherwise she'd just pay another design firm to redo it altogether.

Other than that the yacht was in 'ship shape,' a term that I had suddenly latched onto as the funniest thing I'd heard all weekend.

She explained a bit more about how she'd been feeling,

trying to process through some of the anger and fear with me, yet knowing it was all going to come crashing down on her in a few days at most. Both of us knew this was our only night we'd have together, and we didn't want to ruin it.

She told me she'd be traveling, seeing the world and learning some of the history of some of the places she'd always wanted to visit. I nodded along, knowing this was a wise decision — she didn't have the responsibility of a family and the burden of a job — she needed the time and space to process everything.

We cried, we laughed, and we made it the best damn night I'd had in well over ten years. The next day, we got off the boat and she walked to her car in the parking lot of her new mansion — assuming Truman was right about it all — and I walked to Joey's beat-up sedan. Truman wouldn't let me keep the Bureau's car, and Billy hadn't finished with mine, so Joey had to play chauffeur for a little while.

I had Joey drop himself off at the bar to clean up and prepare for the week, then I took the car and headed out to my spot on the side of the highway.

I carried the package in the same hand the whole way. It wasn't heavy — no more than the weight of three Big Macs, according to Joey — but my grip was struggling against the weight anyway. My knuckles were white, my fingers burning with it by the time I reached the circle of rocks and the little hole on the other side of it.

"Hello," my father said, stepping out from behind the rock.

"Hello," I answered.

I tossed the brick toward him, the paper wrapping snapping in the wind as it fell at his feet.

"What's this?" he asked.

"Your money," I said.

"It's not… it's your money now, son."

I shook my head. "It's your money. You started this whole thing and I got to finish it. I'm out. This is the end."

"It's never the end, son. There's always more —"

"There *is* always more, Dad. But not for me. Not for *us*. You take your money and you go buy someone else."

His face flushed with anger. "I'm not going to stand here and take this —"

I lost my patience about the same time I lost my cool. All the years of taking shit and shoveling it around for this guy. I'd had it. I'd told him so, but I'd never really meant it until now.

"I ain't asking you to, asshole," I shouted. "I'm *telling* you. You find someone else or you retire. Those are your options."

His nostrils flared. I could see him computing, thinking, just like I do, trying to figure out what game I was playing.

I wasn't playing a game. I was pissed, and I was done.

"Here's your money, old man," I said. "Thirty grand, all cash. Just like you gave it to me. A nice little brick of money, ready to spend. I didn't need it."

"Why?"

"Why?" I asked in return. "Because I didn't *need* it, that's why? I don't owe you an —"

"You *do* owe me at *least* an explanation, son. Why? What happened?"

"I cleaned up your mess, that's why. Didn't need to buy a car, already had the firepower. So I didn't need it."

"What about the mortgage on the bar?"

"I'm making money in the bar. I'll get enough, it's just a matter of time. But I don't need to speed things up with your blood money."

He threw his head back and genuinely laughed. "Is *that*

what this is to you? *Blood* money? This is dirty money? This is the reason you're out? Because I didn't follow the rules?"

"You *made* the rules, Dad. You made them, and then you broke them."

"Because I *could*. I made the rules, remember?"

"But the rules make it right. The rules are the only thing separating us from the bad guys."

He was laughing, almost hysterically now, and shaking his head. As if I was the crazy one. As if he had no idea how insane he sounded.

"I'm done, Dad. That's it. Take the money. I don't need it anymore."

He picked it up, making a point of taking his time and staring at me as he did it. He felt it, prodded it, making sure it was what I'd said it was. The weight was right — it had to be, as I hadn't even touched it since I'd taken it from the box — but I waited there anyway. I wanted to see him accept my resignation. I wanted to make sure I was out. I hated that I needed that from him, but I did.

He sniffed it. Like he could smell the amount of money inside just by his sense of smell. Apparently whatever he smelled convinced him, and he looked up at me with those same eyes I shared with him over the top of the brick of money.

"Fine," he said. "You're out."

I nodded, then turned to leave.

"But this type of work always catches up with you."

I nodded again, still walking away. I wasn't going to stop. I wasn't ever going to stop.

"And you can leave this work, but this work can never leave you." He paused, and could feel the weight of the next word even before it was breathed into life off his lips.

"Son."

DEATH MARK

Continue the fun! Turn the page for a preview of the next
Mason Dixon novel, *Death Mark!*

CHAPTER ONE

I HAVE THIS IDEA THAT maybe morality is like death: we can buck and fight against it as long as we want, but eventually it's going to get us. And we're all given a specific amount of morality; a certain flavor of it we can't change or cash in, or alter in any way.

We can mask it, like our faces, but it won't do any good. At the end of the line, wherever that line is, we're as moral as we're ever going to be. We're as good or bad as we're ever going to be, or as 'us' as we ever were.

Okay, enough with the philosophical bullshit. What I'm saying here is that *I have no idea how the world works.*

I don't really care, either, because I know, generally, how *people* work. I get how they tick, what they want, how they intend to get it. I'm good at that part of it. I'm not so good at the part of it where I have to decide what to *do* about it.

You see, I'm good at my gig — I tend bar at a little place I own, and I like it. I love it, actually. The oldies take care of me, and I get to silently judge the younger idiots that come in and ask for things that no bar menu should even *suggest* to offer.

Like light beer.

And I don't mean 'beer that is light,' like a proper Belgian or some of the summer Germans or the pilsners and IPAs that are vying for hipsters' attention out west.

I mean beers that were designed to be tasteless, so men, women, grandparents, and children alike could hate them all the same, pretend they like them, and drink them by the bucketful just for the sheer hell of saying they could drink a bucketful of them.

Those beers are the types I don't anywhere my bar. I've got a few taps, and I keep those taps full of whatever I can get for a reasonable price that comes out of Charleston, or when I'm feeling fancy or festive I might spring for a shipment of kegs of something a little more exotic. But I don't have your typical Applebee's-on-a-Sunday-night fare of brew selections.

So when these youngsters — anyone younger than me, I should say — come in and try to order something like that, I just shrug and serve them whatever I've got on tap in that's in a real beer format.

Want a Coors? I'll give you whatever I've got from Revelry. Have a hankering for a Bud Light? I'll toss you the latest from Tradesman.

The guy that walked in five minutes ago was one of these guys — I could tell by his swagger. There's always a swagger. They come in like they're the coolest cat in town and that I should be *honored* to serve him a 'cold one,' which is 'this guy'-speak for 'crappy beer.'

Sure enough, he sidled up and tucked his legs under the bar top and gave me a nod. No smile, no greeting, no nothing. Just that nod.

I nodded back.

"What can I get you?" I asked.

"Eh, just a cold one," he said.

Of course. Bartender one, this guy zero.

I poured him a legacy IPA from Revelry, waited for the head to peak up above the top of the pint glass, and slid it over to him on a brand-new coaster.

Joey made those coasters — they have a cute little logo of a bearded, mustached man holding a bottle of whiskey in one hand and a pint glass of beer in his other hand. It's green, mostly, but the guy's lumberjack shirt is checkered red and black, and his mustache and beard are a dark brown.

It's sort of a weird logo, but I wasn't on the design committee that made them. The oldies and regulars seem to like the coasters, at least, but I wasn't too thrilled that it was just another expense and not something we could make money from. You can't sell coasters, after all.

Joey, anyway, had printed up a few million or so of these stupid things and placed them in all sorts of strategic locations around the tiny estate of mine. I even saw a handful of them in the bathroom, on top of one of the toilets. I mean really, I guess it's a helpful thing, but I'd just as soon finish my drink *before* I expose it to the nasty shit floating around in the men's room.

"What's this?" the guy asked.

"Cold one," I said, without missing a beat.

"Tastes like shit," he said.

I pulled it back and dumped it out in the sink. "That one's on me, then," I said. "What are you looking for, *specifically*?"

He shrugged. "I don't know, Miller, Coors, Bud, any of those ring a bell?"

I frowned. "Yeah, I've heard of them. Don't have them here."

He looked like he was about to pop a gasket, but to his

credit he held it together long enough to ask the famous question. "What is this, some sort of gay bar?"

I honestly don't know what it is with these guys. Look, if your drink really is a Coors Light, fair enough. I won't get in your way. But if you claim to *not really care* about what type of beer you're drinking, but then you bitch about it when I pour you a craft beer from a small local business that needs your support, I have no patience for you.

And if you top it off by adding some sort of 'color' to your opinion, you're about as good as the coaster that's been stuck to the floor near the drain in the bathroom to me.

"Nope," I said. "Just a bar. But we don't have that sort of stuff here because it's actually cheaper to work with the local places. I get a better deal, and they make more money. Win-win."

"Yeah? Well not for me."

"Well I'm not sure there's anything in this world that will make you a winner at anything, pal."

He looked at me then with those eyes that would have told me I was in trouble, if I thought this was even remotely the sort of guy who could make me feel like there was trouble coming.

Then, as if on cue, he got up and stormed out. The little bell above the door clinked violently as the door slammed shut, but only two or three regulars in the corner took notice.

"Who was that?" Joey asked. He'd snuck up on me, delivering dinner and placing it in front of me at the bar. Fish and chips.

"Just a guy looking for a cold one."

"Huh," Joey said. "Nothing here cold enough?"

"Nothing but the banter, I guess. Fish and chips?"

"Yeah," he said. "Thought we'd keep rolling with that English pub theme for a while longer."

Joey, since I'd made him manager, had done me quite a few favors. One of them was to 'theme' different seasons. We were currently running with an English pub theme, complete with a few English-style ales on tap. I was never a huge fan of English beer, but Joey had done a great job with the theming and menu design.

We're a small operation — just Joey and me — but we're sort of the talk of the town, if you consider that the town is about 800 people. Edisto Beach, in South Carolina. It's the town you run into when you're trying to run into the ocean.

Joey took the helm as planner of all things that needed planning, besides the liquor selection and the mixology. I'd started the place because I'd wanted to bring back the classiness to drink-making. The '-ology' part of mixology. So many younger bartenders were throwing together fruit juices and liqueurs, mixing them in with forty crushed berries and calling it a drink. Sure, it was liquid, and sure, it may count as a drink on a beach somewhere south of the border on spring break, but in my world it was trash.

I wanted the beauty restored to the mixology world. Just like the chefs that were breaking down barriers and expectations, I wanted drink-making to be as masterfully practiced an art form.

Joey got it, and he loved it. But we didn't need two of me — we needed me and Joey. Joey was master of the kitchen, the private chef of the patrons we served six nights a week. He was also in charge of decor, aesthetics, and generally everything else besides the liquor. He did a bang-up job, and I paid him better than anyone else in this town or Charleston.

"So it's working pretty well, then? The pub style?"

"Sure, yeah. Everyone seems to enjoy the beers, and the drinks you've mashed up are a huge hit."

I'd made about five custom drinks to match the English theme, using English gins and genevers, as well as a few specials, like the Cornish Pastis, to round out the palate. I had to admit, they were tasty. I liked creating the drinks, and I certainly liked *drinking* them.

I drank a lot, but never too much. Joey and I were the tasters, purchasers, mixologists, and bartenders, and I always harped on him that we needed to know our stuff. I wouldn't anything without my palate.

"So what's next, then?" I asked him.

"Like for themes?"

"Sure, yeah." I gave him that look he'd come to understand well. *Yeah, but not really. What's* really *next?*

He smiled. "I don't know, boss. You're kind of in charge of that, don't you think?"

He was referring, of course, to our *other* endeavor: moonshining.

CHAPTER TWO

I HAD ALWAYS WANTED TO get into moonshining, but never had the guts. Really. I'd always heard it was a 'good way to get yourself killed,' or 'great if you want to go to prison,' so I'd never really attempted it.

But the truth of the matter was that it's a misdemeanor in most places, and seen as one in all the places. Most cops — trust me, I've asked them — don't really care one way or another. It's when you *sell* the stuff they tend to get all bent out of shape.

I had the stuff all set up in the back area, near the tiny kitchen and against one of the walls. It wasn't much — a couple carboys, a couple large fermentation buckets, and lots of plastic tubing. Joey had figured out how to finagle the whole distillery apparatus onto the kitchen's water spigot using about a hundred adaptors, and a large electric burner served as the heating element.

I'm not interested in breaking the law, necessarily. I'm not really interested in *not* breaking the law, either, but the point isn't about the law. I wanted to start distilling my own stuff, and eventually try to get it sold in the bar, but in order to make sure I knew that I could do it, I had to practice. No point in paying the massive fees and working toward a license if I didn't even like the process.

Hence the tiny distilling operation taking place illegally in the back of my kitchen. Nothing fancy, but enough that Joey and I could get used to the process and try to produce something worth selling.

Joey was excited about our new little experiment, and I often found him in the back trying out a new mash or cooking up something strange. It took time — usually between three and six months — aging the distillate in the tiny oak barrels I'd bought for the purpose, so neither of us knew if our stuff was any good, but it was fun nonetheless.

"What do you have in mind?" Joey asked.

"I don't know, maybe something similar to Scotch?"

Scotch was tricky because, well, we weren't in Scotland. But the premise of Scotch was pretty simple: make whiskey from grain, but smoke the grain over peat before you distill it.

"Sounds hard," Joey said.

"It adds an extra step, but —"

I looked up from the bar just then, interrupting our small talk, and noticed the guy who'd just walked in. He was tall, not as tall as me but tall enough to be noticeable, but he carried himself the same way I did.

Confident.

I gave him a nod, but he kept on staring me down as he walked straight toward the bar. I wasn't entirely sure he'd slow down and stop, and I wasn't entirely sure the bar would be able to stop him if he wasn't.

Finally he stopped. He didn't sit down, and he didn't look down either.

Joey turned to look at me, then he shrugged. He knew

the drill — guys like this came in every now and then. Thinking they were worth someone's attention. Maybe they were, but they weren't worth *mine*.

I waited for him to make the first move. Confidence like that meant he was here for a reason, and that reason probably wasn't drinking.

He reached into his pocket. I moved my hand to the left, feeling the rounded edge of the shotgun's barrel poking out from where I'd mounted it just underneath the bar. I doubted I'd need it, but better to doubt and be ready than to be sure and be caught off guard.

His hand came out, weaponless. He smacked his palm on the bar top and then removed his hand. I looked down at the hard object he'd laid there.

A small, metallic circle. Embossed with some sort of design on the topside of it.

I looked back up at him. "What's that supposed to be?"

The man didn't respond at first. He was waiting, testing. Trying to figure out if I knew more than I let on.

"You don't know what this is?" the man asked.

"If it's money, it ain't going to work in here. Not sure I've ever seen that currency —"

"It's not money."

"Okay, well your *round metal circle* isn't going to get you any beer."

"I don't want beer."

I saw a few oldies shifting around in their chairs, but Joey was off helping a couple patrons near the door.

"Listen, pal, I'm not sure what you're trying to play, here, but I've got *paying* customers — using *real* money — to take care of."

The man nodded. "Go ahead. I'll wait."

I sighed. "Okay, here's how it's going to go down. If

you're waiting for me to suddenly remember where I've seen that little thing, you're going to be waiting a long time. If you're waiting for me to have some time to chat, maybe play 'Antique Road Show' with you, bar closes at 2. That's in…" I stopped to check my watch, "about five hours."

She shook his head. "I want to know what you think of this."

"I don't think *anything* about it. It's a coin, probably from some other country. Why should it mean something to me?"

I shuffled away, grabbing the two beers I'd just poured and an Old Fashioned 'My Way' I'd mixed and placed them onto a serving tray. I swung around the end of the bar and walked them to the customers who'd ordered them.

I took another couple's order and began walking back to the bar.

"Look like your other little coin?"

I stopped in the middle of the bar, examining the man. I was positive I'd never seen him before, yet he looked familiar. Maybe in that 'looks-like-a-lot-of-other-people' sort of way.

"I know you?" I asked.

He shook his head. "No, but you're going to."

"Why's that?"

"This coin was found in a dead man's pocket three days ago.

CHAPTER THREE

I HAD POURED MYSELF A glass of bourbon — Michter's
— and sat down at the bar stool next to the guy. He didn't
want anything but a glass of water, and that was how I knew:
he was a government guy. Paid detective sort.

"You FBI?" I asked.

He shook his head.

"DEA."

"I see. Well, DEA, I'm sorry I can't help with your
investigation."

"Why's that?"

"Well, because I don't know what that little thing is."

"You don't?"

Joey's eyes met mine — he was still behind the bar,
pouring for a few customers who'd just walked in. They were
apparently here on vacation, from what I overheard. Nice
folks, older than me with a son who was about half my age.
They ordered some mixed drinks, and the son ordered a beer.

"I don't. Like I said."

"Got it." DEA-man pulled out a little notebook and
started writing in it.

"You actually *use* those things? What are you, some 1950's detective?"

"No," he said. "DEA."

"Right. So, DEA, how many questions of yours am I going to have to answer before you let me and my patrons be?"

He swiveled around and looked at me after he'd finished scratching in the words 'doesn't know — coin.' "Well, I want to know what you know about this coin, or —"

"I don't anything about that —"

"*Or* any *other* coin you might have seen."

"I've seen lots of coins. This is a bar, you know that, right?"

He sighed. "Look, man. I've got a family. I've got friends, believe it or not. And a life. I don't want to be here any more than you do, but I was told by a... coworker you were the guy to talk to about this thing."

I frowned. "What coworker?"

"I can't say."

"Of course you can't," I answered. "What *can* you tell me?"

"This was found on some dead guy, three days ago."

"Three days ago the dead guy *became* dead, or three days ago you found it on a guy who was *already* dead."

"Does it matter?"

"Not sure," I said. "Does it?"

"He was on his way to a strip club in Charleston."

"Okay, so he was hoping to score with the ladies."

"It was a *gay* strip club. For men."

"So he was hoping to score with the *guys*." I was growing impatient, and I knew he was, too. "Look, pal — you got a name, or should I just keep calling you pal?"

"Jeff."

"Right, Jeff. Look, *Jeff,* I've got a business to run, and I, too, have a life. Tell me who your friend is, or tell me why they think *I* should know what this stupid little coin is in my bar."

"They think it's a copy."

"A copy... of what?"

"A copy of your coin."

I turned and frowned at the man. *Who the hell is this guy? Jeff. Jeff who? Why is he here?*

"I don't have any coins like that."

He sighed, again. It was like a sighing match, and I wasn't sure who was winning.

"I was told you had a little... operation. Something like this, months back."

"Tell me who told you that."

"Can't do that," he said. "But they told me your operation was successful. Then you got out, went clean."

"Okay, so if I'm out of this 'operation,' why would I know about this *other* coin?"

"Maybe they're paying homage to you, you know? Like honoring your legacy by minting another coin, something to track —"

I held up a hand. "Hold on a second, there. *Jeff.* I'm not doing this *thing* you say I used to do, so that means I don't know about anyone *else* doing this thing. Maybe you tell me I'm a suspect and I might be more apt to go along with this story."

Jeff raised an eyebrow, and I found another bourbon in front of me. I nodded at Joey, who'd snuck it in, then looked again at Jeff.

"Okay," Jeff said. "You're a suspect."

I laughed. "Well shit, that was easy. Fine — I'm a suspect. For what? Killing this guy?"

"Yeah, for that."

"Okay, fine. Who's the guy?"

He looked at me, no doubt getting ready to track my reaction and make another tiny note about it in his tiny book with his tiny pencil.

"You Mason Dixon?"

"One and only."

"Okay, Dixon. The man we found dead was identified as your father."

~

Want to continue the story? Grab a copy of *Death Mark* now!

AFTERWORD

If you liked this book (or even if you hated it…) write a review or rate it. You might not think it makes a difference, but it does.

Besides *actual* currency (money), the currency of today's writing world is *reviews*. Reviews, good or bad, tell other people that an author is worth reading.

As an "indie" author, I need all the help I can get. I'm hoping that since you made it this far into my book, you have some sort of opinion on it.

Would you mind sharing that opinion? It only takes a second.

Nick Thacker

ALSO BY NICK THACKER

Mason Dixon Thrillers

Mark for Blood (Book 1)

Death Mark (Book 2)

Mark My Words (Book 3)

Harvey Bennett Mysteries

The Enigma Strain (Book 1)

The Amazon Code (Book 2)

The Ice Chasm (Book 3)

The Jefferson Legacy (Book 4)

The Paradise Key (Book 5)

The Aryan Agenda (Book 6)

The Book of Bones (Book 7)

The Cain Conspiracy (Book 8)

Harvey Bennett Mysteries - Books 1-3

Harvey Bennett Mysteries - Books 4-6

Jo Bennett Mysteries

Temple of the Snake (written with David Berens)

Tomb of the Queen (written with Kristi Belcamino)

~

Harvey Bennett Prequels

The Icarus Effect (written with MP MacDougall)

The Severed Pines (written with Jim Heskett)

The Lethal Bones (written with Jim Heskett)

~

Gareth Red Thrillers

Seeing Red

Chasing Red (written with Kevin Ikenberry)

~

The Lucid

The Lucid: Episode One (written with Kevin Tumlinson)

The Lucid: Episode Two (written with Kevin Tumlinson)

The Lucid: Episode Three (written with Kevin Tumlinson

~

Standalone Thrillers

The Atlantis Stone

The Depths

Relics: A Post-Apocalyptic Technothriller

Killer Thrillers (3-Book Box Set)

~

Short Stories

I, Sergeant

Instinct

The Gray Picture of Dorian

Uncanny Divide (written with Kevin Tumlinson and Will Flora)

ABOUT THE AUTHOR

Nick Thacker is a thriller author from Texas who lives in Colorado and Hawaii, because Colorado has mountains, microbreweries, and fantastic weather, and Hawaii also has mountains, microbreweries, and fantastic weather. In his free time, he enjoys reading in a hammock on the beach, skiing, drinking whiskey, and hanging out with his beautiful wife, tortoise, two dogs, and two daughters.

In addition to his fiction work, Nick is the founder and lead of Sonata & Scribe, the only music studio focused on producing "soundtracks" for books and series. Find out more at SonataAndScribe.com.

For more information, visit Nick online:
www.nickthacker.com
nick@nickthacker.com

Made in the USA
Coppell, TX
16 April 2020

20310385R00215